Shannon Nikole

Chasing Redemption

SHANNON NIKOLE

Chasing Redemption

Copyright © 2023 by Shannon Nikole

All rights reserved.

No part of this book may be reproduced in any form or by any electronic or mechanical means, including information storage and retrieval systems, without written permission from the author, except for the use of brief quotations in a book review.

This is a work of fiction. Names, characters, places, and incidents are either the product of the author's imagination or are used fictitiously. Any resemblance to actual persons, living or dead, businesses, companies, events, or locales is entirely coincidental.

Copy Editor: Word of Advice Editing Services

Proofreading: Ink and Earth Studio

Cover Design: Cat Imb of TRC Designs

Formatting: Ink and Earth Studio

Chasing Redemption

For those who read Finding Starlight and adore Max as much as I do.

And for Jakob, the stranger who walked up to me during the wedding of one of my best friends and asked if I was the "smut writer" before proceeding to ask to be written into a book because of his wife, Erin, who loves romance books. You've made the cut - you're welcome. You better buy a shit ton of copies, dude.

AUTHOR'S NOTE

Dear Reader,

Thank you so much for wanting to read Chasing Redemption, but the most important thing is for you to be informed and comfortable with what you're reading. If you would like to verify the content within Chasing Redemption, please refer to my website where you can find out if this book will be a fit for you.

Thank you,
Shannon Nikole

1

MARLEY

Five years ago...

Tonight was one of the most annoying fucking nights of my life.

A true nightmare, if you will.

Not only was I the maid of honor for my childhood best friend, who was marrying my most recent ex-boyfriend, but they hired me as the event planner.

The planner for my own personal hell.

I forced myself to remain sober all evening since I was technically working the event, but I wasn't sure how much more of this bullshit I could take while wearing a fake-ass smile the whole time.

A hand reached out, touching my shoulder. "How are you holding up, Mar?"

At least it was someone I wanted to see. I turned around and pulled my twin sister, Avery, into a hug. She was the other maid of honor for this shitshow.

"Do I look as miserable as I feel?" I asked.

Avery pulled back a bit, keeping her grasp on my arms

while she examined my face. "I'm sure the average person can't tell. But I'm your sister, and what I see makes me wonder if you've poisoned their wedding cake."

Narrowing my eyes, I stepped out of her embrace and rolled my eyes. "Hilarious. You know I wouldn't last in jail."

She threw her head back, laughing. "Ain't that the truth."

Avery joined me as I finished doing my rounds as the planner. The catered dinner went off without a hitch—the food was delicious, and all the vendors had been paid and tipped. The only thing left was for the wedding to end and for the cleanup crew to do the rest of the hard work. But before all that could happen, I had to deal with the toasts and the endless hours of dancing. And trust me, I had nothing to say in a toast, so hopefully, people would believe the greeting-card-style bullshit I'd be spewing tonight.

As if on cue, the DJ cut the music and announced that the bride and groom would like to say a few words before the toasts began.

Great. Just great.

I stood off to the side, listening as they droned on about how thankful they were that their friends and family could join them on their special day and how blessed they were to find each other.

Gag me.

Avery and I shared a look, our eyes rolling at the same time my name was called on the microphone. Turning my attention back toward the platform the newlyweds stood on, my eyes met with Alison's as she placed her right hand over her heart and addressed me.

"Marley, honey, I want to thank you for not only being in my wedding but for taking on the role of my wedding planner." Her arm gestured to the space we were in. "This wedding would not have happened without you."

Yeah, for several reasons.

Giving a slight nod, I forced a smile. Alison paused and made a show of dabbing the corners of her eyes with a tissue. I'd hoped she'd end it after that, but she had to continue.

"Most importantly, Marley, if you hadn't given up Jerin when you did, none of this would have happened. Your breakup brought Jerin and me together, and I can't thank you enough."

Oh, fuck this.

I turned and sought out a server who was passing out champagne for the upcoming toasts from the bridal party. Grabbing two flutes, determined as hell to get wasted enough to forget I ever heard that, I turned back around in time to raise a glass as the happy couple finished whatever the fuck they were saying.

I downed the entire first flute in one gulp, followed immediately by the second.

Avery sidled up beside me, looking as stunned as I felt, and offered me her glass of champagne. Without even acknowledging her, I snatched the glass from her and threw that back as well. "Best sister ever," I whispered.

Sweat started to bead at my temple as dread formed in my lower belly at what was to come next. Before I knew it, our time was up. The DJ announced my and Avery's names, and we were shoved up onto the platform next to Alison and Jerin, with a new glass of champagne for each of us. I spaced out as Avery delivered some bullshit speech about knowing Alison our entire lives, being so happy for their next chapter, and toasting to what the future may bring.

Avery was damn lucky she had watched so many Hallmark movies, or she would have been shit out of luck with her speech.

"Easy enough," she whispered as she passed me the mic.

Looking between Jerin and Alison, I plastered my golden fake smile on again and raised my glass for my speech.

"To the lovely couple. Alison, hopefully he doesn't cheat on you as he did on me." The wedding guests gasped. "But since he cheated on me with you, maybe you'll be safe?" I shrugged. "Fuck if I know. But enjoy his tiny dick. I know I didn't."

I downed the champagne before handing the mic back to Avery and making my grand exit off the platform.

The crowd was momentarily silent, their mouths gaped open in surprise before the whispers started. Ignoring them, I gathered my belongings and placed them on Avery's seat, hoping she'd take them with her when she left. I listened as everyone else in the wedding party made their toasts while I slipped my phone out of the pocket of my dress and typed Avery a text to explain I needed some fresh air.

My mind drifted back to my toast. For a moment, I thought I'd feel bad about what I said. But the moment passed quickly as I spotted one of the servers refilling champagne flutes. I had a great idea brewing: let *operation get more alcohol* commence.

I mustered up all the elegance I could and waltzed up to the server and helped place flutes on the tray. "Hello, I'm Marley Halligan." I smiled sweetly as I greeted the man. "I'm the event planner this evening."

He looked at me in disbelief. "Looks like you're in the wedding and not an event planner, if you ask me."

Standing taller, I lifted the tray for the man before handing it over. "Yeah, it's a bit unusual, but it doesn't make it any less true."

"Listen," he started, "we're almost out of champagne in the kitchen. Do you know if we have any more somewhere else?"

The corners of my mouth tipped up. "We do. I'll get the bartender to bring some more cases back to the kitchen for you while you make a round with this tray."

I stayed true to my word and sought out the bartender for more booze, but as I turned to leave him, I saw the bride and groom headed in my direction. I picked up my pace and calmly rushed into the kitchen, knowing full well they wouldn't dare follow me in there. On my way to the back door, I noticed another tray of drinks sitting unsupervised on the counter. After swiping a full flute, along with an unopened bottle, I made my way outside.

Suddenly, I could breathe again. The worry that had taken root in my stomach had evaporated, leaving me feeling free. The light feeling could have come from the alcohol, but I chose to attribute it to getting out of that toxic fucking wedding.

And maybe a little came from the alcohol.

The fresh air and the ocean breeze were precisely what I needed. The scent of salt swept by, a sign that the ocean was near, and solidified my decision to go get wasted on the beach alone.

After navigating the backstreets and alleys, I found myself on the boardwalk. I bent down, careful to avoid spilling my drink, and slipped off my heels so I could pick them up. The beach and the boardwalk were deserted, with not a soul or a seagull in sight.

Do seagulls even come out when it's close to dark?

Maybe April was too early for seagulls, or even people for that matter, to visit the beach. It wasn't freezing out, and the alcohol had started to warm me up. I was good to go.

In the distance, a ramp leading onto the sand came into view. With sore feet, I hobbled to the entrance, hurrying to sink my feet into the sand. The minute the soles of my feet landed on the deep, soft sand, instant relief spread and soothed the aches and pains.

"I'm fucking pissed," I declared. I kicked at the sand with my feet as I made my way down the beach. Not only did I come to the ocean to get away from that awful wedding but I came for peace and quiet. But that wasn't the case, because there was one lone busker on the boardwalk, strumming a guitar. "Goddamn buskers. Ruining my peaceful beach moment."

Had I walked by him and not even noticed, or had he just showed up? I wasn't sure I cared enough to leave either way. My eyes drifted shut as I turned my attention back to the ocean. The sound of waves crashing onto the shore was a calming presence, as if it was calling to me, beckoning me further out into the dark unknown of the ocean.

The ocean held mystery and was captivating in all the ways we weren't aware of. The vast body of water scared a lot of people.

But it didn't scare me.

"Do you always narrate out loud like that?" a deep voice called out, practically causing me to jump out of my skin.

When I turned to face the mystery man on the boardwalk, I caught him looking me up and down. His gaze was a mixture of amusement and appreciation. I couldn't blame him for his reaction. I was a mess. I was attempting to hold up the bottom of my dress with one hand—an effort to avoid getting it dirty—while fumbling with my heels and trying to not spill my glass of champagne. Not to mention the unopened bottle underneath my arm.

No wonder he was staring.

"Not usually, but in my defense, I don't even know what I said out loud versus what was in my head." I smirked.

He remained quiet as he propped up his guitar and leaned against the railing of the boardwalk with his forearms. A grin overtook his features before settling into a better smirk than what I'd dished out just moments ago. He chuckled. "You said you were pissed and something about goddamn buskers ruining your beach moment."

Within five minutes of meeting each other, this man had managed to dish back my attitude and then some.

That was hot as fuck.

I threw back the last of the champagne in my glass. "Sounds about right." I frowned as I looked down at the empty flute, as if it would have magically refilled.

"Busker," I exclaimed as I held up the unopened bottle. "Make yourself useful and open this for me, would you?"

One of his eyebrows quirked questioningly as I made my way up the ramp to join him on the boardwalk, holding out the bottle for him to take.

"I have a name, you know," he said.

"Actually," I huffed, dropping my shoes to the ground while letting go of my dress. "I don't know that and don't care. Are you going to open this or not?"

He sighed, grabbing the bottle from my hand a bit too aggressively. As he worked the cork free, he eyed me carefully, taking in my appearance. "What are you doing out here anyway, princess?"

I batted my eyelashes at him. "Thanks for noticing. I *am* a princess."

He opened the bottle and took a long drink before handing it back to me. I grabbed it as aggressively as he had done to me a few moments ago and lifted the bottle to my lips.

"I was the maid of honor at a friend's wedding. I just needed some air."

He held out his hand, gesturing for the bottle.

I shook my head, wrinkling my nose at his request. "Princess doesn't like to share," I replied. I lifted the bottle back to my lips and chugged more than usual as he gazed at the column of my throat, taking in each movement I made. When I pulled the bottle away from my mouth, there was desire in his eyes. Desire that heated his gaze even more when I wiped my mouth with the back of my hand.

The tips of his mouth turned up. "If you're the maid of honor, why are you out here by yourself?" he questioned.

He wasn't alone in his desire. I appreciated what I saw, too.

I hesitated as I contemplated what to tell him. Deep down, I knew I'd never see him again, so what was the harm in being honest? There was just something about him. Maybe it was his devilishly good looks that reeled me in. The sharp ridges of his jaw with a shadow of scruffy beard matched the dark brown hair that was styled neatly, and he had the greenest eyes I'd ever seen.

I cleared my throat, my eyes snapping back up to meet his, and shrugged. "Let's just say that someone else's trash is another person's treasure."

His brow furrowed. "What the fuck does that mean?" Understanding and pity flooded his features as what I meant hit him. "Your ex is getting married?"

I took another long drink. "Yep. My ex-boyfriend is marrying my childhood best friend. He cheated on me with her," I said with a laugh. "Guess I dodged a bullet, though, so I've got that goin' for me."

He stepped closer, reaching for the bottle. I handed it over willingly, and his Adam's apple bobbed as he drank. It was sexy as hell. I couldn't look away even if I wanted to.

He caught me staring and smiled. "It's his loss." He took a few more steps toward me, closing the distance. "You're gorgeous, princess."

"Oh, busker," I said as I pretended to fan myself. "I bet you say that to all the women dressed in gorgeous emerald green formal gowns and drinking alone on the beach at night."

He extended his hand toward my arm, and his fingertips

trailed from my shoulder down to my wrist before he grabbed my hand and laced our fingers. "You're not alone anymore."

My breath hitched as he gave my fingers a gentle squeeze. I tilted my head, looking up at his moonlit face. "No. No, I'm not." I leaned into him, grabbed the bottle from his hand, and took one more drink before placing it on the ground next to us. "Come here, busker."

"You better hold on, princess. I think I'm the one who found the treasure tonight, and I don't plan on letting you go."

Before I could respond, his mouth came crashing down on mine in a frenzy full of need and desire. Everything happened so quickly—tongues dancing, hands exploring every surface of each other's body as if the other held the answers we were desperately seeking.

His mouth moved from mine, navigating down my neck, over my collarbone, and then back up to my already swollen lips. "I hate that you're wearing this fucking dress right now."

"Mm-hmm," I murmured. The anticipation was killing me. "Need you. Now."

He growled as he pushed my dress up to my hips, ripping off my nude lace panties in the process and shoving them into his back pocket. His fingertips trailed downward until he reached my swollen clit, and the stroking of his fingers sent shockwaves throughout my body. My head leaned back as the pleasure erupted. The breeze from the ocean caressed my skin, making my nipples taut and rub against my dress. The sensation was overwhelming and painfully teasing.

He leaned down and whispered into my ear. "This is going to be a night you'll never forget." He pushed his cock toward me, the length of it hitting my stomach. "I'm going to make you feel like no man has ever made you feel before. I'll show you how much of a treasure you are."

His words drenched my already wet core as his length grew

harder against me. He gripped my waist and spun me around before placing my hands on the railing. His lips trailed down my neckline, igniting the spark even more. "You sure?"

"Yes. Treasure me. Make me yours."

I could hear the sound of his belt being undone, the buckle jingling along with the tug of a zipper, followed by the shuffling of clothes being moved out of the way. The head of his cock teased my entrance before he thrust into me and immediately began moving. I screamed out in pleasure, uncaring of who might hear. He was all I cared about. I leaned my head back as he grabbed my hair, tugging me back to him, sliding in deeper than before.

"How does the princess like this?" he growled as he pulled out, flipped me around, and leaned my back against the railing. "I want to watch you as you come apart for me."

In one swift movement, he lifted me and slammed back into me again as my legs wrapped around his waist. He watched me with his emerald green eyes, as if he were imprinting this moment and memorizing the chaos that was us losing control of ourselves.

My muscles began to contract, squeezing around him. Just as I'd been ready to cry out in pleasure, he captured my mouth with his, giving my bottom lip a little tug. The mixture of pleasure and pain coursed throughout my body as he led me over the edge, joining me in our combined free fall as he buried himself deep within me.

Exhausted, I rested my head on his shoulder and slowly unwrapped my legs from his waist. The hem of my dress fell to the ground as he cupped my face, running his thumb over my lower lip, where he'd just bitten, before leaning down to kiss my bruised, swollen lips.

"You are the greatest fucking treasure, princess."

2

MAX

Present Day

Standing in front of my closet, I realized I didn't have the slightest clue about what the fuck to wear to a wedding rehearsal.

My friends, Beckett and Ellawyn, were finally getting the happy ending they deserved, and I was happy for them. But I couldn't deny that it made me wonder if I'd ever find someone to share a life with like that. I hadn't been with someone who lit me on fire since I hooked up with a random gorgeous stranger on the beach a few years back. The worst part was, I still thought of her, and I never even found out her name.

I was a fucking idiot.

The reminders of her were constant. From the emerald green color of her dress to her loosely curled blonde hair and the champagne bottle tucked under her arm. I never hooked up so quickly like that, but with her, the pull was undeniable. I hadn't been able to think of anyone else since.

Pulling myself out of memory lane, I finally caved and

texted Ellawyn to ask what the fuck to wear to her dinner tonight.

Her response was immediate.

> **ELLAWYN**
> Hey, this is Ellawyn's wedding planner. She asked that I respond to you since she's busy right now. Keep it casual. Ellawyn and Beck are going for comfort. You might consider a nice pair of jeans and a button-down. Nice shoes, too.

I hadn't been expecting a reply from a stranger, but at least whoever it was told me what to fucking wear. I thought back to last Christmas and vaguely remembered Ellawyn talking about someone planning her wedding. I responded with a simple thank-you that went unanswered. I went to my dresser and pulled out a pair of jeans before snagging a black button-down to go with it.

Time to celebrate the two most important people in my life.

I PARKED BEHIND MY BAR, Remnant Hearts, and walked the few blocks to The Vault, a local banquet hall where the rehearsal dinner was being held. Since Ellawyn and Beckett weren't getting married in a church and didn't need to rehearse anything, they'd just decided to have a nice celebration dinner for everyone instead.

The Vault building had always been a favorite of mine. I just hadn't ever had a real reason to go inside. It had once been an actual bank, but now it was used mostly for formal events, corporate functions, and sometimes themed nights. But it wasn't a place for somebody to go alone, so I was more than happy to get to check out the inside for once.

The entryway was a high archway with a single light hanging from the center of the arch. The double doors were framed with black accents.

Simple but nice all the same.

When I entered the building, I found Beckett standing near the bartender and joined him. "Hey, man. How's it going?"

I glanced around the big open space. There were two levels. The lower level was the biggest, and the upper level was open and looked out over the lower level. On the upper level, there was a DJ, and the lower level housed all the circular tables for the dinner and the bar. There was also an open vault on the lower level that led into the restrooms. "Where's Ellawyn?"

He nodded up toward where the DJ was. "She's over there with the wedding planner."

Ellawyn stood with her back to us, looking down at something with a blonde woman in a black suit.

"Awesome," I said, glancing around the space once more. "It's nice in here, dude."

Beckett and I spent the next twenty minutes or so talking while we waited for the other guests to arrive. Just as the venue got more crowded, the sound of clanking on glass echoed throughout the room, and everyone's attention turned to the blonde on the balcony above us.

"Attention, everybody. Please find your seats."

The voice registered in my mind as a memory fought its way to the surface, not quite able to break free.

Turning around, I tried to catch a glimpse of the woman, but she'd moved further back on the upper level and had hooked her arm through Ellawyn's as they chatted with the DJ. I forced my attention away from them momentarily and wandered around the room as I looked for a rectangular place card with my name in some fancy-ass script.

Beckett and I found our table at the same time. He pulled out a seat for Ellawyn as she made her way down the stairs toward us. Ellawyn looked lovely in a shimmery gold dress with lace detail. She looked happy, too.

"Thanks, babe," she said, smiling up at Beckett while she took her seat. Ellawyn turned her attention to me next. "Hey, Max," she greeted as she placed her napkin on her lap. "Thank you for coming."

Pulling my attention away from trying to catch the wedding planner, I refocused on Ellawyn. "No thanks necessary," I answered with a smile. Just as I was about to ask who the wedding planner was, she finally turned around and we were face to face.

It felt like I had the wind knocked out of me. The recognition was immediate. The voice and woman staring down at the lower level was the woman from the beach a few years ago. It was the voice that moaned in my ear and screamed as I brought her to climax. The woman I fucked on the boardwalk and walked away from right after.

The one that got away.

As she looked down over the second-floor railing, her gaze drifted over the various tables until her eyes settled on mine. Her jaw dropped as the color drained from her face.

Not necessarily the reaction I'd hoped for. I expected her to visit our table, even if it was just to use Ellawyn as an excuse to get closer to me, but she didn't. Instead, she organized a shit ton of gift bags before heading down the stairs and handing the bartender an envelope. She gracefully darted between tables, careful not to get too close to mine, and grabbed her coat from the rack before slipping out into the dark streets of Quimby Grove.

I wanted to chase after her, to see if she was all right. Reluctantly, I turned to Ellawyn. "Who is the wedding planner?"

A big grin spread across her face. "Funny you should ask," she started. "She's the woman that won a date with you at the Mr. Claus function last winter." She wagged her eyebrows at me, a mischievous smile forming on her face. "That's Marley of Events by Halligan. She's an event planner from New York City."

"Then why is she here?"

Ellawyn's eyes narrowed. "Well, I liked her work and begged her to help plan my wedding." She studied me for a moment. "Is something wrong?"

I shook my head. "No, I'm sorry." I looked toward the door that she'd just exited from. "She just looks familiar and I can't place her," I lied.

Not too long ago, I'd confided in Ellawyn about the woman from the beach all those years ago and how much regretted letting her leave the boardwalk without so much as a name. Hell, Ellawyn had even painted the scene for me after hearing my story. She didn't seem convinced by my answer now, but she decided to play along anyway.

"Maybe you two can chat and see if there's any overlap. She left to go decorate Starlight Books for tomorrow, but you can talk with her then. Plus, you owe her a date."

What are the odds that the woman who ended up bidding on me for a Mr. Claus contest would end up being my mystery woman? Pretty fucking slim, I'd say.

"Sounds good," I said to Ellawyn as I picked up my beer. I took a sip as thoughts of my beach bombshell continued to fill my mind.

I barely recognized Starlight Books when I walked in for the ceremony. The entire bookshop had been transformed. The tables, chairs, and couches that had always been in the café had been removed for the evening.

In their places were about fifty black velvet chairs with metal gold-finished legs. They were divided in half by a small aisle going down the middle. The ceiling was adorned with so many strings of twinkle lights that when they flickered, it created a starry night type of setting. At the end of the makeshift aisle stood a tall wedding arch that had been covered in dark vines and more twinkling lights.

The back section of the bookshop had been set up with round tables that had black tablecloths draped over them. In the middle of each table was a stack of books with an arrangement of flowers made out of book pages. Each place setting included a name card that resembled a library card, and the area was sprinkled with confetti made from the pages as well.

It was impressive. Even more so now that I knew who was responsible for all the small details and hard work that went into creating this night for Ellawyn and Beckett.

It was beautiful and unique, much like the woman who had made it happen.

Beckett came up behind me, clapping me on the back. "Showtime," he said.

The ceremony had been quick and painless, unlike some of the other weddings I'd been to throughout the years. Ellawyn's parents had traveled in from Moon Harbor, and her father walked her down the aisle while her mother had sobbed in the front row. Ellawyn cried right along with them, just like

Beckett had cried when he first saw Ellawyn walking down the aisle.

While it was nice to watch my two best friends get married, my eyes stayed glued to the blonde event planner as she worked her magic, making sure the ceremony went just as planned. The downside was that she'd avoided looking at me at each opportunity she got. When our gazes would meet, she'd avert eye contact.

It was starting to piss me off. I spent the entire reception trying to figure out why the fuck she wouldn't acknowledge me.

Maybe she regretted our night together.

I pushed my food around my plate, glaring down at the table and ignoring everything around me. How could she be in the same room as me, yet ignore me after the moment we had shared?

I tapped my foot, feeling a headache coming on.

"What's the problem? Is the food bad?" Beckett asked as he deposited himself into the seat next to me.

"No," I grumbled in response. "The food is fine." My fork fell to the plate before I turned to Beckett to explain. "I think I hooked up with the event planner a few years back. She's been ignoring me all night."

Beckett laughed. "You realize she's *working*, right?"

I glared at him as I picked up my beer and took a drink. "So?"

He sighed. "Let me put it to you this way. If an old hookup showed up at the bar while you were busy, would you stop everything to go catch up?"

Honestly, I wouldn't. But I wouldn't have pegged princess —I mean, Marley—as the type to compartmentalize like that. I picked up my beer and finished it as I let the revelation sink in that she probably wasn't ignoring me to be rude but rather because this was her business and she was working.

I could respond to that. I didn't care for it, but I could respect it.

The rest of the evening was spent moving on from Marley and enjoying myself with Ellawyn and Beckett. We danced to stupid music, drank a shit ton of beer, and played board games in honor of Benji after things had settled down a bit.

As the folks at my table started to set up a game of Scrabble, I felt her eyes on my back. I craved her attention. I grabbed my beer bottle and twisted my body so I could see her. Keeping my eyes on hers, I brought my beer to my lips and smirked as I took a drink, then wiped my mouth with the back of my hand just as she had done all those years ago.

A pink hue spread across her cheeks. If I had to guess, I'd bet she was thinking back on our night together, too. She reached up and tucked a piece of hair behind her ear before pulling a notepad out of her purse and jotting something down. She slid the note over to the cash register before grabbing her coat and purse.

When our gazes met again, I gestured to the empty seat next to me, hoping she'd join me. Instead, she ignored me and walked into the bookshop's kitchen. I stood from the table and went to the cash register to find the note she'd left. Unfolding the paper, I hoped it was meant for me, but it was for Ellawyn, wishing her a happy wedding and letting her know she'd be in touch tomorrow.

I slid the paper back onto the register for Ellawyn to find later before going into the kitchen, hoping to catch her. But she was already gone. When I stepped outside the back door, there was no trace of her.

Just my damn luck.

3

MARLEY

Wandering around the streets of Quimby Grove on a Sunday morning was not as productive as I would have hoped. It felt kind of nice, though. Quimby Grove had that small-town charm I read about in books or watched on television.

It felt like what I'd always imagined a small hometown would feel like.

Quimby Grove Square was the hub of the town. A gorgeous white church with stained glass windows sat directly on one of the corners of the square, along with two courthouses on two of the other corners of the square that were right across from each other. One is what locals have dubbed the old courthouse, whereas the other is the new courthouse. The last remaining corner of the square had another lovely church.

All the streets of the square were lined with small businesses. Standing at the corner of the old courthouse, I could see a retro-looking theatre with a marquee that was lit up down the street, along with tattoo parlors, a wine bar, and restaurants and shops galore.

It was lovely.

Uncertain of which direction to go, I headed down the opposite street toward one of the churches and in the direction of Starlight Books. I'd decided to venture out this morning in hopes of running into a certain someone who had been a constant on my mind for these past two days. The only problem was, it was difficult as fuck to accidentally run into someone when I didn't know their name, where they lived or worked, or literally anything about them besides the fact that he'd given me the best sex I'd ever had.

And that was just a quickie against a railing on the boardwalk with our clothes on. Imagine what we could have done if we'd had time on our side.

Letting out a groan, I kept walking toward the bookshop.

Running into my hookup from years ago had not been something I'd have thought would happen. Had I dreamt it would happen? Yes. Had I hoped to find him? Also yes. Would finding him have made my life so much easier, allowing me to live with myself a little better? Yes. One hundred percent yes.

No questions asked.

Except I should have asked at least one question last night. Such as, oh, I don't know, maybe what his fucking name was would have been a nice start.

Whatever.

As I made my way down the block, I appreciated small-town living. Each person that passed me on the street said hello and smiled at me. The gesture was so surprising that I couldn't help smiling back and returning the greeting.

When I got closer to Starlight Books, I saw that the light was on inside and picked up my pace. When I reached the door and lifted a hand to knock, the blinds opened, and Ellawyn's smiling face appeared.

She flipped the lock and held the door open for me. "Good morning, Marley," she singsonged.

"I'd ask you why you're in a good mood, but I already know." I winked at her as I stepped inside, sliding my coat down off my arms. "I have a weird question for you."

She pinned me with a smirk. "Let me guess." She strode toward the back of the shop, pulling me with her toward the kitchen. "You want to know who the guy was that practically eye fucked you last night?"

"Ellawyn!" My cheeks flamed. "Uh, yeah, actually," I said, unsure of how much to share. "He looked familiar."

"His name is Max, and he's Beckett's best friend." She clapped her hands together. "And he's who you won a date with at the Christmas fundraiser!"

Oh hell.

"Oh. Max, is it? Do you know where he works or if he'll be around today?"

While I wished I could stay and get more intel on Max from Ellawyn, I had a train to catch soon and didn't have much time to waste. A quick chat would have to suffice for today.

A playful smile stretched across Ellawyn's mouth as she passed me a blueberry lemon scone. Waiting for her to respond, I tore a piece off and popped it into my mouth.

Damn, the pastry was amazing.

"He works across the street at Remnant Hearts Bar." She waited a moment. "You going over there to ask him out?"

The scone caught in my throat. "What? No, of course not," I muttered, practically choking.

She rolled her eyes and slid over a bottle of water. "He's probably over there already. He does the prep in the morning." When I didn't respond right away, she continued. "He's alone if you did want to go check him out."

Visiting Max was a necessity, not a social trip. I exhaled and tried to keep my tone casual as I slid back into my coat and threw my purse over my shoulder. "I am going to go visit, but not for that reason."

"All right, but come say goodbye before you head to the train station, okay?"

"I will," I promised.

Sure enough, as soon as I stepped out of Starlight Books, I saw Remnant Hearts Bar right across the street. It was hidden right under my nose this whole time. Holding my head up high and squaring my shoulders, I took off toward the corner of the block and pressed the crosswalk button. Cars slowly drove by, the drivers smiling as I waited. They looked carefree and happy, while I was about to walk into a man's bar and alter the course of his life forever.

The crosswalk sign changed from a red hand to a green person walking. The countdown started at twenty, a vicious reminder that my time was up.

I hurried across the street with just a few seconds to spare, took one last deep breath, and opened the door to step inside Max's space. It was quiet as I eased the door closed behind me before moving further into his bar.

Remnant Hearts, much like the man from years ago, had its distinct vibe. There was an old red telephone booth against the far wall of one side of the room. In a corner sat a full suit of armor. Like, armor that a knight would wear. The rest of the walls were decorated with vintage metal signs, old photographs of the town, and local memorabilia.

This felt like the man from four years ago.

"We're closed," a voice called out from behind me.

Jumping at the sudden noise from behind the bar, I turned around to face him. His features softened as he took me in, his eyes trailing from my face and moving downward until they worked their way back up again. "Hi, busker."

He threw his head back, laughing. "Princess."

"Mind if I sit for a moment?"

"Not at all." He gestured to a barstool in front of him. "Water?"

Max looked even better than the past two nights I'd seen him. Even more handsome than when we had hooked up, too. His emerald green eyes shone brightly. His hair was cut shorter but a tad messier on top. He had a little scruff, but not too much. His broad shoulders filled out the fitted long-sleeve button-up that left his tattooed forearms on display because he had the sleeves rolled. He wore a black apron to protect the front of his shirt and his dark denim jeans.

He was still fine as hell.

"Marley? Did you hear me?"

I slid onto the barstool in front of him and shook my head no while my mouth betrayed me by saying yes.

"Which is it?" he questioned, his brow furrowing.

"I'd love some, thanks."

He grabbed a glass from below the bar and filled it with that bar hose thing that bartenders use and then slid the drink to me instead of just setting it down in front of me. "Why didn't you come to talk to me last night?" He leaned forward, resting his forearms on the bar. "I was hoping you would."

A straight shooter. A no-bullshit kind of guy. I took a drink of my water and hoped like hell that he'd appreciate the same straight shot I was about to lay on him soon.

"Sorry about last night. And the night before that. I wasn't expecting to see you, and you knocked me off-kilter a bit." I wiped the condensation off my cup with a finger, drawing a heart in the process. "And I was working. I was trying to remain professional."

That explanation was mostly true. I do strive for professionalism while working, and I refused to have this conversation with him while at a client's wedding, even if the client was his best friend.

He didn't respond right away. Instead, he took a rag over the top of the bar and started to refill the glasses underneath the bar. "I get that." He turned away, grabbed a rolling cart full of clean utensils and napkins, and started to roll silverware. "I heard your name was Marley Halligan."

"It is. And you're Max something."

"Quinn," he said with a wink. "Max Quinn." He turned his gaze downward, rolling more silverware with a line forming between his eyebrows.

He didn't continue speaking. I'd have thought he'd been happy to see me this morning, based on his persistence last night.

"Did I come at a bad time?" I couldn't stay much longer, not if I wanted to catch my train on time.

"I'm glad you're here. I was just trying to figure out what you're doing here so early in the morning. It seems like you've got something on your mind."

Time for that straight shot. "Max, you're a dad."

The silverware he'd been about to roll fell straight to the floor, and the clattering noise sounded louder than it should have. Then the silence took over, and Max didn't move an inch. He stood so still that I was concerned he wasn't breathing at all.

After what felt like an eternity, he placed his hands on the bar and straightened his arms out, as if to maintain a distance between him and the piece of wood between us. "Marley, is it?"

His tone was laced with disbelief and condescension. It took every fiber of my being to not roll my eyes at this man and lash the fuck out. But I knew that wouldn't get me anywhere productive.

"Yeah, and you said it was Max, right?" My quick comeback caught him off guard enough that his head snapped up to meet my gaze, hitting me with a glare.

"We were only together one time," he snapped.

Now this bullshit was getting harder to tolerate. "One time is all it takes," I argued back. "And I don't recall us using a condom, unless you were a magician and pulled one out of a hat. But the cum running down my leg that night would indicate otherwise."

Max's pupils dilated as he processed what I'd said. "I thought you were on the pill."

This wasn't going as planned. In my head, he was more understanding and caring. While I had expected shock, I hadn't anticipated him being this much of an asshole about it. But I guess I didn't know him much at all. "I wasn't," I bit back.

He rounded the corner of the bar, coming around to stand next to me. "Are you sure I'm the father? How can you be sure?"

I gave him my infamous *you've got to be fucking kidding me* face as I took a step toward him, getting close. "Well, considering I don't typically fuck strangers on the boardwalk, and given I can do basic math, I know you're the dad."

He stared at me, stunned and silent.

I checked the time on my phone and noticed I was dangerously close to being late. I exhaled, trying to remain calm and levelheaded. "Listen, I've got a train to catch so I can get back into the city on time." I held out my phone for him. "Why don't you add your number so we can get in touch sometime this week to talk?"

He scoffed. "I'm not giving you my number." He grabbed my dirty glass and walked it back around the bar to the busboy container. "I want a paternity test."

"Shocker," I mumbled as I slid my phone back into my

pocket. "I'll have one shipped to the bar. You can do the test at home and then mail it back to the lab."

"Good. Because until anything can be proven, I don't want anything to do with you," he growled.

"Awesome, busker. Just awesome." I wasted no time leaving the bar and letting the door slam in my wake. With only one stop left to make before heading to the train station, I went to Starlight Books with a fake-ass smile plastered on my face and high hopes to not return to Quimby Grove anytime soon.

Max Quinn could go fuck himself.

4

MAX

Marley waltzed into my life, threw a curveball, and walked right back out. As soon as the door slammed closed, I rounded the bar and sat down in a chair as the news sunk in.

I'm a father.

Marley's voice replayed in my head on an endless loop. She'd just come right out and said it. No pretenses, no softening the blow or anything. Just a matter-of-fact statement.

Had she been lying?

Despite me being a colossal dick, I hadn't gotten the vibe that she'd lie about that. But I guess it was a possibility. A chance that she'd learned I owned a bar and decided to pick me as the father of her kid because I'm a business owner.

But that didn't make any fucking sense either.

Marley was a business owner, too. At least I thought so. The chance to ask her about herself was nonexistent. Shit, I couldn't even tell her how nice it was to see her after these years or the fact that I hadn't stopped thinking about her since our time together.

No one had ever measured up to her fiery personality or had come close to lighting a match to how beautiful she was.

I'd always considered her the one that got away. I'd have given anything to go back in time and get her name and phone number. To spend more time with her. To know her.

And when I finally saw her again, I fucked up and made her out to be a liar.

I threw a rag across the bar, letting it hit the wall and leave a streak of water as it slid down onto the floor. Resting my head in my hands, I closed my eyes while I tried to make sense of everything that had just happened.

The sound of the door opening and closing wasn't even enough to get me to open my eyes and greet whoever was inside. I ignored them, listening to the footsteps as they grew closer to where I was sitting. Suddenly, something wet hit me on the shoulder. My eyes flew open, focusing on the figure standing in front of me—Beckett.

"What the fuck?"

"Just came to chat," he said with a shrug. He pulled out the barstool that Marley just vacated and sat down. "Marley just came to tell Ellawyn and me goodbye before heading back into the city."

"And?"

Beckett scanned my face, his eyebrows raising. "And she looked pissed off. I heard she was over here beforehand. What happened?"

I reached for a glass, filled it with beer, and took a drink. "She told me I'm a father," I said, just as blunt as she did.

"You knocked her up that one time you hooked up years ago?" He ran a hand through his hair before resting his head in his palm. "Damn."

"Apparently," I said, looking down at my beer. "I just told

her I didn't believe her and want nothing to do with her until I know that the kid is legally mine."

It sounded harsh, even to me. I knew that and I heard it when I told her I wanted a paternity test. It was a moment of instant regret. But at the same time, my defenses had been up. Should they have been? Maybe not. But I needed some time to collect myself.

"That was a dick move. I do know she has a kid, though. I've heard her say things about having to go pick them up or hearing a kid in the background."

The weight of the news settled onto my shoulders, along with how I'd treated her. I pushed the beer away and filled a glass of water instead. "What do I do, man?"

"Well, first, you stop being a shitty bartender and give me a beer."

I grabbed a clean glass from the shelf under the bar, almost wishing I'd finished my drink before switching to water, and filled it with beer. I set it on the bar in front of him. "Anything else?"

Beckett smirked. "How about some of those little boats of peanuts?"

"Fine," I grumbled as I headed into the kitchen to pour some peanuts into a little paper serving dish. "Here," I said, dropping them next to his beer as I sat back onto my chair.

Beckett chuckled as he popped a peanut into his mouth. "Do you not believe her?"

"I might have been a dick at first, but yeah, I think I believe her." My only excuse for being such an ass boiled down to my being afraid and thrown off guard. The woman I'd desperately wanted back had waltzed into my bar and dropped a hell of a bomb.

She was ballsy, I'd give her that. It wasn't what I'd expected her to say, even though I wasn't sure how I had envisioned us reconnecting. But that just wasn't it.

I was a dick, though, and there was no excuse for it.

Beckett laid his forearms on top of the bar, leaning forward slightly. "Either you do or you don't." He sat back, arms crossed over his chest. "Which is it?"

"I believe her," I said without hesitation.

"Then there's only one thing left to do." Beckett wrapped a hand around his beer and took a long drink.

I sat up straighter. "What?"

"Go get your girl."

IF I EVER MADE ANOTHER impromptu trip to New York City, I would not take the goddamn train again, that's for fucking sure. I ended up driving to Harrisburg to catch the next train into the city. Which meant three hours in a noisy train car filled with people who talked way too loudly on video calls with their significant other without wearing headphones. Or the people who talked and laughed too loudly with the person they were seated beside.

It was enough to drive me crazy.

After arriving at Penn Station and fighting my way up to street level, I realized I had no clue where to find Marley. In retrospect, I should have spent some time on the train looking up some information. I pulled my cell from my back pocket and searched for Events by Halligan. The first website that pulled up looked promising, so I clicked on the link and, sure enough, Marley's face popped up on the corner of her website.

Damn, she looked gorgeous in that photograph.

Her long blonde hair was styled in loose waves, lying over her shoulders and coming down her chest. Her ocean-blue eyes were polarizing, with a depth I could drown in. Her lips were a glossy shade of pink that shined in the photo. But the best part was her smile, stretching so wide that it met her eyes.

I'd lose myself in her image if I wasn't careful.

Scrolling to the bottom of her website, I found an office location in the footer section: *913 W Hudson Street, New York, NY.*

Score.

"I just need to know where I can find her," I explained for the umpteenth time.

The receptionist rolled her eyes as she continued filing her fingernails. "Sir, I'm not just going to give out my boss's location." She scoffed. "I ain't about to get fired for you."

The woman had become a thorn in my side and a pain in my ass. If I had to guess, I'd bet she was in her late teens and more concerned about her manicure and cell phone than with me. She also brought a shit ton of attitude to the conversation.

She must get it from her boss.

"And as I've told you, I'm the father of her child."

She scrolled through her cell phone, liking photos and videos that popped up on the screen. "That's interesting. She told me the father of her *child* dropped dead," she quipped.

Between wanting to pull my hair out and yelling at the receptionist, I was amused that Marley had told her I'd dropped dead this morning. If I hadn't been so annoyed with the woman sitting in front of me, I may have laughed at that. "She only said that because she was pissed at me."

"I wonder why. But that doesn't help your case." Her cell phone buzzed on her desk, causing the receptionist to glance at the caller ID and then back to me. "Excuse me. I have to take this."

When she turned her back to me, I glanced down at her planner that was lying open on the top corner of her desk and searched for today's date. She'd noted Marley's exact location. Marley was at a sweet sixteen party at the eagles recreational building.

That was almost too easy.

"I'm just going to count my losses," I said to the back of the receptionist. "Thanks for your time."

She waved me off with a flick of her wrist without so much as a glance in my direction. I headed back down the hallway and left Marley's building while mapping out where exactly the recreational building was. Thankfully, it was within walking distance, but I'd arrived before I was mentally ready to go in and face her. After all the shit I'd said today, I wouldn't be surprised if she made me get on my knees and beg for forgiveness.

The longer I stood on the sidewalk outside of the building, the more nervous I became. After wiping my palms on my jeans, I pulled open the door and followed the sounds of pop music blaring from inside. The large room where the party was being held had been filled with teenagers. Bodies upon bodies were in the middle of the room, dancing all over one another as they sang the lyrics to some song I didn't know.

The room was decorated with pink and black decorations with gold accents. Twinkle lights hung from the ceiling, along with a chandelier made of crystals. Even the cake table had been elegantly decorated, and the cake itself looked like a work of art.

Marley had done a damn good job on this party.

Trying to remain unseen, I circled the perimeter of the room while I searched for Marley. I'd almost missed seeing her.

She was shorter than a lot of the teenagers in attendance. She was in the opposite corner standing alone, watching the party unfold from the sidelines as she bobbed her head to the music.

I made my way across the dance floor so I could talk to her. But when she noticed me, she crossed her arms over her chest, and I stopped dead in my tracks.

Because that girl looked *pissed*.

5

MARLEY

After a horrible confrontation with Max this morning, I had to head back into the city to set up for the biggest sweet sixteen gig I'd ever been able to land.

This teenager, I shit you not, was worse than a bridezilla. She changed her mind on the theme at least seven times, had multiple cake tastings with all the well-known bakeries within the city, and had been rude to every single vendor I used for this party. I'd taken it upon myself to send handwritten thank-you notes to each one, begging them not to hold this party against me.

That's how bad this teenager was. Her future husband would be in for a real treat when the time came.

Despite how horrible the planning and execution of this party had been, the result was stunning. Everything turned out as we'd planned. From the chandelier to the twinkle lights and floral arrangements, it'd all come together perfectly. I was obsessed with the setup and even made sure to snag plenty of pictures for my portfolio before the party kicked into gear.

I'd been in awe the entire time I'd been a wallflower tonight.

Typically, I hung around for events I'd planned, ensuring everything went smoothly and to help facilitate cleanup. Considering this party would end at nine this evening, I'd be in for a long night. Killing time at these events after everything was in full swing could be difficult.

So I did what I do best. I people-watched.

There was just something so intriguing to me about watching people in their environment when they were unaware they were being watched. I could easily pinpoint those who were truly happy or those that were just trying to fit in. As someone on the sidelines, I got to watch it all play out in front of me.

I enjoyed watching people's stories unfold.

I placed myself in a dimly lit corner of the room and positioned myself so I could see everything that was happening without being too obvious. Unfortunately, there wasn't much to see. The dance floor was packed with sweaty teenagers who tried to show off their dance moves as if they were the best dancers to grace this party.

My gaze drifted from the dance floor to the perimeter of the room, searching for anything of interest. The adults were mingling, watching their kids dance, and one man was walking around the room, alone.

Focusing my attention on him, I craned my neck to get a better view as he came closer. But I didn't need to see much more. Because I knew that man. That man, wandering around a sweet sixteen party, was Max. I stood straighter, plastering a scowl onto my face as I crossed my arms over my chest while he made his way toward me.

"What are you doing here?" I asked.

He frowned. "I deserved that."

I sighed. "Come on." I grabbed him by the arm and led him out of the main room and into a small one across the hall that had a few chairs, along with a couch. I settled into a spot on the couch and pulled my legs up onto the cushions before stretching them out. He watched me get comfy and then followed my lead, opting for the recliner closest to me.

"You can't just show up to my events. How did you even know where I was?" I paused a moment as I reconsidered. "Actually, I don't want to know. But I'm betting my receptionist was involved."

"She wasn't much help," he muttered as he reached down and tugged on the lever of the recliner to let his feet go up. "I'm sorry that I said I didn't believe you." His eyes were focused on mine, unmoving. "I do believe you, and I always did. But a part of me just couldn't believe *it*, you know?"

That was a feeling I knew all too well."Yeah, I get that. I'm sorry, too. I could have delivered the news better than I did. It just didn't come out the way I'd rehearsed."

"I can't even imagine trying to plan a conversation like that. But as soon as you left, I regretted how I handled it and knew I couldn't wait a moment longer to talk to you. So I came to you, hoping we could talk and that I could take you out to dinner tonight."

"Wait, what?"

Did Max just ask me out to dinner after how badly earlier had gone? "You realize it's almost dinner now, right? And that I'm stuck at this party?"

While he considered what he was asking, I took a moment to soak him in. He'd changed out of his long-sleeve button-up and into a black V-neck T-shirt with a white logo for Remnant Hearts. The logo was kind of cool. It was focused around two hands, both holding a beer that met in the middle to tap the bottles together in a 'cheers' type of fashion. The T-shirt was tight and pulled across his chest in a way that outlined all the peaks and valleys of his muscles. His jeans fit him like a glove. The look was simple, but it worked for him.

He was just as handsome as I remembered.

Max's voice pulled me away from ogling him. "Can someone cover for you?"

"Oh." I sat up on the couch, tucking my legs underneath me. "Is dinner tonight really that important to you?"

"Yes," he said without hesitation. "I have to be back in Quimby Grove to open my bar tomorrow morning. I would have tried to work something out so I could stay longer, but I didn't have the chance. Plus, I heard I owe you a date from Christmas."

He was here, wanting to talk. I couldn't say no to that and potentially isolate him. "Yeah, you do owe me a date." I pulled out my cell and sent a message to my receptionist to come and cover for me. "All right, we'll go to dinner. My receptionist is coming to take over for me, so I have to go let my client know."

We both stood, heading toward the door. "Great. Where should we go for dinner?"

"McGee's Pub." I had a gut feeling that tonight's dinner wouldn't go too smoothly, so going to my favorite restaurant seemed like a small win. "I'll meet you there around eight."

"Can I pick you up?" he questioned, holding the door open for me.

"Maybe next time." I smiled as I stepped past him and headed across the hall. "See you at eight," I called over my shoulder before I disappeared into the main room where the party was.

"You're going on a date," Avery crooned and then lowered her voice to a whisper. "With the father?"

"We're just going to dinner. It's not a real date." I huffed. "Now shut up and help me figure out what to wear."

Avery followed me around my apartment as I looked for my favorite pair of black boots. I tore apart my bedroom while she went into my walk-in closet and came back out holding my favorite knee-length boots.

"Thank you." I snagged them from her and tossed them onto the bed before going to my dresser for a pair of black tights. I threw them onto the bed as well. "Do I dress more casually or more businesslike?"

She shrugged. "Does it really matter at this point?" She tilted her head, eyeing the boots she'd just brought out from the closet. "Are those mine?"

I glanced back at the boots. "No, those are mine," I said as I pulled out a pair of high-waisted shorts from my dresser. "You just borrowed them forever ago and didn't give them back until recently." I snagged a black belt and tossed it onto the bed with the rest of my outfit. "I just want to make a good impression."

A shirt—I needed a shirt. I dove back into the trenches of my closet and found my favorite long-sleeve black shirt. It was casual but hugged my curves like a second skin. I laid the outfit on my bed and turned to Avery. "What do you think?"

Avery paused at the foot of my bed before sitting down on the storage ottoman. "I think you're stressing too much about dinner with a man you've already boned." She patted the spot next to her. "Mar, come here."

Slumping down next to her, I laid my head on her shoulder. "It's not about me. I'm going up to bat for the loves of my life," I exhaled. "I feel like I'm making a sales pitch."

She threw an arm over my shoulder and pulled me closer. "The outfit looks great. It's stylish without trying too hard. It's completely you." She kissed the top of my head. "You'll look beautiful, as always."

Feeling thankful for my sister, I pulled her into my arms and hugged her tight. "Thanks, Avs." With renewed confidence, I gathered my clothes from the bed so I could shower and get ready. Before entering the bathroom, I turned back to Avery and found her lying on my bed reading a magazine and laughing at the articles. "For your loving sisterly moment, you may *borrow* two items and one dress from my closet."

"Oh my god." She dropped the magazine and rushed into my closet. As I turned on the shower, all I heard were her squeals and the sound of her jumping up and down.

When my cab pulled up to the curb outside of McGee's Pub, I spotted Max standing on the sidewalk right outside the entrance. I stayed in the cab a little longer than I should have and admired him from a distance. He truly was handsome. He must have gone shopping, because he traded in his bar T-shirt for a new black button-up and held a small bag that was likely carrying the old shirt. It was adorable and had me smiling from ear to ear as I exited the cab. When he hadn't noticed me getting out, I called out to him.

"Hey, good looking. You new around here?" I tried to sound casual, playful even. I hadn't wanted him to see how much this dinner was stressing me out. I wanted to remind him of the woman he met on the beach.

His head whipped around, and a huge grin spread across his face. It was a smile that lit something up inside of me. One that had the nerve to wake up the butterflies that had been dormant for all these years.

The warm, fuzzy feeling was nerve-racking as I made my

way toward him, willing those pesky butterflies to go back into hibernation. "Glad to see you found my favorite Irish pub."

Max met me in the middle, his eyes assessing me up and down. "Yeah," he said, shifting his eyes back down my body once more. "You look amazing."

"Thanks," I said as I yanked on the door and held it open for him. "You're not so bad yourself. I like your shirt."

He paused and rubbed at the back of his neck. "Marley." He stepped behind me, took hold of the door, and gently urged me inside ahead of him by placing his band on the small of my back. "You'll always come first."

The touch was electric. Sparks shot all throughout my body, lighting up my entire being. I hadn't felt like this since he had last touched me. It was as if my entire body was on fire, and he was the only one who could extinguish the flame and contain me.

I shivered at the thought.

"This place is awesome," Max shouted over the TVs while he looked at a menu.

"What are you drinking, busker?" I asked as I pursued the drink options myself. When I looked back up at him, I noticed that his eyes were focused on my mouth. Without thinking, I licked my lips as my cheeks heated. "I think I'm going to have the S.O.B. drink," I said, returning my attention to my menu.

"The S.O.B. drink?" He flipped his menu over, looking for the drink selection. "Oh, vanilla vodka and cola. I've never tried that mix." He shifted in his seat. "But don't worry, I know you don't share," he said with a wink.

If I hadn't known any better, I'd have thought he was flirting with me. But he couldn't possibly be. I was the mother of his two kids. Men like Max weren't interested in being with single mothers, even if he was the father of said kids.

Right?

The waitress came, took our orders, and returned with our drinks right away. While I had ordered the S.O.B., Max settled on a drink called The Naked Man, which was some sort of whiskey concoction.

We waited on our food and made small talk about New York City and the sweet sixteen party I'd planned. He went on about how impressed he had been and how everything at the party had looked so nice. He said he'd never seen anything like it.

I had to admit, it felt damn good to have my hard work noticed.

Especially by Max.

"I appreciate the compliment. Thank you." I rolled out my napkin and placed it onto my lap. "My job is very important to me. I've worked hard to make a name for myself as an event planner in the city."

He nodded, understanding showing on his face. "I feel the same way about the bar. It's special to me, and I've put a lot of work into making it a staple in my small town. It's not New York but—"

I cut him off. "If you thought I meant to insinuate that my business is somehow superior to yours, I didn't. I'd never think something like that."

"I know," he said. "I'm just nervous. I never got the impression you'd be someone to say shit like that." He combed his fingers through his hair before leaning on the table. "I think I just want to dive into the elephant in the room if that's okay."

Now it was my turn to be nervous. "Sure." I waited, letting Max be the one to steer this conversation. I couldn't imagine how much was on his mind.

"I'm a father," he mumbled, mostly to himself. "The kid is about five?"

"Yeah, you're a dad," I said and laughed. I took a drink and then continued. "They're four years old. Turning five in December."

He grabbed his phone from his pocket and typed something out. "Okay, turning five in December. What date?" His fingers flew over the screen as he typed out his questions and the answers.

"Are you taking notes?"

He looked up, his eyes wide like he'd been caught stealing cookies from the cookie jar. "I don't want to forget anything."

Okay, that was sweet. Too sweet considering the butterflies in my tummy had woken up again. "December thirteenth is their birthday."

His fingers raced across the screen again as he wrote down the new information. Just as he had opened his mouth for another question, the waitress appeared with our food.

We went back to our small talk as we ate and enjoyed our meals. As the silence took over the table again, I could tell that Max still had a lot on his mind, so instead of throwing information at him, I took a few steps back and continued letting him come to me with questions as he processed all of this.

After we finished eating, Max insisted on being the one to pay for our dinner. "Listen," he started. "I know our dinner wasn't the most productive, and I have to go back to Quimby Grove tonight, but I was wondering…"

"Wondering what?" I pulled out my phone and requested a ride on an app as he continued talking.

"Can you visit Quimby Grove for a weekend? We could get to know each other properly, and I could learn about my kid."

My phone almost dropped to the ground when I comprehended his question. I pinched the bridge of my nose as I tried to think this through. A few weeks out of town could be doable. I only had consultations and planning sessions lined up for the rest of the month anyway, and I could do those things remotely. It truly felt like the perfect time, if we were going to do it.

And I owed it to my kids to do this.

"Yeah, I can most likely arrange that. Give me a week or two to figure out my work schedule and move some things around, then I'll give you a call at the bar to let you know when we're coming. I'm sure the kids would love spending time in Quimby Grove."

Max's shiny eyes locked on mine, the relief evident. "Awesome." He extended his phone toward me. "Call your phone from mine so we have each other's numbers."

"Wish we would have thought of that back then," I joked, grabbing his phone and dialing my number. When my phone rang, I hung up and handed it back to him just as my ride pulled up. "I'll be in touch," I promised, and slid into the back of the car.

When I looked back at him out of the rear window, his eyes were waiting for mine. He smiled and waved goodbye.

6

MAX

Two weeks had passed since my trip to New York City to see Marley.

That night, back in New York after we'd had dinner, I spent the entire train ride back to Harrisburg thinking about this new reality I'd been thrown into. Marley hadn't mentioned what she expected of me now that we'd reunited, but I knew it all boiled down to one thing.

Acceptance.

Accepting Marley and my... my kid.

It was never a decision. There was no way I'd be able to walk away from my kid. It was all I'd thought about since returning home to Quimby Grove.

Would the kid like me?

Would Marley introduce me as dad right away?

How involved would Marley want me to be? I knew I wanted to be as involved as possible. A thousand questions swirled around my head at all times. It had been hard to think about much of anything else, sleep included.

Beckett and Ellawyn had stopped by the bar to check in.

They'd been great about giving me my space, and they hadn't bugged me with a single question. But I knew that would change tonight.

They'd invited me to dinner at the bookshop so we could hang out and catch up. But I'd known exactly what they wanted to catch up about. Marley and me. I pulled the door open, the bell over it chiming, and entered the shop.

"Lock the door behind you." Ellawyn's voice carried from the kitchen.

"Got you," I shouted as I locked up and pulled down the blinds. I'd just flipped the open sign to closed when Beckett came in from the kitchen.

"Hey, want a drink?"

"Sure. Water would be great." I headed toward our usual table and sat down. "Anything I can do to help with dinner?"

"Nope." Ellawyn walked over to the table with three bottles of water in hand and sat down beside me. "How're you, Max?" She handed me a bottle and placed the other two on the table for her and Beckett.

"Things are pretty good. How about you, Ellie?"

"All good. Can't complain. I just got married to the most amazing man, and business is going well here in the shop."

"Steady business is worth celebrating, for sure. Can't complain about mine either," I added.

Ellawyn had been monumental in getting my business back up to speed and helping it grow. She designed a new logo and even helped brainstorm ideas on how to get more buzz around the bar.

I was eternally grateful.

Beckett appeared from the kitchen, carrying three plates and utensils. He put a plate in front of each of us. "Dinner is served," he said, and grinned as he sat down.

"Ellawyn." I laughed. "Did you have Beckett make us all grilled cheese sandwiches?"

She raised her chin. "You bet I did." She took a big bite and held a hand in front of her mouth. "They're delicious."

They were, indeed, delicious. We chowed down on our food and enjoyed one another's company. The three of us had been through so much. It felt nice to spend some time with them again. Two weeks without their company had been far too long.

Ellawyn had just finished eating and had propped up her head with her fingers laced together under her chin, staring right at me. She cleared her throat. "Have you talked to Marley lately?"

I shook my head. "No, but she's supposed to come visit for a weekend soon."

Ellawyn turned her head, looking guilty as she gazed anywhere but in my direction. "Um. She's coming... tomorrow."

That got my attention. "Tomorrow?" I sat up straighter. "As in tomorrow, tomorrow?"

"Yeah. They're staying in my old apartment while they're in town," she explained.

You've got to be kidding me. My... well, I didn't know what Marley was to me yet, but she didn't even bother to tell me she was coming to town tomorrow.

"I've got to go," I announced, gathering up my dirty dishes and taking them to the kitchen sink.

Beckett followed me, bringing his and Ellawyn's dishes with him. "She wasn't sure if you knew or not."

After throwing my water bottle into the recycling bin with a bit too much force, I turned to him. "It just sucks that Marley didn't bother to tell me about it herself. I have a right to know."

"I agree."

"I'm going to head out and try to get out of this annoyed mood before they get here," I said flatly.

Instead of going back to the bar to help close, I decided to bypass it, along with my truck that was parked out back, and just walk home. I didn't feel like dealing with drunk people, and I'd probably be in too much of a bad mood for the customers anyway. Besides, a long walk could help clear my head.

Once I got home, I couldn't help but think that this was the last time I'd view my home as one of a single man without a family, and it'd been a long time since I felt connected to someone in a familial way.

Tomorrow, everything would change.

Tomorrow, I was no longer in it by myself.

IN CASE MARLEY showed up early this morning, I made it a point to be at the bar earlier than normal. If I weren't a stubborn man, I'd have sucked it up and asked Ellawyn when Marley planned to arrive. But I was still a bit bitter last night and refused to ask.

After I had pulled my head out of my ass last night, for the most part anyway, I looked around my house and tried to envision what it would look like with a kid. Would I be the type of parent that made them have a playroom or the type that would let toys be wherever they ended up?

I pictured colored pages on the refrigerator and melting crayons in the oven, turning them into fun shapes. I pictured hugs each morning and night, along with forehead kisses and tummy tickles. I pictured running through the yard playing tag and chasing fireflies at night. I could even picture the first time I punished them and the apologies that would come after.

I pictured it all. I *wanted* it all.

But right now, I needed to focus on work until they arrived. I'd been behind on my usual tasks all morning. I went into the kitchen and loaded the dishwasher so I'd have clean glasses for tonight.

The door to the bar opened, and then a female voice called out my name. I rushed out of the kitchen and into the bar, but my steps faltered once I saw Marley standing in front of me, smiling.

She was wearing an emerald green sundress with her hair in a bun on top of her head. She looked beautiful. The fact that she chose the same color she'd worn the night we met wasn't lost on me either.

I stared at her unabashedly for another beat before moving my gaze downward. What I saw made my breathing halt. Because I saw not one but *two* children.

Had Marley mentioned there were two kids?

She cleared her throat. "Max?"

"Hey, Marley." I closed the distance between us and crouched down to greet the children. "Who do we have here?"

A little hand shot out in front of me. "Hi. I'm Izzy Mae Halligan, and I'm this many." She smiled brightly as she held up four little fingers.

She was adorable and almost a spitting image of Marley. Izzy had curly blonde hair with the most dazzling green eyes. Staring into her eyes was like looking in a mirror. She wore a tie-dye dress with pink leggings underneath and little sandals.

Taking her hand in mine, I gave it a gentle shake. "Hi, Izzy Mae Halligan. It's nice to meet you. My name is Max." I pointed to her dress. "I love your outfit. It's so colorful."

"Thank you!" She beamed with pride. "I can never decide between colors, so Mama says this pattern fits best."

Marley ran her fingers through Izzy's curls, laughing.

My attention turned from Izzy to the little boy next to her. "And who is this?"

Izzy was the one who spoke up again. "This is Jax Luke Halligan. He's also this many." She held up her four fingers again. "Jax is what Mama calls *shy*," she said with a hand in front of her mouth, as if she were whispering. Her volume stayed the same, though.

My laughter couldn't be contained. She was cute. "Hi, Jax. I'm Max and I'm so happy you're here."

He didn't answer me, but one side of his mouth tipped up a bit. He had blonde hair with a bit of a wave to it, along with those same piercing green eyes as his sister. The same eyes as *me*. He was dressed nicely with a black button-up shirt and khaki shorts.

This kid could be my damn twin.

Suddenly, it dawned on me. I looked up to Marley for confirmation. "Twins?"

She nodded. "Yep. They're my little munchkins." She took both of their hands and led them over to a booth and got them settled in beside each other. "Here are your favorite coloring books and the best crayon packs from home." Marley placed the identical items in front of each kid and gave them each a kiss on their forehead. "Mama is going to grab us all drinks, okay?"

I rounded the bar and continued watching as she interacted with her children. Our children. I could tell she was a great mother and loved them both so much.

She joined me at the bar a few moments later. "You were great with them."

"They're cute. I wish I'd known I had twins instead of just one kid," I teased. "But they're adorable, princess. You've done an amazing job as their mama."

A blush crept up Marley's cheeks. "I'm sorry. I thought I

mentioned it at dinner that night. But it was a crazy twenty-four hours. I didn't want to overwhelm you."

"Makes sense." I grabbed four plastic cups and filled them with water. "I take it twins run in your family."

"They do," she said as she wrapped her hands around two of the cups. "I have a twin sister named Avery."

"Oh god, there's two of you?" I joked with a wink.

She rolled her eyes and led the way back to the table to join Izzy and Jax. Marley and I slid into the opposite side of the booth, our arms brushing as we interacted with the kids. Each time, a jolt of electricity passed through us, and we shared a knowing look.

The connection was undeniable and alive as ever.

"Are you our daddy?" Izzy asked as she rooted through her crayon pack.

The water I'd just thrown into my mouth almost came flying out, but I managed to choke it down. "I see you have your mother's no-nonsense approach to life."

Izzy's face scrunched up as she pulled out an orange crayon. "Huh?"

When it came to expectations of how this moment would go, I had none. I'd only hoped that when the time came for us to tell them, they were happy with the news. But Izzy asking during our first meeting had thrown me for a loop. I could tell it'd thrown Marley, too. Marley looked at me, questioning if we should tell them. I gave her a nod of approval.

"Izzy, Jax," she started, waiting for the kids to pause their activities. When their crayons stilled, she continued. "Max is your daddy."

My breathing halted as I waited for their reaction. But nothing happened. They both just said okay and continued with their coloring pages as if the question hadn't been asked to begin with.

One of the hardest parts of this had just gone without issue. We spent another hour or so coloring together. Izzy and Jax had both pulled out the last page of their coloring books so that Marley and I could color matching pictures with them. We colored an image of a unicorn with a rainbow, while Izzy and Jax worked on an image of trolls under a bridge in the forest. They giggled as they chatted with Marley, and she joined in on their laughing fits as if she hadn't a care in the world.

The envy was real. I was eager to have that relationship with them, to catch up and become a constant in their lives like she was. But that relationship would take some time to cultivate.

But for them, I had all the time in the world.

The door to the bar opened, and in walked a customer. Reluctantly, I left our booth to wait on the customer while the little family I'd just met continued playing. But even as I served the customer, my eyes tracked each and every move they made, and I felt like I was missing out on something really special.

After taking the customer's order, forcing myself to give him my full attention like I'd do any other day, Izzy suddenly appeared at the barstool next to the customer. I chuckled, watching her try to climb up onto the stool and then was proud when she finally made it on her own.

"Hey, Iz," I said with a big smile. She placed her water cup onto the bar. "Would you like some more water?"

She nodded eagerly. "Yes, please."

I grabbed the cup and filled it halfway with water and placed it in front of her. "Here you are, sweetie."

"Thanks, Daddy," she said, sliding down from the barstool. When she landed firmly on her feet, she carefully picked up the cup with two hands and held on tight. I kept my attention on her the whole time, and I didn't notice Marley approaching.

"Busker," she whispered. "Did Izzy just call you Daddy?"

I nodded, my eyes welling up with tears.

Marley laughed. "She warms up quickly. But I wasn't sure if she'd do that with you, too." She looked back over toward the kids and smiled. "It's a relief, you know?"

Only Marley had no idea just how much of a relief it was. She'd always had the affection of the children, as she should. But I was a stranger walking into their lives. They didn't have to welcome me with open arms, but Izzy had. She had accepted me already.

"I really liked it," I admitted to Marley. "It...it fit."

Marley crossed her arms over her chest, watching as our kids behaved alone. "I'm glad you're okay with her calling you that," she said over her shoulder.

"Thanks, princess," I said, tugging on the ends of a few strands of hair. "Do you guys want to eat lunch here? I can grab a menu."

"Oh shit," she said, glancing down at the watch on her wrist. "I actually have to meet Ellawyn over at Starlight Books for lunch with the kids. The three of us are staying at her old apartment, and she's giving me the keys over lunch.

"Oh. That makes sense." There was so much I wanted to say at that moment. I wanted to beg them to stay for lunch. I wanted to drive them back to my house and get them settled there. I wanted them imprinted into every facet of my life. Ultimately, I wanted more time with them. But I knew I was being greedy, and I just had to remind myself that there would be plenty of time for that in the future.

"Let me help you get the kids ready," I said instead.

Marley and I joined the kids back at the booth, and the four of us worked together to clean up all the crayons that were sprawled out on the table and those that fell onto the floor.

"I'll get them off the floor," Izzy exclaimed before diving under the booth and hitting her head almost immediately. "I'm okay," she shouted from underneath the table, a giggle following her right after.

Jax focused on the crayons on the table, packing up his box first and then starting with his sister's box before neatly stacking the coloring books on the table.

Once everything was packed up, I knelt in front of the kids. "Thank you both for visiting me and spending some time with me today." I held out my arms, feeling hopeful. "Can I get a hug goodbye? But only if you want to."

I was hoping for a lot with this. But Izzy had me on cloud nine ever since she called me daddy.

The twins grabbed each other's hands and laced their fingers together before stepping forward into my embrace. Two little arms squeezed tightly around my neck as I hugged them back and gave them a little squeeze before releasing them.

"Thank you for the hug."

When I turned to the side, I saw Marley standing behind us, beaming with happiness, her hands clapped together in front of her mouth. "Come on, kids. Let's grab some lunch and get the keys to where we'll be staying." She stepped up, coming to my side, and lowered her voice. "Come by after work?"

"I can, but it'll be late."

"That's fine," she said, grabbing the kids' hands.

After we all said our goodbyes, I held the door open for them and watched as they crossed the street. Only when they were safely inside Starlight Books did I look away and go back to work.

7

MARLEY

The hype of Starlight Books was real. My kids were obsessed with the entire shop. They loved it all. The books, food, drinks, the couches, the big windows, the board games, and back to the books again. They were in their glory.

They especially enjoyed meeting Ellawyn and Beckett. When they learned that they'd be sleeping at her apartment this weekend, they were ecstatic. I wasn't sure if they thought her place would be just as magical as the bookshop or what, but they were thrilled.

The best part for me was watching my kids adjust to Quimby Grove. It would make coming back here frequently an easy adjustment.

Ellawyn's apartment had been a pleasant surprise to us all. It was within walking distance of Quimby Grove Square, which meant we could walk to Max's bar whenever we wanted and essentially just walk wherever we needed to. The apartment itself was way better than I'd imagined.

I must have been used to small New York apartment buildings being the norm.

Ellawyn had a lovely two bedroom apartment with an open floor plan. Once you stepped inside, you were right in the middle of it all. The kitchen, a dining room table, and the living room all filled one huge living space. It wasn't cramped, though. Each section had plenty of space. The master bedroom had a king-size bed, and the second bedroom had a queen.

The kids and I worked together to settle into our new home for the weekend. The kids claimed the smaller bedroom, which was adorned with colorful paintings, while I placed my suitcase in the master suite.

Once we were somewhat organized for our stay, we decided to order a pizza from a local shop called Georgie's Pizza and stayed in for the evening. I was exhausted after a long day of travel.

The kids cheered from their temporary bedroom as the sound of the doorbell echoed throughout the apartment, signaling the arrival of our pizza.

"Time to wash up for dinner," I called out to them as I went to answer the door. After paying for our food, I deposited the pizza onto the dining room table and went into the kitchen. "Where the fuck are the plates?" I said under my breath, hoping the kids didn't hear me as I opened cabinet after cabinet. I'd been about to give up when I opened the cabinet over the stove and found them.

"Aha. There they are." I internally cheered as I grabbed three.

"Hi, Mama," Jax said, coming up to my side in the kitchen. "Can I help?"

"Of course, love bug. Why don't you take these plates to the table and set them at three of the chairs for us?"

He happily grabbed the plates and raced into the dining room, where he set each plate down with a thud.

"Not so rough in there, please," I called to him as I grabbed three bottles of water from the fridge and a handful of napkins. "Izzy, come eat, please."

Izzy rushed out, wearing a different dress than she had on previously and a bow clipped to her hair. "Do you think Daddy will like this dress?" She grabbed the fabric at her sides and held it out, slowly spinning in a circle.

"Of course. He'll love it. You're very beautiful." I pulled out a chair for her and waited for her to get situated before scooting it closer to the table. "But remember, Daddy has to work tonight, so he won't be joining us for dinner."

Her smile dropped, and instantly, a frown took its place. She pulled the bow from her hair and pushed her bottom lip out, pouting. "When will we see him?"

Jax sat next to his sister and took her bow from her before placing it onto the table and grabbing her hand. "When, Mama?"

Hearing Jax ask about Max almost had tears of joy forming. My reserved little man was asking about his father when he hadn't said much about the situation all day. "We'll see him again tomorrow morning," I promised. "Let's eat before the pizza gets cold."

The rest of the evening was spent cuddling on the couch and watching movies together until it was time for Izzy and Jax to have their baths before bed.

And they *loved* bathtime.

Ellawyn's apartment had a huge vintage clawfoot tub in the master bathroom. Beside it was a homemade makeshift ladder that had been used to hang towels. Leaning against the wall was a bathtub tray I certainly planned to make use of while we were here. It was simple, yet elegant.

The kids each took a turn pretending to swim in the tub, soaking up every minute of it. By the time they were finished with their baths, I'd been met with heavy eyes and big yawns. I led them into the second bedroom and helped them get settled together under the covers of their big bed. I tucked the blankets tight around their bodies, shoving my hands underneath them to get the covers in there really good.

"Snug as a bug in a rug," I teased.

They giggled at the comment.

I shrugged. "We like being silly around here." I gave them each a kiss and got their little kisses on my cheek to return the 'lovins,' as they called it. "Sweet dreams. I love you."

"Sweeter dreams. Love you," Izzy replied.

"Sweetest dreams. Love you, Mama," Jax added.

That sweet dreams trio had become our ritual over the years. The words were comforting. I knew that no matter what changed, no matter what we'd have to endure, we'd get through it because we had one another. As I pulled their door shut slowly, I listened as Jax and Izzy each told the other they loved each other and said goodnight.

Yeah, I'd get through anything as long as I had my munchkins with me.

A KNOCK on the door woke me from a deep sleep. I rose from the couch and went to the door. "Who is it?"

"Max."

I glanced down at my outfit, making sure I was decent enough to answer the door, and was pleased to see I was wearing flannel pajama pants, bunny slippers, and an oversized men's graphic tee that had a cat on it, along with text that read 'let's get weird.'

At least a boob wasn't running rogue and popping out of a tank or something. Not embarrassed in the slightest, I opened the door, groaning at the bright lights that lit the hallway. Max was nothing but a silhouette because I couldn't see shit.

"Come in," I mumbled before going into the kitchen for a drink.

Max followed me into the apartment, closing the door behind him and locking it. "Were you asleep?"

My eyes darted to the microwave, and I noticed it was eleven thirty. "Uh, yeah." I pulled a can of Pepsi Zero out of the fridge, thankful I brought some with me from home. "Want a drink?"

He smiled down at my Pepsi. "Sure, I'll have what you're having." I gave him the can I'd just pulled out of the fridge and then grabbed myself another one. "Since you were asleep, do you want me to leave?" he questioned, cracking open his can of soda.

Shaking my head, I cracked mine open too and took a drink. "I'd like it if you stayed. And I knew you were coming. I should have stayed awake," I said and laughed. "I just didn't realize how late a bartender would be. How dumb."

I walked into the living room and sat down on the couch. Max followed behind, laughing, and it was like music to my ears. He sat down on the couch, leaving a space between us.

"Not dumb," he said. "I'm the idiot who said I'd stop by after work. If I worked a normal nine-to-five job, it wouldn't have been as late."

"But I'm the one who invited you, busker."

We fell into easy conversation. It was effortless. We talked about how his night at work had gone and what the kids and I had done earlier in the evening. When Max's stomach growled, I warmed him up some leftover pizza, but he scolded me and gave me a lesson all about how room-temperature pizza is superior to warmed-up pizza. We ended up testing his theory, at his request, and afterward, I conceded and agreed with him.

Max surprised me by clearing his dirty plate and the rest of my dirty dishes. He rinsed everything off and placed them into the dishwasher while I got cozy underneath one of Ellawyn's blankets that she'd left here.

"It's weird being here again," Max said from the kitchen.

He'd been here before? He never mentioned it.

"How do you mean?" I asked, sitting up straighter on the couch.

My mind raced as I tried to figure out any scenario that would have involved Max being in Ellawyn's apartment. Had they dated before she met Beckett? Or was it just a friendship sort of familiarity?

Max walked in and joined me on the couch, sitting a little closer this time. "Well," he started as he pulled part of the blanket over his legs, "Ellawyn had a stalker for a while, and that fucker had broken into her apartment and knocked her unconscious."

"What the fuck, busker?" I twisted my body to see him better. "How could you not have mentioned this to me?"

He shrugged. "I wasn't sure if Ellawyn had mentioned it to you or not. And I didn't want to say anything in front of the kids in case it'd scare them."

Oh.

Well, that made sense. "So what ended up happening?"

Max continued to recount what had happened between Ellawyn and her stalker. Apparently, the stalker had ended up being Beckett's grandfather, Benji's, neurosurgeon. He'd expressed an interest in Ellawyn when treating Benji, and she had declined his requests to date him. That led to the stalker becoming obsessed and going after Ellawyn in her own home. Max and Beckett managed to get to Ellawyn before anything worse had happened to her.

Scary things could happen in even the smallest of towns

that seemed otherwise safe. I was incredibly lucky to be where I was in life, even with the hand I'd been dealt.

"I had no idea you were such a hero for the town of Quimby Grove," I teased, shoving him playfully on the shoulder.

"Beckett was the hero of that story," he insisted. His gaze went to the ground, hesitantly, before looking back toward me. "There's only one woman I'd risk everything for, princess." His eyes were serious, filled with such devotion and conviction.

My cheeks flushed, and I ducked my head. "I should go to bed. It's late and the munchkins are early risers." I rose from the couch, leaving the blanket on Max's lap. "Feel free to sleep on the couch... if you want. The kids were promised they'd see you first thing in the morning anyway."

He toed off his shoes, laughing. "Anything for you and those munchkins."

"Night, busker," I said, lingering in the bedroom doorway. He lay down on the couch, an arm slung over his face as he got comfortable on the sofa.

"Sleep tight, princess."

His face looked relaxed in the dim light of the moon, a slight smile lingering before he rolled over, turning his back to me.

I WAS deadass tired when my alarm went off at six thirty. I made sure to wake up before it was humanly possible for Max to be awake. Part of me was worried he'd left in the middle of the night. The thought soured my stomach. The kids wanted him here, and I found myself feeling the same way. I peeked my head out into the living and found him still sleeping, with an arm thrown over his eyes. It was adorable.

Once satisfied that he was fast asleep, I checked on the twins and then hopped into the shower and got myself ready for the day. When I returned to the living room, Izzy and Jax were standing directly above a sleeping Max. I moved into the kitchen and started a pot of coffee.

"Hey, kids," I whispered. "Come here, please."

Izzy and Jax held hands and tiptoed their way over to me. I bent down and wrapped my arms around their waists and picked them up and placed them onto the counter. Soon, they'd be too big for me to pick them up at the same time. My babies were growing up. "What are you two doing over there?"

Jax giggled. "Watching him."

My shy little man was certainly coming out of his shell. The way children treated people always blew my mind. So full of hope, so innocent. I hoped they didn't lose that as they grew up. "Do you want him to wake up soon?"

"Duh," Izzy said, looking over her shoulder toward Max. "He needs to do stuff with us, Mama."

A part of me should have worried about how quickly they were getting attached to Max. But I wasn't. It just felt right, as if a piece of our puzzle had been missing and we suddenly found it, realizing it was the perfect fit.

"Why don't you go wake him up?" I suggested. After all, being woken up by kids was part of the parenting territory. It was Max's turn.

Their little eyes grew with excitement. I lifted them both off the counter and poured myself a cup of coffee as they walked over to the couch and peered down at an unknowing Max.

"Do it, Jax," Izzy urged.

Jax had a big smile, with only a hint of mischief, plastered on his face as he leaned over Max and tried to shake him awake. When Max didn't budge right away, Izzy moved over and worked on shaking his legs with as much force as she could muster.

Max woke up, practically jumping out of his skin, and looked between Izzy and Jax. "What happened?" he asked, running a hand over his face.

"Time to wake up," Jax said. "This is your two-minute warning."

"Yeah, or you'll go into time-out," Izzy continued.

Laugher erupted out of me as I doubled over, laughing my ass off. "Oh my, that was hilarious."

Max sat up on the couch, glaring at me. "Ha, ha," he teased. "I take it you've been a bad girl a time or two, Marley? Have you ended up in time-out?"

My eyes went wide as my cheeks tinged with embarrassment.

He smirked and changed the subject. "What's on your agenda today, Mar?"

The kids climbed up onto the couch and sat next to Max, one on each side of him, practically gluing themselves to his sides. The man didn't have an inch of space to spare for himself.

"Will you take us out?" Jax asked.

"Take you out..." Max looked at me, his eyes pleading for help.

I grabbed a cup of coffee for Max and brought it with me into the living room. "Here you go," I offered before going to sit down on the recliner. "They want you to spend time with them today. Like to go into town or just do something together."

Max nodded as he took a drink of coffee. "Yeah, I can probably do that. I just have to go to the bar first so I can get the prep going. I can probably pick you guys up here around lunch?"

"It's fine if you have to work today. We understand that this was a last-minute thing. Don't we kids?" I glanced over at the twins, watching their faces turn down in disappointment. Neither responded.

Max watched their reactions too and wrapped his arms around them. "Yeah, it's last minute, but if I go start things now, then I'll be able to take the rest of the day off." He gave their shoulders a light squeeze. "Do we have a deal?"

Jax was the first to respond. "Deal. See you at lunch, Daddy."

Followed by Izzy. "I guess lunch isn't too far away," she said.

"I wouldn't miss it for the world," Max said.

And somehow, I knew he meant it.

8

MAX

Spending the weekend with Marley and the kids just felt right. Despite being nervous over this huge life change we'd all been thrown into, I finally felt as though my life had more of a purpose beyond Remnant Hearts.

Marley, Izzy, and Jax—they were the pieces I'd been missing but hadn't known. Izzy and Jax had quickly become my whole world. Hell, before I even met them, I knew I'd be all in and try to give them everything I had. I wasn't just Max to them. I was already their dad. In a way, it almost felt like it was too soon but not soon enough at the same time.

It was like they knew I fit in with them, too.

The weekend had flown by and had been filled with showing the three of them the sights of Quimby Grove and all it had to offer. The kids loved the slower pace of the town, and Marley had a smile glued to her face the whole weekend as she watched the kids enjoy themselves in my world.

Unfortunately, the weekend had come to an end. My newfound family was scheduled to leave this afternoon because Marley had been called back to the city due to a work situation.

I'd been next to Marley when she'd received the call, and the look she'd given me had been one full of disappointment and apologies.

Since we only had today left, I decided to take Marley and the kids to the bar for a quiet lunch together, where we wouldn't be interrupted every five minutes.

I loved Quimby Grove, but one of the downsides to small-town living was that everyone knows everybody, which meant a lot of people stopped us whenever they saw me. On a normal day, I wouldn't have cared, but today was one of goodbyes, and I was being greedy. I wanted them all to myself.

Last night we spent time packing up their things, hoping to savor every spare minute together today. After we loaded up my truck, we decided to take our time and walk the few blocks to the bar instead of driving.

"Ready, gang?" I asked before leaving Ellawyn's apartment.

"Ready," the kids shouted in unison.

Marley laughed as she ruffled their hair. "Good, I'm starved."

"Remember when we first met and you hadn't eaten anything at all? You'd just been *so* damn thirsty." I bumped her shoulder.

Her face turned crimson. "Hush, you." She leaned closer, whispering so only I could hear. "Although I do remember feeling full by the end of the night."

"Still the same dirty girl, even after all these years," I whispered back with a smirk. If only I could get her alone like that again. My cock stirred in my jeans at the mere thought of being inside Marley again. Pushing the thoughts of a sweet, naked Marley away, I refocused on the task at hand.

"All right, let's go," I said, ushering everyone out of the apartment and locking the door behind us.

We took our time walking through Quimby Grove Square.

We stopped in front of stores that Marley and the kids were intrigued by, and they peeked through the windows. Izzy and Jax were thrilled to find a retro candy store and made Marley and me promise to bring them back soon. And Marley was over the moon about an edible cookie dough shop. She practically drooled on the front window.

It was adorable.

All three of them were.

I wrapped an arm around Marley's shoulders, and we continued our way down the block in the direction of the bar, when a voice shouting her name interrupted us.

Izzy tugged on Marley's hand. "Mama, someone called your name."

We stood on the sidewalk, the four of us searching the surrounding area as we tried to find the source.

"Jakob," Marley said to a man that was coming toward us. "What are you doing here? Hell, how did you even know I was here?" She placed her hands on her hips, waiting for a response.

Jakob smiled at her, opening his arms. "Is that any way to treat your boyfriend?"

The declaration surprised me. Marley hadn't mentioned a boyfriend, although I definitely picked up on some tension between the two. Jakob was tall, with a bit of muscle and a closely shaven head. It was clear as day that he'd used intimidation tactics on women to try to get whatever he wanted. This was a man that wasn't used to being told no.

Marley rolled her eyes at him, taking a few steps backward. "You seem to keep forgetting the *ex* part of ex-boyfriend," she mumbled. She turned toward the kids, grabbed their hands, and continued down the sidewalk until she was in front of Starlight Books. "Be right back," she called over her shoulder before disappearing into the shop.

"What are you doing here?" I crossed my arms over my chest as I waited for his response.

"Came to bring Marley back to New York."

"How did you even know where she was?" That was the part I really wanted to know.

"Her sister told me she was in some town in Pennsylvania called Quimby Grove." He widened his stance. "She needs to come home."

Marley stormed back out of Starlight Books and walked over to where Jakob and I stood. "Jakob, go home. You can't just follow me around like a lost puppy dog."

"You need to come back to the city," Jakob sneered, "where you belong." He looked me up and down, a dismissive laugh erupting from him. "You belong with me, not whoever the fuck this is."

"Watch it," I said, stepping toward him. "You don't get to come to my fucking town and disrespect Marley like that. And definitely not in front of our kids."

Jakob looked between Marley and me. "This is the guy that fucked you and then disappeared?" He scoffed. "This is the guy you left me for?"

"Do you have amnesia?" Marley asked. "I dropped your ass two months ago because you cheated on me. That had nothing to do with him," she said, gesturing over to me.

Jakob's expression softened a bit. "Marley, it was an accident. I told you that."

Marley glared at him. "So what you're telling me is that your cock accidentally slipped inside that other woman over and over again?" Marley cocked her head to the side. "How does that happen?" She scratched her head before turning toward me. "I don't think it works like that, do you, Max?"

When she turned to me for an answer while feigning

confusion, I had to laugh. This woman was as sassy as I remembered. "No, I don't think it happens like that either."

"It's over, Jakob. It's been over."

"We were meant to be together," the man started. "This town has nothing for you."

Jakob's comment made my blood boil, and I could tell that Marley was just over this dude and probably creeped the fuck out. I took a few steps toward Jakob again and placed myself in front of Marley. "You need to leave my town. Leave Marley and her kids alone and just fuck off. If I find out that you continue to harass her, there will be hell to pay."

Jakob looked at Marley. "You'll regret breaking up with me," he warned before storming off down the block, toward the bus station.

It wasn't until Jakob rounded the corner that Marley's shoulders finally relaxed and unhunched. I pulled her into me, wrapping my arms around her as if to protect her from this bullshit.

"An ex-boyfriend, huh?" I questioned as Marley wrapped her arms around my waist.

She exhaled and removed her arms from me. The loss was felt instantly. "Definitely not my proudest moment, that's for sure."

"I think we have a lot to catch up on."

"Yeah." Marley sighed. "Me too."

After the run-in with Jakob, we headed into Starlight Books to get Izzy and Jax and take them to Remnant Hearts for our lunch. As we settled into what Izzy has now deemed our 'family table,' which was essentially just the closest table to the bar, a loud police siren sounded as a herd of police cars sped by.

My muscles tightened at the noise.

"Wee woo," Jax called out, trying to mimic the sirens while Izzy giggled at her brother.

Marley looked up at me, her lips pursed. "Do you think everything is okay?"

A bad feeling settled in my stomach, taking root as all the worst-case scenarios played out in my head. Was Beckett and Ellawyn okay? Did someone get hurt? Quimby Grove was generally a very safe town with a relatively low crime rate. While police sirens weren't unheard of around here, the amount of commotion that just sounded on High Street made me concerned.

"I'm sure everything is fine," I responded, mostly to myself. "I'll go start lunch." I disappeared into the kitchen, letting myself fall into the routine of cooking. It didn't take long for my quick lunch of cheeseburgers and fries to be done.

Just as I was plating the food, my phone buzzed in my pocket. When I glanced down at the screen, it was Beckett's name that flashed across. I answered it, listening as Beckett told me that the Quimby Grove Bakery had been vandalized.

Our small town never saw vandalism to businesses like this. Even the teenagers knew that was a line not to be crossed. Not to mention that the Quimby Grove Bakery had been a staple in our town for decades. It was a treasured small business, with a sweet elderly woman named Charlotte running it all these years alone. She'd known me since I was a baby.

Wanting to go check on her, I grabbed three of the plates and delivered them to the table to Marley and the kids. "A local business was vandalized down the block," I said as I sat a plate down in front of each of them. "I've known the elderly owner for years, I'm going to go check on her quickly if that's all right with you." My eyes darted to Marley's, waiting for a response.

"Of course it's all right," she said, practically shooing me out the door. "Do you need me to do anything?"

I shook my head. "I don't think so. I'll be right back." I rushed out the door, heading toward the square.

A handful of police cars were parked outside of the Quimby Grove Bakery, the street filled with dozens of spectators. The closer I got toward the shop, the harder it was to get through the people. Beckett spotted me from right outside of the bakery and waved me over.

"Hey, what..." My question trailed off as I took in the destruction in front of me. All the front windows were smashed in entirely. The glass in the door had been broken as well, and the door practically hung off its hinges. But the inside was worse.

The display cases were destroyed, broken glass littered the floor, and pastries were thrown across the shop. The tables were flipped and broken. The booths were slit open, completely ruining them. Anything that could be ruined, was. Nothing survived the assault on the business.

"Is Miss Charlotte okay?" I asked instead.

Beckett nodded, his jaw ticking with anger. "Yeah. She was at the bank, doing her daily deposit. Somebody did this within a half hour window." He paused, glancing around him, before he pulled me away from the crowd. "Where has Marley been?"

A tightening twinged through my chest as my eyebrows hunched together. "She's been with me all morning. She's currently at the bar, waiting for me."

"Apparently Officer Barclay wants to question her," Beckett said, voice low.

I wasn't following. "Why? She didn't do this." I gestured to the colossal mess just up ahead. "She was with me the whole morning, literally."

Not only was it impossible for Marley to have done this but she absolutely wouldn't have done this. Officer Barclay was losing his goddamn mind. "You don't think she did it, did you?"

Beckett held his hands up in surrender. "No, not at all. I

think it's just because she's the new face in town this week, and we don't usually have issues with vandalism."

I rubbed a hand over my jaw and exhaled. "It's just a coincidence." I took one more look at the wreckage, wondering where Miss Charlotte was. I'd have to stop by her place and check in on her, make sure she's okay. "Thanks for the heads-up. I've gotta get back to the bar. Marley's train leaves soon, and I'm not missing my goodbyes."

Beckett nodded. "Just let her know that she'll probably receive a phone call at the least." He clapped me on the back and then took off toward Starlight Books, while I turned and went back to Marley and the kids, feeling thankful it wasn't my business that'd been destroyed but feeling brokenhearted over the Quimby Grove Bakery.

S*AYING* goodbye to them was a lot harder than I had thought it'd be.

Despite only having a few days with Izzy and Jax, I felt such a deep connection to them. An invisible tether coming from my heart to theirs. Love taking root and blossoming between us. Everything about them—about us—felt right. Even things with Marley felt right, like we belonged together on a level I hadn't even known existed.

It physically pained me to let them go.

After I returned from dropping them off at the train station in Harrisburg, the activity at the bakery had subsided. It was almost as though the incident hadn't even occurred.

I hadn't told Marley about Officer Barclay wanting to question her. and I wondered if I made a mistake. It was purely coincidence. I'd hoped that the police realized this and just left her alone, especially when I'd been with her all day.

My phone dinged, alerting me of an incoming text from Marley.

> **MARLEY**
> Just letting you know we made it back to the city safely.

I smiled down at my phone, typing out a response.

> Are you and the munchkins actually home safe and sound?

Her response was instantaneous.

> **MARLEY**
> Yes!

A split second later, a photo message came through. I opened the image to see a smiling Izzy and Jax while they ate their dinner. More like devoured their dinner. Their faces were covered in pizza sauce as they each held up a large slice, pausing from eating to undoubtedly say 'cheese' to the camera.

The sight of my kids made me happy and caused me to miss them even more. I pulled up my camera app on my phone and flipped it around so I could take a photo of myself. I stuck out my tongue, making a silly face at the camera, and hit the capture button. I inspected the photo and then sent it off to Marley and the kids, along with a message of how much I wished I were there with them instead of working at the bar tonight. Now that I finally knew they were home safe, I slid my phone away and went back to work.

The night flew by until Officer Allen Barclay sauntered into the bar around midnight. He walked over, pulled out a barstool, and waved to me as he sat down.

"On or off duty?" I asked as I made my way over to where he sat.

He smirked. "A little bit of both." He loosened his tie, freeing his neck a bit. "But if you're asking if I'd like a beer, the answer is yes."

"Rough day, I take it?" I poured him a beer and set it in front of him before I went back to wiping the counter around us.

Allen Barclay had to be here because of my connection to Marley. This man hadn't stepped foot into my bar in years. He wasn't a big drinker.

"Yeah. The Quimby Grove Bakery was badly vandalized today." He paused, gulping down some of his beer before continuing. "But you knew that."

"That's correct." I moved further down the bar, wiping the counter as I went. I wondered what he'd say to me, if he'd outright ask if Marley had done it or ask for an alibi.

He studied me for a few moments before relaxing and lowering his voice. "I'm going to have to question that woman that was with you all weekend. See if she has any... information on this case."

"So you admit that you know she was with me all weekend," I said, throwing the rag underneath the counter and into a bucket. "She didn't do this."

His eyes were locked on mine as he lifted his beer and took another drink. "Interesting. I hear you're the father of her two kids, too."

Officer Barclay could be a real fucking tool. He was a younger cop, not brand new but not as seasoned as most of the police force at Quimby Grove. He was used to getting his way with most things and had gone through a lot of the women that resided in town. Basically, I couldn't fucking stand him.

"If she's a true person of interest, then why isn't the sheriff here talking to me instead of you?"

Allen Barclay's jaw ticked at my comment. Apparently, I'd

struck a nerve. "It must just be a coincidence that the first time she was in town for an extended period, one of our town's shops were destroyed," he answered, ignoring my question about the sheriff. He finished his beer and pushed the glass toward me before he rose from his seat. He rapped his knuckles on the bar and straightened his tie again. "I'll be in touch with her either way." He walked out of the bar and right into his patrol car.

"Son of a bitch," I muttered to myself as I pulled out my phone to fill Marley in.

9

MARLEY

I'd be lying if I said I hadn't lost a little bit of sleep since Max filled me in on the vandalism in Quimby Grove that happened when I'd been in town a few weeks ago. But what I couldn't wrap my mind around was the fact that the local police wanted to question *me* about it. It was the most ridiculous thing I'd ever heard, plus I'd been with Max that entire weekend.

Once we returned home, and after Max brought me up to speed, I'd thrown myself into my normal work routine and spent any free time with the kids. But it wasn't easy.

I used to find comfort in routine and having a familiarity to my day. But now it was the hardest fucking thing. Not just for me, but for Izzy and Jax, too.

The kids missed Max.

Hell, I missed Max, which was something I hadn't expected. I'd figured that the kids would develop a quick connection with him. They were the most loving four-year-olds in the world. Their bond had been almost instant, and I knew that Max had felt the same way about them.

A small part of me had been worried that they wouldn't hit

it off right away. The kids never connected to Jakob in that way. But that was different. Jakob hadn't been around the kids too much, and never alone. Maybe the kids connected with Max so well because they knew he was their dad, and they trusted in that.

Maybe that bond knew no limits or bounds. Maybe that was how real families were supposed to be. I wasn't sure I'd ever understand that type of relationship.

Avery and I never had a relationship with our father. He was barely around when we were growing up. The earliest memory I have of him was from whenever we were five years old.

I'd hidden Avery in our bedroom closet because our parents had been fighting again and she'd been crying. Avery never liked fighting, especially the kind that resulted in shouting. So I'd hidden her away, hoping she wouldn't see or hear anything. When I'd walked outside to where my parents had been fighting, I'd watched as my dad went to his car and put a suitcase into the trunk. He'd slammed the trunk down hard and said his last words to me. The words that forever lingered in my head, stuck on repeat. He pointed a finger in my direction and told me that Avery and I hadn't been worth whatever he'd been going through. He'd gotten inside the car, slammed that door too, and drove away.

I'd never seen him again after that.

And I'd never told Avery what he'd said. I kept that secret and carried the burden for all those years as we grew up. I wouldn't change a damn thing, though. If Avery had known, it would have destroyed her. And I'd have done anything to protect my sister.

So I did feel lucky that Max and the kids had developed a good relationship so quickly. And despite having left Quimby Grove, I knew they wouldn't be without him for long. I also knew that Max was nothing like my father, and he'd never leave his kids behind.

My kids would never know what it felt like to be a burden, for they would forever be loved and cherished.

Staying away from Quimby Grove was difficult. At first, I stayed away because of the whole vandalism investigation. I wondered if I somehow had vandalized the bakery and just had amnesia about the whole thing.

Anxiety was a bitch.

Eventually, I reached out to Officer Barclay after he'd called me with a few questions, and we chatted about my time in town. It was uneventful, and he agreed that he didn't truly think I had anything to do with the incident, but he was doing his due diligence since I was a new face. Which I guess was fine. It was still weird as hell, but it was over now, and I could finally move on from the stress of that situation.

After that, my workload at Events by Halligan was heavy. Consults were back to back for weeks, for events that had been planned months ago, before any of this had happened with Max.

Guilt started to settle in. It felt terrible about being unable to take the twins back to Quimby Grove these past few weeks. And I knew Max felt the same way about the bar. He couldn't just up and leave the bar that he owned.

We were stuck, torn between our livelihood and trying to foster his relationship with Izzy and Jax.

But Max never let those obstacles get in the way of what we could accomplish. Each night, Max would video chat the kids to say goodnight and ask about their days, and each morning, he'd call again and wish them a good day while they chatted over breakfast.

We both wished for more, but this seemed to work for us in

the meantime. It wasn't ideal, but it was better than nothing. We had to work with what we got.

But today... Today had been an excellent day so far. It was early morning on a Friday, and my only client appointment for the day had canceled because she'd called off her wedding. It was a bummer for her but a victory for me. Not only did I now have nothing else planned for today but I also had the entire day off tomorrow, which was rare for an event planner.

Feeling overly excited, I shot Max a text about the good news and then sent a message to Avery, demanding she come over for some twin time. She responded right away with the heart-eyes emoji and two coffee emojis.

My sister was coming *and* bringing coffee. She knew me well. The day just kept getting better and better.

As I waited for Avery to arrive, I picked up the house and tried to ignore the feeling of sadness that soured my stomach when Max didn't text back. We'd gotten closer over the last few weeks. At least I thought we had. Maybe it was really the bond with the kids and not me.

No, we definitely bonded... I think.

The doorbell rang and I shoved my doubts away before I took off running toward the door. Whipping it open, I was met with a barefaced Avery, dressed in an oversized sweatshirt and leggings. Her appearance was concerning. That was not how my sister dressed, even on her bad days.

Not that this was a bad outfit. It was actually quite cute. But it wasn't Avery. Not in the slightest. "Hey, Avs," I said, pulling her in for a hug.

She laughed as she tried to hug me back with hands filled with coffees and a bag from the bakery down the block. "Hey, Mar."

"I hope there's food in that bag." I let her go, ushering her inside and closing the door behind her. "The kids ate all the waffles this morning."

She handed me a hot coffee. "What kind of twin would I be if I showed up to your place miserable *and* without treats?" Avery bypassed me and headed straight for my bedroom.

Whenever we were kids, we always had our most important talks in our beds. We'd climb under the covers and lean against the headboard while we had our drinks and snacks. Talking while cozy provided a level of comfort we had always craved growing up. The habit just sort of stayed with us into adulthood, too.

With a frown, I followed her into my room. We both placed our coffees onto the nightstand tables and pulled the covers down so we could slide into bed. Once we were comfy enough, we pulled the covers up to our laps and grabbed our coffees again before turning to face each other.

Well, I turned to face her. Avery's head was cast downward, gaze focused on her lap.

"Avery, what's wrong?"

She was quiet at first, her hands fidgeting with her paper coffee cup as she ran her fingernails over the sticker that was slapped onto the side of the cup. When she finally turned her head to look at me, my heart nearly broke. Tears fell down her cheeks, leaving a wet trail in their wake. Her eyes were puffy and tinged red like the hue of her cheeks.

"I feel so lost." She said it so low, I almost missed it.

I reached for her coffee and gently pulled it from her hand before placing it on the nightstand with mine. When I turned back to my sister, she launched herself into my arms and cried. If it wasn't for her shaking body and my T-shirt becoming damp, I wouldn't have known she was crying. She always cried so quietly, always suffered in silence, alone. I tightened my hold on her, squeezing her tightly as I kissed her hair.

"It's okay, Avery. I'm here. Let it out." I repeated the words as if they were a chant, as she continued to break down.

It always took her a long time before she'd confide in me and let me be there to support her. I hated seeing her in pain. When she would eventually let out what she'd been holding in, it was always like this.

If I could, I'd take all her pain away. I hated this for her.

Avery pulled herself off me, sniffling and wiping her eyes as she righted herself on the bed. "I feel like I'm constantly making moves but going nowhere." Her bottom lip trembled as she fell back into my arms. "I just want to belong," she choked out in between sobs.

"Avery, you do belong," I assured her. "You belong with me."

"I know but even that is evolving now that Max is around." She looked up at me through her wet lashes and frowned. "But it's more than that. Nothing I do ever fits, even when it comes to a career."

Avery always had a hard time finding her place whenever it came to careers. She'd always been a wanderer of sorts, going from job to job, not because she was flighty, but because she'd always aimed for a job that would make her feel good and bring her happiness.

That's all she ever wanted, to feel happy and fulfilled in her career. She just hadn't found that one thing that brought her that yet.

"Oh, Avery. I know that's always been tough for you." I swiped away the strands of stray hair that had fallen onto her face and tucked them behind her ear. "What things make you truly happy?"

She thought for a few moments and sat up in bed. "I don't know." She sighed. "How pathetic am I?"

"You're not pathetic at all."

"But you have your life figured out," she huffed.

I smacked her on the arm. "It's not a race. There's no trophy for figuring out what makes you happy in life. It's a process. A journey. Everyone is on their own timeline."

My life may have been figured out career-wise, but everything else had been a complete shitshow, especially lately. "My life isn't a picnic, Avery. Everyone has their own shit they need to deal with. I happened to get knocked up by a stranger and have twins with him without ever knowing a goddamn thing about him. You..." I pointed at her. "You just aren't sure what you want to spend your time doing and what truly fuels your soul. And that's okay."

"Thanks, Marley." Avery sniffled, wiping her eyes with her sleeve.

"You'll figure it out, Avery. I promise. And I'll be your biggest cheerleader when you do."

Avery waved me off, clearly done talking about herself. Whenever she did choose to open up, it was always over way too soon. She truly was on her own timeline with things.

"Enough about me." She pulled a donut out of the bakery bag for each of us and handed me one. "What's going on with Max?" She took a bite of her donut as she waited for my answer.

Over the next twenty minutes, I filled my sister in on everything that had happened and how great he was with the kids but how difficult it was to be so far apart.

Avery rolled her eyes. "The solution is easy," she said casually as she finished off her donut and reached across me for her coffee. "You need to move," she said matter-of-factly, as if it were the most obvious choice.

My mouth dropped. I couldn't believe she'd suggested that. "Avery. I have my own business. I can't just up and move."

"You really could." She tipped her coffee cup to her lips while I stared at her in disbelief.

"I need to work, you know," I protested.

"Oh... do they not have events in Quimby Grove that need planned?" Her eyes narrowed on me, her tone laced with sarcasm.

"Fuck if I know. But that's not the point. I have about six months of work events here in *this* city that are already booked. I can't just cancel those contracts. I'd be out so much money."

She tapped her lips as she pondered my dilemma. "I've got it." She snapped her fingers. "Hire someone to work the events here while you're in Quimby Grove starting the business down there."

"I... Well..." I stammered because, damn her, she made some sense. "I don't have anyone with that kind of flexibility that I'd trust to run my company."

A grin stretched across her face. "You have me." Avery rose to her knees, facing me as she got more excited at the prospect of covering for me. "I could totally handle the business up here for you. I've helped with enough jobs over the years to know the ropes."

"I don't know..." It's not that I didn't trust Avery, but what would happen if this didn't make her happy? She had just been talking about feeling so lost.

She grabbed my hands, holding on to them tightly. "I know what you're thinking. But it'll give me the sense of belonging I've been after. It'll give me time to really think about what would make me happiest in the future." She dropped my hands and placed hers together in front of her chest, pleading with me. "Please, please, please, Marley."

Just as I was about to respond, the doorbell rang. "I'll think about it," I promised as I hopped off the bed and headed into the living room, with Avery following behind me.

"Do more than just think about it," Avery insisted as I opened the door to find a very handsome Max standing at the threshold. He looked between Avery and me and laughed.

"Guess I know where the twin thing came from," he joked.

Avery shot out her hand. "I'm Avery."

He shook her hand, smiling. "Nice to meet you, Avery. I'm Max."

"Oh, I know." She smirked. "I'll leave you two alone." She turned to me, pulling me in for a hug. "I bet you'll think about my offer now," she teased.

"Shut up," I shot back. "Call you later. Love you."

Avery echoed my words and took off down the hall toward the elevator bank. After she stepped into an open elevator, I ushered Max inside.

He stepped in, glancing around my space, taking it all in. "It's different to see it in person instead of through a cell phone camera as a four-year-old holds it upside down." He laughed.

"Yeah, they haven't quite figured that out yet." I walked over toward the couch and took a seat. My heart raced as he sat down next to me instead of opting for the love seat or recliner. Suddenly, I felt warm. Was it getting hot in here? I fought the urge to fan myself in his presence and decided on casual conversation instead. "I'm so surprised to see you, you know. You didn't tell me you were coming to town."

"I wanted to see the kids," he said, pausing momentarily. "And my princess."

Our gazes locked. His eyes were full of desire and laced with heat as he placed his hand on my thigh. If it inched up any higher, I might've combusted just from this form of stimulation.

"You missed me," I repeated as I fought to bring my feelings to the surface. "Busker, I've missed you since that night on the beach," I said honestly.

As soon as the words left my mouth, Max hauled me up

onto his lap, my knees on the outside of his thighs as I straddled him on the couch. I gasped as his mouth lowered onto my neck, gifting me with desperate kisses as I gripped his strong, broad shoulders.

"When you told me you had the day off, I knew I couldn't be away from you any longer," he started right before his mouth claimed mine. He traced his tongue over my lips, begging to be let inside and to explore every possible inch. "The need to be near you is fucking undeniable."

He followed the trail from my mouth to my cheek, inhaling as he went, before peppering my neck with kisses, his lips exploring my skin as he made his way down my body. "A gravitational pull so fucking strong that there's no chance in hell of me not chasing your light."

I reared back at his declaration. Did Max just basically tell me that he wanted to be with me and would chase me? My breath hitched as I searched his face. "You'd chase me?"

He brushed the hair from my shoulders, letting his hand rest on my neck before he pulled my mouth down to his. "I'm hoping I won't have to chase you much longer. But I'd chase you for eternity if I had to."

My heart raced. I'd chase him, too. To the ends of the world and anywhere in between. I needed him like my next breath. I captured his mouth in mine as I moved my pelvis across his hardening dick, the friction of his jeans driving me wild. "I want you," I whimpered into his ear. "I need you."

Max growled, lifting me off his lap and depositing me onto the floor right in front of him. He unzipped his jeans and pushed them down with his boxers, his dick springing free from his clothes. He kicked them off to the side before reaching for me. His hands dipped underneath my skirt and roamed up my thighs, caressing the skin as he glided up to the waistband of my underwear. With his gaze locked on mine, he slowly dragged them down over my hips and let them drop to the floor. He slid a finger through my slit, coating himself as he let out a groan.

"Fucking drenched, princess." He groaned. "Come give me a taste."

He yanked his shirt over his head before tossing it aside with the rest of his clothes and lying down on the couch. "Come here." He held out a hand, leading me closer to him as he helped me get settled onto the couch so that I was straddling his head. He gripped my hips, lowering me down onto his face and sucking on my clit.

My head fell backward and I whimpered. My fingers latched onto his hair as his fingers slid into me, curling and hitting the spot that drove me wild.

The man was driving me insane. His vicious pattern of licking, sucking, and biting had me teetering on the edge of release while his fingers worked their magic inside me, getting me close and then bringing me back down right before the climax.

He was the cat and I was his mouse, chasing my orgasm before he caught me. "You're so fucking perfect," he said, granting me a moment of reprieve as I caught my breath. "Hold your skirt up, baby. I want you to watch."

Lifting my skirt to my waist, I held it in place with one hand while the other gripped the back of the couch, steadying me as Max's tongue ran through my pussy. He looked so fucking good with his tongue inside me. I moved my hips, riding his face as his tongue returned to my clit and his fingers slid back inside me, pumping me hard and fast as I found my climax, exploding on his tongue as I shouted his name.

My legs shook as I fell over the side of the couch. Max gripped my hips, holding me still as he lapped up my orgasm and licking me senseless until he lifted me and slid out from underneath me, pulling me into him as we both caught our breath.

Max tipped my face up to him and traced his fingertips over my bottom lip before pressing his lips to mine. His tongue eased into my mouth, my essence still on him as I leaned further into him, twisting my body and climbing on his lap to straddle him. He grabbed the hem of my sweater, yanked it up over my head, and tossed it to the floor.

"Mm," he said, kissing my neck. "No bra." His hands moved over my breasts, his eyes roaming my nearly naked body as he pinched a nipple between his fingers. He dipped his head, dropping his mouth to my breast as he swiped his tongue over the pebbled nipples. "I need to go get a condom, princess," he said as he moved to my other breast, repeating the attention there.

My chest heaved as I arched into him, begging for more. "I'm on birth control this time," I assured him. I reached my hand behind me, grabbing his hard cock and running my hand up and down his length. "Can I have you like this?" My body trembled, my desire for him growing. "There's been nobody since you."

Max looked into my eyes, silently asking a question about my ex-boyfriend. I shook my head no.

"Me neither." He groaned into my neck, his restraint breaking as he gripped my hips and lifted me above his cock before slamming me down onto him. A scream of ecstasy escaped as he filled me completely.

"Oh, fuck," I whimpered as Max held on to me, guiding our rhythm as we met each other thrust for thrust.

If I ever had any doubts about Max being the man for me, they would have vanished in this instance. The man was cherishing my body and savoring it as if it were his last meal. It was easy to get lost in all that was Max. I hadn't felt this desired since the first time we'd hooked up. I knew it wasn't just a hookup. It was the prologue to something much more lasting. It had been everything, even back then. More so now. I'd always known he couldn't be replaced.

"Get there, baby," he said through clenched teeth as he pounded into me harder and faster than before.

My nails dug into his shoulders, leaving scratch marks as I moved my hips with his. My head tipped backward as his lips devoured my nipples. "Max," I murmured.

He slid a hand between us, trailing over my swollen clit. "Marley," he moaned.

And together, we shattered into a million pieces.

Being with him felt like the most natural thing in the world. It felt damn near perfect.

"Tea?" I offered as Max exited the shower.

"Coffee?" he countered, sauntering over to me and wrapping his arms around my waist. "Kiss," he demanded playfully.

After our little rendezvous on the couch, I'd probably give the man anything he asked for. I leaned in, grazing my lips against his as I wrapped my arms around his neck. "Coffee it is," I said, nuzzling my nose against his.

Max gave me one more kiss before pulling away and heading over to the dining room table to sit down. "I was thinking we should talk."

I froze. A million thoughts rushed to the forefront of my mind. Did he already regret what happened between us? Did he have bad news about the kids? Did he not want anything to do with us anymore? With *me* anymore? I cleared my throat.

"Oh yeah?" I said, trying to come across as nonchalant. I grabbed our drinks and joined him at the table, choosing to sit across from him instead of beside him to maintain some distance. A boundary of sorts, in case that was needed.

Placing a warm mug in front of him, I studied him as I wrapped my hands around my cup, taking comfort in its warmth. "Do you regret what just happened between us?" I spat out the question so quickly, I couldn't stop it even if I wanted to. Mortified, I waved it off. "Forget I said anything."

Max reached over, laying a hand across my arm. "I'd never regret you in a million years, princess. It was like a fucking dream come true." He rubbed his thumb over my wrist, smiling. "I've been waiting far too long to have another taste of you, to savor you. No fucking regrets, *ever*."

His words meant more than he'd ever know. To feel cherished is something I'd never felt before him. I wanted to keep those feelings protected, safe and sound, buried deep within me.

"I do have a question for you, though." He took a drink of his coffee, winking at me as I stared at him from across the table, unmoving. "Okay, what is it?" I questioned.

He hesitated. "What if... What if you and the kids come to Quimby Grove for the summer and we see how things go? We can give parenting together a real chance. Give *us* a real chance."

Before I could open my mouth and respond, he cut me off.

"It's a big ask, I know. But you could start your business in Quimby Grove and see if you get any traction in the small towns surrounding it, too. I wish I could come to you for the summer, but I just can't do that yet. I'm willing to work toward that, though."

I quirked an eyebrow at him. "Have you been talking to Avery?"

"Avery? Your sister?" He rubbed a hand over his chin. "How would I have talked to her? I just met her today."

This was exactly what Avery had been telling me just hours ago. What were the fucking odds that the two of them would say practically the exact same thing? It felt like a huge sign from the universe.

"I was just talking about something like this with my sister this morning, right before you showed up. She was trying to convince me to move to Quimby Grove, start my business there, and she'd stay here and finish up with my current clients."

A wide grin spread across his face. "And what do you think? I think the stars are aligning for us, Marley." He planted both of his palms on the table, drumming his thumbs over the wooden surface while wearing a boyish grin. "Summer is only a few weeks away, too."

Avery and I had always played things safe when we were growing up. We didn't cause trouble, and we tried to do what was expected of us. I couldn't think of a time that we'd ever taken a big risk that required such a huge leap of faith.

I grabbed my coffee, brought it to my lips, and took a big drink. Warmth coursed throughout my body, and I wasn't sure if it was from my coffee or from the way Max was making me feel.

"Well..." I leaned back in my chair, exhaling as I gathered my thoughts. "I think it makes a lot of sense for us to try to figure out a way to parent together for Izzy and Jax." I paused, fidgeting with my hands, which were restless in my lap. "Things between us are moving quickly, and I'm afraid to get my hopes up." I kept my gaze laser focused on my lap, avoiding his awaiting eyes.

"You can get your hopes up," Max said, the smirk evident in his tone. He stood from his chair and came to my side of the table, where he settled in next to me. "I want you and the kids in Quimby Grove. I want to see you all every single day. I want to make plans for our future, together. I want meals at the dining room table each day and bedtime stories at night. I want it in my house, where we're all under the same roof."

A couple of tears slid down my cheeks, and I swiped them away as I stared down at my coffee. I'd always wished for a relationship like this. The kind that was written in books and made women everywhere gush over them. I'd never known this kind of feeling truly existed, or if it had, it certainly had always been out of my reach.

I raised my chin, my eyes finally meeting his. "Are you sure?" I questioned. "Because you don't have to do this with me if it's not what you want. It's okay for you to just want the kids. I'm not an obligation."

He needed to see me, to know that I meant what I was saying. That he wasn't trapped with me because we had two kids together. I wouldn't expect that of him. He had a choice.

It would hurt like hell, but he had options, even if I wasn't one of them.

Max grabbed the side of my chair and pulled me closer to him. "Marley, I'm all in," he said, grabbing my hands in his and squeezing.

"I'm all in," he repeated.

10

MAX

Marley and the kids had taken the role of tour guide seriously while I'd been in town these last few days.

Izzy and Jax gave me a grand tour of their bedroom. They shared a room by choice, and each had their own bed. The walls were white, with a black accent wall behind their beds that was covered in stars. Hanging from the ceiling were glow-in-the-dark planets and some moons. Above each bed hung a framed painting of their names. The letters of their names had characters painted on them; each character had been assigned to a letter. For Izzy, princesses were painted with the letters, while Jax's name had superheroes.

The other walls were adorned with framed pictures of quotes, superheroes, and Disney characters from the movies that were popular whenever I was a kid. A small bookcase was nuzzled between the two beds, acting as a nightstand. On top, a heart picture frame held a photograph of Marley with the kids on her lap. Marley and the twins were midlaugh. They looked so happy.

A feeling of longing pierced through my chest.

I wanted that with them.

The first four years of their lives had passed me by, but I was here now and ready to step up to the plate.

During the rest of the tour, which felt longer than a walk through a fancy museum, I learned that Izzy and Jax had always dreamt of having bunk beds and bean bag chairs. They chatted nonstop about them.

"Mama said soon," Izzy exclaimed as she wandered around her room searching for something. "And Mama always keeps promises." She plucked up a stuffed elephant that had fallen off her bed and held it out to me. "This is Effie, my stuffed elephant."

Nodding, I crouched down to her level and inspected the stuffed animal that she clearly loved so much. "I'm sure Mama will keep her promise, too." I reached out and ran a hand down the back of the elephant. "Effie is adorable. And soft," I added right as Jax tugged on my other hand, pulling me to my feet and toward his bed. "My turn," he insisted.

"What should we do, buddy?" I sat down on the edge of the bed, waiting as Jax went and scoured the bookshelf, the tip of his tongue peeking out of his mouth as he concentrated on the task at hand.

He must have found what he was looking for, because he quickly grabbed a book and rushed back to my side. "Will you read Seuss to me?" He stuck his bottom lip out and gave me puppy dog eyes.

"Of course," I said, and chuckled. I scooted up toward the headboard so I could lean against it. Jax crawled up onto the bed and sat right next to me, leaning in close enough to rest his head on my arm.

The corners of my mouth tipped up as I gazed down at him and cracked open the book. Overcome with emotion, I cleared my throat and started to read. *"Oh, the Places You'll Go* by Dr. Seuss."

"Oh!" Izzy jumped up from her bed and ran over to Jax's and snuggled in close to her brother. "This is my favorite," she said, leaning over her brother's shoulders while she pulled Effie into her chest. "Continue, Daddy."

By the time I finished reading the book, Jax had fallen asleep on my arm and a sleeping Izzy was sprawled across my legs, Effie still clutched her in hand. And I had zero desire in the world to move from my spot.

This was what I'd been missing. The precious moments where all I wanted was for time to stand still. Still enough for me to absorb the moments and commit them to memories I'd cherish forever.

The sound of a photo being snapped caught my attention. Looking up, I was met with a smiling Marley leaning against the doorframe as she lowered her phone.

"That was sweet," she whispered. "Do you want me to move them so you can get up?"

Shaking my head, I glanced back down at the munchkins and soaked it all in.

Marley gave me a wink and waved goodbye before gently closing the door, leaving me to treasure my last night for a while with the two newest additions in my life, who had grown to mean so much to me.

This was a snapshot I never wanted to forget.

A COUPLE WEEKS had passed since I returned to Quimby Grove from my spontaneous trip into the city to visit Marley and the kids. Before I left, Marley and I had sat the kids down and told them about spending the summer with me in Pennsylvania and asked if they'd like that.

They were overjoyed. Both of them had eagerly nodded their heads and rushed into my arms for a hug. Marley and I had decided that the three of them would join me in Quimby Grove once she was able to loop Avery into the business and the kids finished preschool for the year.

That gave me a couple weeks to make sure everything was situated at my place. Which, as it turned out, was not a lot of time whenever you owned your own bar and had to do a lot of cleaning and reorganizing in order to prepare for kids.

Who knew.

Ellawyn and Beckett had been enlisted to help. Every spare moment any of us had, we worked together so we could revamp my five bedroom house that was right outside of town. The first room we tackled was the bedroom for Izzy and Jax.

I ordered a set of bunk beds that were kind of tiered, with plenty of drawers underneath, a ladder, and a little cubby on one side. Ellawyn was able to find some white-and-gray striped bedsheets she insisted would look amazing with the bedroom set.

She was right.

Their names hung perfectly centered above their bed, cut out from wood I'd had lying around. Once they arrived, I planned to give them the option of decorating their names or leaving them like they were.

Beckett, a self-proclaimed king of bean bag chairs, went out and picked up four of the best he could find. Two were about six foot long, and the other two were sized more normally. We arranged them on the opposite side of their room, close to a spacious horizontal bookshelf that served as the focal point of that area. I even managed to score some classic children's books to get their Quimby Grove collection started.

We put the finishing touches on it with two new dressers, a wooden toy box, and a rug, and I knew the room was perfect for Izzy and Jax. They'd love it, I had no doubt about it.

Marley's room, on the other hand... hadn't gotten the same level of attention. After we finished the twin's bedroom, there wasn't any extra time to make it special for her because they were due to arrive that evening.

Her room did have a brand new bed, though.

And a dresser.

So I'd say the necessities were there. But deep down, I knew Marley would be fine with it because the kids always came first. And soon enough, I'd be able to put Marley first and make sure she received the attention she deserved. I did do a deep clean on my own bedroom, just in case Marley ended up between my sheets where she belonged.

Shoving that fantasy aside, I focused on my next task: groceries. I headed into the kitchen, pulled open the fridge, and surveyed the inventory. I was faced with a damn near empty fridge. There was a carton of expired milk, three bottles of water, and a bag of rotten grapes.

Shit.

Leaving the water bottles in the fridge, I grabbed everything else and tossed it into the garbage before wiping down the inside of the refrigerator. I grabbed my phone from my back pocket and shot off a quick text to Marley, asking what type of food we should have on hand for the kids.

Because I had no fucking clue.

> **MARLEY**
> Just normal kid food should be fine!

That was it? That was all she had to offer? What the fuck was "normal" kid food? Deciding not to respond, I swiped my keys from the counter and headed to the supermarket in town.

When I arrived, the place was packed with people. I couldn't turn down an aisle without being stopped by someone who wanted to say hi and catch up.

It was exhausting.

I found myself standing in an aisle full of shampoo and body wash with an empty cart.

This was as good a place to start as any, I guessed.

After grabbing a bottle of my normal body wash, I moved throughout the aisle in search of kid stuff and managed to find a bottle of something or other with some cartoon characters on it. That was a win in my book. I grabbed a bottle and tossed it into the cart as I moved further down the aisle, where I spotted a two-in-one shampoo and conditioner in a bright bottle that raved about being tear-free.

Score.

Into the cart it went.

By the time I was done scouring each aisle of the supermarket, I had an overflowing cart filled with all sorts of things.

Cereal? Check.

Fruit? Check.

Fresh milk? Double check.

Other random shit that looked good? Check.

Feeling satisfied, I went to the front of the store so I could get the hell out of there.

Grocery shopping was for the damn birds.

AFTER RETURNING HOME, I did a final walk through the house and made sure everything was in order. The nerves started to settle in the closer it was to their arrival time. The house looked good; it usually did. But it was single-man level clean before today. Now it was clean enough for a family.

It had been too damn long since this house had been a home.

The house used to belong to my dad. It was where I grew up and lived for my entire life—mostly, anyway. It was always just me and Dad. My mom had passed away during childbirth, so I never had the privilege of knowing her, but my dad never let me feel as though I were lacking. He raised me in this house and did a damn good job. I always hoped to follow in his footsteps and open a bar, just like he had.

Dad had found joy in running his bar; I'd say he was married to it. I spent many days there with him, too. Some might say it was no place for a child, but there was no place else I'd rather be.

And it had nothing to do with the food or access to booze.

My dad was my best friend, and that bar, my refuge.

When he had passed away shortly after I graduated from high school, I'd been devastated. After dealing with months of extreme grief, I had pushed forward and decided to stay in my childhood home, took over the bar, and renamed it to something that would allow it to be mine.

The bar was my safe place. It was where I felt closest to my dad. It was the most important thing to me, and I'd cherish it forever.

And now I'd get to raise my two kids here and pass down the warmth that encompasses this home and my bar. Memories would be made here this summer, and I couldn't wait.

A car door slamming shut, followed by another, tore me away from memory lane. I walked outside the house and stood on the front porch while Marley unbuckled the kids from their car seats. They spotted me instantly, and they took off toward me as soon as they were freed from the car. They barreled up the porch steps, smiling wide as they rushed into my open arms.

I wrapped them into a hug and gave them a squeeze. "I

missed you two munchkins," I said, dropping a kiss to each of their heads.

They both squeezed me back. "I missed you too, Daddy," they said at the same time.

Izzy stepped back and batted her eyelashes at me. "Did you get us any presents?"

"Izzy Mae," Marley scolded from behind the car. "We do not expect gifts. She placed her hands on her hips and gave our daughter a stern warning. "Apologize, please."

Izzy frowned, her shoulder's slumping forward. "Sorry," she mumbled before skipping over to her mother and jumping into her arms. "We never expect gifts," she echoed her mother's words, nodding her head in the process. "But they are always welcome." She beamed.

My shoulders shook with laughter. I looked down at Jax and ruffled his hair. "Should we go help the ladies with the suitcases, little man?"

He nodded, taking my hand in his and pulling me toward the trunk of the car. He reached inside, unable to properly see, and attempted to find a suitcase. There was a superhero duffel bag just out of his reach. I stepped forward, waited until he wasn't looking, and inched it forward for him as his little hand frantically continued his search. He latched onto it and tugged it over the edge of the trunk and out onto the grass.

"Got it," he said proudly while he looked up at Marley and me.

"Thank you, sweetie." She gave him a high five. "Can you go put it on the porch for us?"

"Yes, Mama." He grabbed the bag by the handles and dragged it over to the porch. When he reached the steps, he carefully stepped up onto each one and took his time until he made it to the top. His face broke into a smile as he placed it by the door.

"He fell down the stairs once when he slipped on his blankie and has been skittish of them ever since," Marley whispered into my ear and then clapped me on the back. She reached into the car and grabbed Izzy's duffel bag with a stuffed Effie sticking out of it and then handed it to her before lifting out the last two suitcases. "He's just very cautious now."

"Makes sense." I grabbed the suitcases from her so she could go and pay the ride share driver.

As I made my way to the porch, I couldn't help but realize that this moment was a pivotal one for us. This was the moment that would change everything. A moment that could alter the course of our lives forever, even more than how they'd already been changed.

When I reached the door, I turned around and took in Izzy and Jax's eager expressions, and Marley's anxious one. "This is it," I said, gripping the doorknob. "Are you ready to see your home for the summer?"

11

MARLEY

When Max swung open the door to his home, it was as if the nagging anxiety that had taken root in my stomach magically faded away. All signs of nervousness disappeared once I crossed the threshold of his sanctuary.

It was as if I'd always belonged here. Almost like everything that had happened in my life had led me to this very moment. A feeling like I truly belonged here.

I haven't ever felt like this before, and I couldn't explain the feeling either. It just felt natural.

I made my way through the foyer and continued into the family room as Max chased the kids up the stairs. The room was massive in size and completely breathtaking. The walls were painted a deep blue, and a velvet sofa had been placed in the center of the room. The far wall had built-in bookshelves that had become the home to many books. Knickknacks adorned the shelves alongside the books, when there was space. A Fabergé egg was on display next to the classics, and a glass trinket box had been perched up on a higher shelf.

My gaze swept past the bookshelves and settled on the fireplace that sat directly in front of the sofa. Above it, a shelf mantel hung on the wall that held three picture frames. Stepping close, I took in the moments that had been frozen in time.

The first was a black-and-white photo of a beautiful woman who appeared to be pregnant. Her long dark hair was braided and hung over her shoulder. She wore a floral summer dress and was all smiles as she looked at the camera and gracefully held her baby bump.

Max's mother.

I found myself reaching out toward the photograph, my fingertip trailing over the edge of the frame before I gently grazed over the woman's face.

A throat cleared from behind me, and I snatched my hand back as Max strode toward me. "Sorry, I was just looking around—"

"It's okay. After all, this is your home too." His gaze left mine as he took in the photos on the mantel. "That's my mother." He picked up the photo of the woman I'd just been admiring.

"She's beautiful. Will we get to meet her?"

He looked down at the photo of his mother with a pained stare. "I'm afraid not." He placed the photograph back onto the mantel and then shoved his hands into the pockets of his jeans. "She passed away during childbirth." He shifted his body away from me, his hand going back to the photograph for another light touch over the image of his mother's face.

"Oh, Max." I stepped closer to him, placing a hand on his arm. "I'm so sorry. I hadn't realized."

"It's okay." One of his shoulders hunched up as he gave me a half-smile. "This photo..." He pointed to the frame in the center. "This one is of my dad. He's gone now too, but he was amazing." He stepped toward the far side of the mantel and gestured toward the last photograph. "This is one of us together at my high school graduation." He picked it up, admiring his late father. "It was our last photograph together." He sighed. "One of my biggest regrets is that we didn't take more together."

The photograph had a slightly younger version of Max in it as he looked up at his dad with a grin spread across his face. His red graduation cap sat askew on top of his head, and his dad's head was tilted back in laughter.

"It's a wonderful picture, Max."

Max ran the tip of his finger over the photograph, the gentlest of touches to his dad's happy, carefree face. "It is." He placed the photograph back and nodded toward the staircase. "The kids insisted they wait for you to come up. They won't see their new room without you." He chuckled as he ran a hand through his hair. "They've thoroughly inspected every other room, though."

"Mama," Izzy's excited voice carried down the stairs. "Hurry," she pleaded.

"Coming," I called. "One second." Just as I went to leave the family room, something on the wall caught my attention—a painting. I stepped closer, feeling Max's heat behind me. The painting was of a beach in the evening, the moon reflecting on the ocean's surface. A woman with long blonde hair blowing in the wind was dressed in an emerald-green gown and standing on the sandy beach. In the background, a man with a guitar stood on the boardwalk. "Max..."

His hand landed on my shoulders and gently eased me backward until I was flush against his chest. His hands snaked around my waist, his chin settling on my shoulder. "I'd shared our story with Ellawyn once, telling her all about how we met at the beach and how much I regretted letting you walk away that night. A couple of months after I told her, she gifted me this beautiful painting." He dropped a kiss on my cheek. "In a way, it was like I found you on the beach all over again. My beautiful, rare treasure."

The painting was beautiful and looked perfect on his wall. "It's beautiful, Max." I turned in his embrace and wrapped my arms around his neck. "I can't believe you hung it on the family room wall."

"It deserved to be on display, not tucked away somewhere like a lost memory or a secret." He bent down, his lips grazing mine in a tender kiss. "Come on, princess. Let's go upstairs before the kids combust with excitement."

We took off toward the staircase and followed the sounds of our giggling children until we found them at the end of the hallway. "Okay, okay, we're here."

"Daddy," Jax called out.

Max stepped out from behind me. "I'm right here. Go on in, kiddo."

Izzy and Jax stepped closer to the closed door and shared a look before joining hands. As they started to count down, Izzy's hand lifted to the doorknob. On the count of one, she twisted the knob and pushed the door open.

Gasps escaped their mouths as they ran inside their bedroom. Their excitement was contagious. I found myself growing excited with them as we took in the space.

"Mama, look," Jax exclaimed.

"Bunk beds," Izzy screamed with joy as she climbed up the ladder to the top bunk while Jax cozied up on the bottom bunk. "We've always wanted bunk beds, Mama."

"I know you have." Turning my attention to Max, I crossed my arms over my chest. "How did you know about this?"

"Uh..." He shifted on his feet. "Well, they told me when I was last in the city. I hope you don't mind."

My pretend annoyance slipped away immediately. I smiled

and playfully shoved at his shoulder. "I don't mind at all. They're your kids, too."

"Oh my goodness." Izzy jumped down from her bunk and ran across the room. "Jax, there are so many bean bags to sit on."

"And lots of books," Jax answered as he plopped down onto one of the larger bean bags with his sister. "Mama, come join."

I approached the bean bag area and pulled out my phone so I could capture the moment with a photo. I felt such adoration at Max and the work he put into the bedroom for our kids. "Look at you two, all piled together in a bean bag." I crouched down to their level. "Is it cozy?"

"Yes," they responded.

"Thank you, Daddy," Izzy called out.

Max crossed the room and leaned up against the wall as he watched the kids giggle and roll around. "You're very welcome."

I never expected him to do all this. I grabbed a picture book off the rack, handed it to the kids, and then moved closer to Max. "You didn't have to do all this, you know," I whispered.

"I know." He turned his head, his gaze focusing on mine. "But I wanted to. I want to take care of them. And you. I know it seems sudden, but you three are everything to me."

My breath hitched. "The feeling is mutual," I admitted.

And it was. From the moment we met on the beach all those years ago, I knew Max was special. Deep down, I knew he was made for me. But back then, I figured he was mine just for that moment in time, a small snapshot of our lives intertwining. I never thought I would find my way back to him. That he'd even want me.

But I did.

And he does.

Max reached out, grabbing my arm, and steered me away

from the wall and toward the door. "I'm going to show Mama to her room. We'll be just down the hall."

The kids mumbled their acknowledgment as they explored their room more while Max led me down the opposite end of the hallway. "With this being decided on such short notice, I didn't have enough time to make your room as special as the kids'."

I waved him off. "The kids come first, you know that. I don't need anything special."

He levels me with narrowed eyes. "I've seen your place in New York, you know."

My hands go to my hips. "Just because I have things a certain way up there doesn't mean I won't be happy with something different. I'm not that hard to please."

He smirked. "Oh, I know you aren't hard to please."

With my eyes rolling hard, I gripped the doorknob and twisted it open. The room was huge, albeit modestly decorated. But it was cozy. The walls were painted a slightly darker shade of olive green, which looked lovely with the sunlight shining in through the windows. The bed was centered against the furthest wall, with a floral painting hanging above the bed. Two light wooden nightstands sat on either sides of the bed, housing two small houseplants. A matching dresser was placed on the opposite wall.

Simple, yet welcoming.

I loved it.

"It's perfect." I went further into the room, going directly for the bed, I let my fingers trail lightly over the crocheted blanket. It was a lighter shade of green and comfortable. "I think this is just what I needed."

And it was the truth.

New York City was perfect in its own way, but it was busy. It was chaos twenty-four seven, and sometimes that could be exhausting. Quimby Grove was much more relaxed and leisurely. The vibe of the bedroom was perfect—a reminder to pause and to revel in the simplicity of small-town life.

"I also might have done something else for you." He came over to the bed, took a seat, and gently pulled my hand down toward him. Turning toward the nightstand, he reached into the single drawer and pulled out a wide square book. "Here."

I took the book from him and flipped it over, seeing that it was a planner. "You got me a planner?"

"Yes, and inside you'll find a list of potential new clients that are looking for an event planner here in Quimby Grove and the surrounding cities. There are names, contact info, and addresses. I wasn't sure if you wanted to work while you're here, but I figured it wouldn't hurt." He brushed my hair out of my face. "I just didn't want you to have to start from nothing."

Flipping through the beginning pages of the planner, I saw that there were at least forty names and businesses listed. "You did this for me? This must have taken a lot of time for you to put all this together."

"Of course, I did. You're worth it."

Clutching the planner to my chest, I closed my eyes and allowed myself to remember this moment. Another snapshot of time that I'll commit to my memory forever. The moment when someone did something so selfless for me, simply to make my life easier. "This means so much."

Max reached out, brushing his fingers against my chin as he turned my face toward him. He leaned in, slowly closing his eyes, and moved for my lips just as I did the same. The moment our lips brushed, the door to my room swung open, and in ran the munchkins.

Pulling away was a tragedy, but I stood from the bed and crouched down to meet my kids. "Tired of your new bedroom already?"

"No," Izzy answered.

"But our tummies want ice cream," Jax added.

"Then ice cream is what we shall have," Max chimed in as he rose from the bed. "Let's go, we've got to celebrate your first night here, and I know the perfect spot in town."

The kids jumped up and down and barreled down the steps.

Grabbing Max's hand, I pulled him behind me as we followed the kids. "Come on, you promised ice cream."

CONSIDERING THE HEAT, we decided to drive to the ice cream shop instead of walking into town. Max assured us we would be having the best ice cream we'd ever tasted.

The kids were excited, but I was skeptical.

After a few minutes in the car, Max turned into the parking lot for Leo's Homemade Ice Cream. Walking in, it seemed like any other local ice cream shop, with a black-and-white checkered floor and ice cream freezers lined up with the day's available flavors. The one thing that was a little bit different, though, were the stands of fresh-baked goods.

Izzy's eyes went wide when she took in the array of cookies and ice cream. "Mama, look." She grabbed my hand and led me over to the cookies that caught her eye.

"Hey there, Max," an older woman behind the counter greeted. "The usual?"

The woman had long gray hair that was twisted into a bun at her nape. Her light blue dress brought out the color of her eyes. She reminded me of a grandmother I never had. She seemed sweet.

"You know me too well, Diane."

Jax scooted up behind Max, gripping his hand while peeking around his legs.

"Hey, little man." Max reached down and picked up Jax. "Look at all these flavors. What's your favorite?"

"Green." Jax laid his head on Max's shoulder, eyeing the woman behind the freezers.

"Ah, the mint chocolate chip? That's one of my favorites, too. Do you want it in a cone or a bowl?"

"Cone."

"Diane, can I get a scoop of mint chocolate chip in a cone for my boy here?" Max shifted Jax onto his hip and turned to where Izzy was eyeing the cookies. "Is my Izzy a cookie monster?"

Her giggles filled the room as she jumped up and down, nodding. "Can we take a cookie home?"

"Of course. Want to come and see what the ice cream flavors are first?"

When she said yes, Max picked Izzy up. He placed her onto his other hip and took her over toward the ice cream. Once she picked a flavor, which was black raspberry, Max put the kids down. They scampered off, trying to play hopscotch with the floor tiles.

"Babe, what do you want?" Max pulled his wallet from his back pocket while he waited for my response.

"Cookies and cream, please." I turned to Diane, who was scooping the kids' ice cream into their cones. "Thank you."

After Max paid, we all went out behind the ice cream shop and found a table to sit at outside. Armed with napkins and wet wipes, the kids devoured their ice cream. By the time they were finished, Jax had green all over his face, while his sister was covered in purple.

They were full of giggles and pure joy.

Though, it could have just been the sugar.

After cleaning them both up, we headed back toward the car so we could go back to Max's place. "I noticed you have two vehicles," I mentioned to Max as I buckled the kids into their car seats. "One looked like an old truck?"

Max nodded from the driver's seat as I slid in next to him. "Yeah. The truck was my dad's. I couldn't part with it. So I use it to run back and forth to the bar most days." He gestured toward the vehicle we were in. "This jeep is a few years old but perfect for Pennsylvania winters and hauling around two munchkins." He winked.

"Are we going home, Mama?" Izzy questioned from the back seat, her voice sounding sleepy.

Were we going home? It was on the tip of my tongue to correct her, to say we were going to Max's house and not our home back in New York. But I knew that wouldn't be the appropriate response. Max's home was their home. He'd proven that with the changes he made to his house for us. To me, though, the man himself felt like home.

"Yes, munchkin. We're going home."

"Good, I like it there," she murmured.

Within a minute, both Izzy and Jax were passed out in their car seats, right before we pulled into Max's driveway.

12

MARLEY

The first night in Max's house went surprisingly well for both kids. Hell, it even went well for Max and me.

I wasn't sure what to expect when it came down to co-parenting with the father of my children, who had missed the first four years of their lives, but so far, it had been going seamlessly. It was as if our lives had melded together instantly.

When bedtime rolled around last night, we did our routine as a newly formed family of four. Max and I both helped with bath time, and the four of us ended the night curled up on the bean bag chairs reading books.

When the munchkins fell asleep, we carried them into their respective bunks and tucked them in.

It was nice not to have to do the routine alone for once.

Whenever it was just the three of us, I never minded doing everything alone. Sure, I had help from my sister, but for the most part, I shouldered everything. Even when I'd been in a relationship with Jakob, I never off-loaded my responsibilities.

A man wasn't needed to help with the kids, but damn it was nice to just have someone there. Someone to talk to.

Someone to help without me feeling weird about asking. We were establishing a partnership in all this. We could lean on each other already, which was a relief.

Once we slipped from their bedroom, Max and I ended up parting ways for the evening. He insisted I take some time for myself and decompress. I would have been annoyed if it hadn't ended up being exactly what I needed.

Damn him.

As much I wanted to be in bed with the man, sometimes I needed my own space. I needed my space a lot of the time. Alone time was my favorite form of self-care, and I'm so touched that he recognized that and made it okay for me to be myself in his home. He took care of me in a way that nobody ever has.

And while today started out well, Max left early for work, and then it was just me and the kids after about eleven in the morning. But even in an unfamiliar house and a new town, it almost felt like it did back in New York.

We stuck to our routine, playing outside before making some lunch. The kids adored Max's huge backyard. Living in the city, we didn't have open space like that to run around. We played freeze tag, hide-and-seek, and red light, green light before it was time for the kids to eat and catch a nap.

With naptime underway, I found myself not knowing what to do with the free time. Back home, I would have either tidied up the house or done some remote work for Events by Halligan.

But here, Max's house was immaculately clean, and I didn't have my company to keep me busy. But I guess I kind of did. With the planner full of leads Max had given me, I guess I could branch out and start to consider taking on some work for the summer. I went into my bedroom and grabbed the book from the dresser, then went downstairs to the family room and nestled into the couch, flipping through the pages and looking over the notes Max had left me. He even managed to write down a few comments of what type of event the client was planning.

There was a lot of potential within these pages.

I plucked my phone from my pocket and then tapped on my sister's contact.

She answered on the first ring. "Mar, one sec." The sound of loud music and shuffling came through the line, until the volume decreased substantially. "How are you? When are you coming home? I miss you."

I couldn't help my laughter. That was my sister. My heart ached at how badly I missed her, too. "Avery, I just left yesterday."

She scoffed. "And it feels like it's been forever."

"I miss you too, though. I need your advice."

"Sounds like story time. Let me grab a drink and get comfy." I heard the pop of a bottle of champagne in the background.

"Drinking already?" I pushed the button to change the call to a video chat, and her face filled the frame of my phone as she poured herself a small glass.

Her green eyes rolled. "Don't act like you wouldn't be partaking if you were home right now. It's my day off." She grabbed her glass, and the phone, and relocated to her bedroom. When settled within the comfort of her bed, she held the phone out so she could see me. "Your job is exhausting, by the way."

Don't I know it. "That's kind of what I wanted to talk to you about. Should I work while I'm here for the summer?"

She pondered my question as she sipped her drink. "I know you aren't hurting for money, but Events by Halligan is in your blood. You fucking love it." She put her glass down and yanked a blanket up over her shoulders. "You couldn't stay away even if you wanted to."

I did love my work. But I wasn't sure how to do that kind of work here without a support system. I sighed into the phone. "Max actually gifted me a planner last night with pages upon pages of potential event planning leads for this area." I pinched the bridge of my nose. "But Av, I don't know how to make it work here without the help I have back home."

Back home, if the kids weren't in preschool, they were with my sister. If I had to schedule a meeting, I held it in my office. I had a quiet place for business calls.

I had everything figured out. But here, I felt so far out of my element.

I might have had leads, but I didn't have relationships and connections.

"Marley, you're making this too complicated. You might not have me physically, but Max is there. He can help. And you know that bookshop owner from the wedding. I bet you could go to her shop to meet new clients and make some calls."

"You have a point about the bookshop. That would be an ideal meeting spot. Thanks, sis."

"Anytime. Let me know how it goes."

After hanging up with Avery, I went through the planner once more and pulled a few clients that lived in Quimby Grove and gave them a call. Each person I spoke with was more than eager to meet with me today.

I wasn't used to that. Back home, meetings would be scheduled weeks, sometimes months, in advance. I had two hours until my first meeting at Starlight Books. Which meant I had practically no time to find an outfit professional enough and get the twins up and ready to head into town.

WITH FIFTEEN MINUTES TO spare until the meeting, I made it to Starlight Books with the munchkins in tow. After explaining to them what we were doing, I set them up at their own table close to mine and gave them their coloring books and crayons.

Just as I sat down, my first client arrived to discuss the potential of hiring me to plan her wedding that would take place in two months. Thankfully, I had the thought to bring my Events by Halligan portfolio with me to Quimby Grove, because it was a huge help in winning her over. I was able to go over some examples of my work on previous weddings, and the bride-to-be was in awe.

She hired me on the spot and took one of my contracts home with her, where she'd review it this evening with her fiancé and email it over once she filled it out.

I was on cloud nine.

Before my next client meeting, I checked on the kids and bought them a drink and a cookie for an afternoon snack. As we were paying, Ellawyn came out of the kitchen and came over to visit.

"Hey, Marley!" She pulled me in for a hug and then bent down to greet Izzy and Jax. "How are my favorite kiddos today?"

"Good," Izzy answered. "Mama brought us here for some meetings today."

"We're coloring," Jax added.

Ellawyn stood up and gave me a puzzled look. "Meetings?"

"Yeah. Max thought it may be good for me to work on some events down here and build a client base. I took the plunge today on short notice and ended up scheduling meetings while Max is at work." I glanced down at my children. "Had to bring them with me."

Ellawyn's eyes went wide with excitement. "Oh my goodness. Marley, that's amazing. Why don't I help keep the kids occupied while you meet with clients?"

I flicked my wrist. "You don't need to do that. I know how busy you are. Plus, I only have two left."

"Nonsense. I'd love the company. Please let me help." She tilted her head and gave me puppy dog eyes.

I arched an eyebrow. "Does that work with Beckett?"

"Not at all." She laughed. "So I thought I'd try my luck here."

I shook my head as I chuckled at her silliness and caved to her offer. "Okay, fine. Thanks, Ellawyn."

"Anytime, lady. Now go and work your magic."

Ellawyn stepping in was a sign of fate. Not only did my two meetings go well but I ended up going over the anticipated length of time with both, as they had decided to sign the contracts right then and there and pay their deposit.

After saying goodbye to my last client, I went back into the kitchen of the bookshop to check on the kids. Their giggles drifted to my ears as I pushed the door open.

My smile couldn't be contained at the sight before me.

Both Izzy and Jax were covered head to toe in flour. Izzy's hair had patches of white, and Jax's face was as white as a ghost. Both had yellow icing on their faces. "Looks like you three are having a ball," I called out from the doorway.

Ellawyn shrugged her shoulders as she turned around to face me. "What can we say? We love to bake."

She looked as bad as the kids, with flour in her hair and on her clothes.

I strode over to where they were and gave both kids a kiss

on top of their head, but they had other ideas when they wrapped their flour-covered bodies around my waist for hugs.

"Oh my goodness," I teased. "You got flour on me." I chased them around the kitchen for a moment as their playful screams filled the room.

"How'd the meetings go?" Ellawyn hopped onto the counter, cupcake in hand, and started to unwrap her treat. "Come on up here, my little helpers."

"It went so well. Both signed contracts today and paid their deposit." I picked up my kids one by one and sat them onto the counter, one on each side of Ellawyn. "Do you mind if I run across the street and tell Max the good news?"

She handed each of my munchkins a cupcake. "Go ahead," she responded. "I've got things covered here."

"Covered with flour and filled with sugar." I placed another kiss on my kids' cheeks. "Sweet as can be—just the way I like it."

With a wave goodbye and a promise to be right back, I grabbed my belongings from my table and hurried out of Starlight Books and toward the crosswalk at the end of the block. After I pressed the button to cross, I glanced across the street and eyed the rows of shops on that side. My eyes flitted across the alleyway between two of the shops, and my gaze caught on something that had me looking again. It was a dark figure that appeared to be crouched onto the ground, slumped against the outside of one of the buildings.

The crosswalk light switched, signaling my turn to cross the street. I strode across, narrowing my gaze as I tried to determine if it was a person in the alleyway or something else. A nauseous feeling formed in my stomach the closer I got.

I felt like I was going to be sick.

As I made it across the street, panic started to take over, along with adrenaline as soon as I saw that the figure was clearly a man. I jogged down the alleyway and took in the bloodstained T-shirt and the pool that had started to form on the concrete beneath him. "Sir." I shook his arms gently.

"Sir, wake up." When I glanced down at where my hands were, they were covered in blood. I wiped them on my jeans and pulled my cell phone out of my pocket to dial 911. The operator picked up immediately.

"Hello," I said. "There's a man in an alleyway in Quimby Grove. On High Street, by Remnant Hearts Bar. I think he's been stabbed or something. There's a lot of blood. Please hurry."

The man was unresponsive. I shook him once more. "Please wake up," I pleaded.

Placing my phone on speakerphone, I put it on the ground away from the man and gently removed his hands from his abdomen. His T-shirt was sliced and drenched in blood.

I yanked off my sweater, then rolled it up and used it to apply pressure on the wound. "I'm sorry," I offered. I didn't think the man could hear me, but the deep sinking feeling in my gut told me I couldn't give up. I couldn't leave him. He may be dying, or perhaps already dead, but I wouldn't walk away and not try something.

Sirens could be heard, but they sounded so far away. Everything seemed so out of place. Time stood still as I leaned on this man, hoping I was helping him as best I could.

The sirens grew louder.

I took a hand and moved for the man's neck. Pressing two fingers to his neck, I found a barely there, faint pulse right as the medic hopped out of the ambulance parked outside the alleyway.

"He's badly wounded," I called out. "He barely has a pulse."

The medic ran over to where we were and took my place. "Okay, I've got it from here."

Moving out of the way, I went further down the alley and sunk down onto the ground as I watched the medic work on the man.

More first responders showed up, and the medic began speaking loud enough for me to overhear. "Victim has been stabbed repeatedly in the abdomen. Pulse faint."

Tears tracked down my cheeks, falling onto my chest as I continued to watch the paramedics and police work the scene. I didn't know what to do. I couldn't leave; the police would need a statement from me.

At least I thought so.

A man in a suit glanced in my direction as he spoke with some of the officers on the scene and jotted something down in a notebook before he bent to pick something up off the ground.

Wiping the tears from my face, I stood up and started to walk toward the group.

The suit stuck a finger into the air, signaling for me to wait.

Turning around, I went back to stand along the wall where I had been sitting previously. When I looked back over to where the man had been lying on the ground, all that was left was a pool of blood beginning to dry as a stretcher was being lifted into an ambulance.

The once bright spots of blood on my hands were now darkened and dried. The warmth now turned cold. My body shuddered as the door to the ambulance slammed shut.

"Ma'am." The guy in the suit stalked toward me. "I'd like you to come down to the station with us for a few questions."

I nodded my head, unable to find the words as I followed him toward his unmarked police car. Another uniformed officer opened the back door and gestured me inside.

"Oh, wait," he called as he rummaged in the glove compartment of the car. "Here are a few wet wipes to get that filth off your hands." He tossed a box in the back seat.

Filth.

Rage boiled deep inside. "It's not filth. It's the blood of a man who may not be with us much longer." Ignoring the wipes, I crossed my arms over my chest. "You're being incredibly disrespectful."

The officer rolled his eyes.

"Have some respect, Barclay," the guy in the suit chimed in as he settled into the driver's seat while officer dickhead took the passenger seat. "I apologize for him, Marley."

I didn't acknowledge his comment or any other comments the two made on the short drive toward the station. They probably thought I was being ridiculous, caring for a random man, but that man was still a person. He was someone's son, friend, maybe a brother or a uncle. He was a person.

He didn't deserve hateful comments.

When we arrived at the station, Max was already waiting outside. When the officer opened my door, Max rushed over and pulled me into his arms. "Are you okay?" he asked as he held me tightly.

"I'm okay." I clenched the back of his shirt with my fists. "Go to the children. I'll meet you at Starlight when I'm finished here."

His grip lessened as he pulled back to look at my face. "You're sure?"

The suit cleared his throat behind me. "It's time to go inside," he said as he gently grazed my elbow, directing me toward the double doors ahead of us.

I nodded to Max before turning back toward the man and following him inside the station. He led me down a long corridor. The walls were navy blue, decorated with portraits of prior officers, detectives, and other personnel. When we reached the end of the hallway, he opened the door to a bland room with a table and a few chairs on each side.

"Wait here," he instructed before leaving me alone.

My body ached as I deposited myself into a hard plastic chair. Every muscle in my body was sore, the ache almost unbearable. I didn't even know what I had done to cause this kind of pain but, fuck, did it hurt.

My mind flashed back to the man on the ground in the alleyway. The blood pooling beneath him. The stickiness on my fingers as I applied pressure to his wounds, hoping help would arrive.

But it was too little too late, I could tell. Something inside me knew the man had passed away.

I couldn't help but feel as though his blood were on my hands—not just literally, but figuratively too. Maybe I could have done something more to save him. Perhaps he could have had a fighting chance if someone more experienced had found him instead of me.

The door to the room opened, and the suit walked in with a woman dressed in uniform. "Marley, this is Officer Juni."

The woman smiled warmly as she sat down across from me. "Hi, Marley." She glanced down at my hands before her eyes snapped back up to meet mine. "Thank you for coming in. Could you please write down exactly what happened for us?" She slid a sheet of paper toward me, along with a pen.

"Sure." I gripped the pen between my shaky fingers and wrote out exactly what happened and how I found the man as the suit sat down next to her and opened a manila folder.

"Marley, I don't recall if I introduced myself properly. I'm Detective Goodhart," he said.

Setting the pen down, I pushed the paper away. Despite how little I wrote for my statement, it was truth. It wasn't some long-ass story full of drama.

"You didn't introduce yourself," I responded to Detective Goodhart flatly as I replayed the events in my head. "And I don't recall telling you my name either."

The detective pressed his lips together firmly. "I didn't have to ask. That information was abundantly clear on the scene."

"What does that mean?" I crossed my arms over my chest. "How was that clear?" I couldn't piece it together. I hadn't told the 911 operator my name, and nobody ever asked on the scene.

"Marley," Juni started gently. "We found these at the scene of the crime." She pulled out a transparent evidence bag and flipped it over to reveal half a dozen business cards with my name and face on them. "They were scattered all around the victim."

My stomach coiled in disgust while I leaned closer to the bag to get a better look. It was definitely my picture, but it was impossible these were mine. "Those aren't mine," I protested calmly. "My real business cards don't have my photograph on them."

"These do," Detective Goodhart commented, tapping on the evidence bag. "This photograph is from your business website, correct?"

"Yes, but that doesn't mean I put it on business cards and then spread it around a potential murder victim. Come on now, that's idiotic."

They had to have thought I murdered that man in the alleyway. My chest was tight, my breathing morphing into quicker, more shallow breaths as the room started to blur.

"Marley, how about some water?" He questioned and then immediately addressed the female officer in the room. "Juni, could you get Marley a bottle of water?"

"Sure," I mumbled, nodding my head and shutting my eyes. If I could just get the room to fucking stop spinning, I'd feel a hell of a lot better. The sound of the door opening and shutting caught my attention. Officer Juni must have left.

As my vision came into focus again, the seat across from mine scratched against the floor as it was slid out. The detective lowered himself into the chair and rapped his knuckles on the table. "Marley, I'll be straight with you. I don't think you did this, but someone is trying to make it seem as though you were involved."

My head snapped up, meeting the asshole detective's gaze. "What?" I breathed in deeply, trying to calm myself down and keep my anger at bay. I closed my eyes and counted to ten. "You made it sound like you did."

"It's very unusual," he admitted. "But I don't think you could kill someone even if you wanted to." He closed the folder and ran his hands over the top. "But it is strange. Quimby Grove doesn't have a high violent crime rate, or it didn't until these past few months. Do you know anyone who would try to throw you in the middle of this?"

My answer was automatic. "No, I truly don't. I only know three people in this town and none of them would do this."

Detective Goodhart leaned back in his seat and sighed. "It could just be an elaborate ploy to try to throw the investigation."

When I looked at him, I could tell he didn't believe I had anything to do with this. But I could also tell he didn't have any other lead. His eyes were red-rimmed, with dark circles running deep underneath. He was an older man, probably mid-fifties if I had to guess, and the wrinkles on his face were a mixture of laugh lines mingled with frown lines.

But overall, he seemed like a stand-up guy.

"Listen, Marley, you're free to go for now, but if you think of anyone who would want to try to involve you, please reach out."

He rose from his chair, extending his hand. Following suit, I stood and went to place my hand in his until I saw the dried blood and pulled back. "Thanks, Detective Goodhart. I'll keep you posted if anything comes to mind."

Shoving my hands into my jeans pockets, I made the journey back to Starlight Books to pick up my kids and put this horrible experience behind me.

13

MAX

Days had passed since the devastating incident in the alleyway. After I left Marley at the police station for questioning, I went back to the scene and tried to have a few words with Officer Allen Barclay, one of the responding officers on the scene.

But every question I'd asked, he brushed off with a nonanswer or an inability to comment. While understandable, it was also frustrating when your girlfriend was tossed into the middle of town drama.

The increased crime rate was concerning, especially with my kids in town. But based on everything I'd heard so far, there were far more questions than answers.

Marley had been silently suffering ever since. She put on a strong face when the kids were around, but the moment she was alone, her frown would reappear as her smile slipped away. When she washed her hands, it was like she was transported back to the scene of the crime, even hallucinating, seeing the man's blood dripping off her hands and going down the drain.

It wrecked me to see her like that, so distraught and unsure of what was going on. I'd do anything to get my Marley back.

And now that the kids were in bed, it was my time to strike.

Marley was curled up on the sofa in the family room as she stared out the window, looking out into the night.

"Hey, Mar." I lifted her feet from the couch to sit down and placed them on my lap, massaging the soles of her feet one at a time. "I was thinking it was time for you to dive into your event planning work again. It could help get your mind off things."

She sighed into the cushions of the couch. "I don't know if it'd help."

"It can't hurt."

"You're right, but what about the kids?"

Little did she know, I'd already taken care of that. I'd rearranged the schedule at Remnant Hearts to have someone else come in to prep and open the joint while I'd work the night shift and close the place down. It'd be a bit of an adjustment, but if it allowed Marley to work with her clients, then that was a sacrifice I was willing to make.

It took a bit of convincing, but after laying out the plan, she was on board, except she wanted to put an ad out for a sitter for a few days a week so we wouldn't have to work opposite shifts all the time.

With no disagreements from me, we submitted an ad to the *Quimby Grove Gazette* before we settled into our respective rooms for the night with the promise of a better tomorrow.

WHEN I WOKE up the next morning, I found a smiling Marley in the kitchen making blueberry pancakes with the twins.

"I already have a sitter interview lined up for later this afternoon," she cheered. "I feel so much more positive about this new arrangement." She flipped a pancake over and moved to the fridge to grab a little milk carton for each kid before placing them in front of where Izzy and Jax sat at the table. "I've decided to put the incident behind me and really try to move on."

I walked over to the kids, ruffled their hair, and bent down to place a kiss on their foreheads. "Morning, kiddos," I greeted before turning my attention to the woman making us breakfast. "That's great, Mar."

She waved the spatula around, motioning for me to join her by the stove. "Kiss?"

Happy to oblige, I joined her and planted a kiss on her soft lips. "You are in a good mood this morning. I like it." I took the spatula from her and plated the pancakes that were finished cooking while Marley grabbed the butter and syrup.

"So what time is the interview?" I questioned as I sat down next to Jax and started to cut his pancake for him while Marley did the same with Izzy.

"Um, three thirty, I think. I was hoping to drop the kids off at Starlight Books with Ellawyn for a snack while I met with the interviewee at the coffeeshop on the square."

"Sounds like a plan."

I spent the rest of breakfast watching as Marley interacted with our children. I couldn't wrap my head around the fact that I had missed out on so much of their lives while Marley had handled everything by herself. If I'd just asked for her name or phone number that night on the beach...

I never should have let her leave.

It was my biggest regret, even before we were reunited. And now that I knew kids were involved, it was something I'd never forgive myself for. I'd spend the rest of my life making it up to them, hoping they'd eventually forgive me.

Forever didn't feel long enough to redeem myself, though. But it was all I had to give.

AFTER BREAKFAST and some time with the kids, I went into Remnant Hearts to open the bar one last time for the next few weeks. Today, I'd work from open until close and hopefully get to see Marley and the munchkins after the nanny interview.

The bar was all but empty as the day settled into the typical afternoon lull. The only person left was Old Man Woodford, who usually rode out the slow periods at the bar. If I were a betting man, I'd bet he was in his early seventies, with white hair and wrinkled features. He was a good guy, rarely drunk, just nursed a beer or two throughout the day.

I think he was just lonely and in need of company sometimes.

He sat at the bar, staring at the news channel that was currently on the TV. "Looks like it's going to thunderstorm later tonight." He jerked his head toward the screen.

"Oh yeah?" I wiped down the counter, careful to avoid his space. "We could use a good storm. It's been a minute."

"It has."

The conversation stalled as Woodford unfolded his daily newspaper and flipped through it for his favorite sections. I was just about to go to the back, when I heard shouting coming from outside. The voice sounded a lot like Marley's.

"Woody, I've got to step outside for a second. I think Marley may be in some trouble." Not waiting for a response, I opened the door to the bar and stepped out onto the sidewalk. Across the street, a few shops down from Starlight Books, stood Marley with her back to me. She was facing a tall blond guy who had his arms folded aggressively across his chest as Marley sternly told him to go home.

Not waiting for the crossing signal, I jogged across the street and joined them. "Hey, what's going on here?" I placed my hand on the small of Marley's back, a silent gesture of support, as I recognized the man.

Marley's hand went to her forehead as she tipped her head backward. "Max, remember Jakob, my ex-boyfriend from the city?" She leaned back into my touch ever so slightly. "He was the one who applied for the babysitting job. I told him absolutely not."

He huffed. "There's no reason not to let me. I've been around those kids for months. I've practically helped raise them since their dickhead of a father could never be bothered to."

A pounding radiated within my ears, my blood boiling at his comment. My hands clenched into fists as I tried not to lay this fucker out right here on the square.

Marley stepped in front of me, blocking my shot. "Jakob, enough. That situation has never been any of your business, nor did I ever make it your business. You were good to my kids. I won't deny that. However, for you to step in and watch them now is no longer appropriate or wanted."

My jaw clenched as I restrained myself from stepping around Marley.

Jakob eyed me suspiciously before looking back to Marley. "The deadbeat dad is a bartender, huh?" He shook his head, laughing. "A bartender, Mar? Really? You can do better than that. Fuck, you had better than that."

Wrapping an arm around Marley's waist, I gently pulled her back, placing her so she'd be standing off to the side. A playful smile pulled at the corners of my lips as I shook my head in amusement right before I cocked my fist back and aimed it straight for his fucking nose. The douchebag stumbled backward a few steps as he tried to stop the blood from traveling down his face.

"Stay away from my kids," I spat. Grabbing Marley's hand, I led us back toward Starlight Books.

Hours later, the knuckles on my right hand were still red and swollen from the punch I delivered to that fuckface, Jakob. I hadn't punched someone square in the nose like that since high school.

I took pride in being able to control myself, in my personal life and in my business. But the last straw was when he called me a deadbeat dad. I don't give a fuck about being looked down on because of my job. He hadn't been the first person to insult me about my career, and he certainly wouldn't be the last, but ever since I'd found out about Izzy and Jax, I'd been involved.

Sure, things were a bit rocky in the beginning, but we had all bounced back from that. Those kids were my whole world now.

So, fuck that guy.

I snagged a clean rag from underneath the counter and placed a handful of ice in the middle before wrapping it up and placing it on my bruised knuckles. Thankfully, the bar had been dead tonight because of the weather. Old Man Woodford hung around until about ten o'clock this evening, and since he'd left an hour ago, the bar had been empty.

A crack of thunder roared outside as the rain came down harder. Just as a flash of lightning struck, the door to the bar opened, and in walked a soaking wet Marley.

She was drenched from head to toe. Her blonde hair clung to her face in thick, wet strands. The dark red long-sleeve T-shirt she'd been wearing clung to her body in all the right places. Getting my mind out of the gutter, I arched an eyebrow in her direction. "What are you doing here?"

She moved further into the bar and pulled out a stool. "After the whole mess with Jakob, Ellawyn and Beckett offered to let them sleep over at their house so we could have some time together tonight. Plus, the kids could tell that something wasn't quite right, so a distraction helps." She shrugged. "But mostly, I just couldn't turn down the offer to have you all to myself for once."

I wouldn't have turned down the offer either. Ever since Marley had moved into my house, we'd kept our distance from each other. We both slept in our separate bedrooms as we let the kids adjust to a new house.

It was the right move for us, but it fucking sucked.

The last time I'd had Marley had been back in New York. I was hungry for her touch but ravenous for her taste.

"Remember our time together on the beach?" Marley spoke up, pulling me from my thoughts. "You kept calling me princess."

I flicked the switch on the open neon sign that hung in the window, turning it off. "I do. And I happen to recall you calling me busker and making me open your champagne."

She smiled. "You were the best thing to happen to me that night, you know. I never forgot it."

"Neither did I, for so many reasons," I admitted back to her.

She hummed. "Tell me more."

"Well, I never went to that beach expecting to fuck someone on the boardwalk. That was a first for me. But I also never saw someone as breathtaking as you. Yeah, you were dressed up in that fancy emerald dress, but it was more than that. You didn't look beautiful because of the dress. You just were. You had a fire that was ignited inside of you that night. You were a force to be reckoned with. I didn't stand a chance."

"It wasn't just fucking." The words trailed from Marley's lips in barely a whisper.

"No." I walked around the bar, joining her on the other side. "It wasn't. It was always something more. Something bigger than what we ever could have imagined."

"What would you say if I told you that I wanted you? Right here, right now. Like that time on the beach—rough, hot, and passionate. Make me yours."

"What would you say if I told you that I'd fuck you so hard that you might think I've broken you by the time we're finished?"

"I'd say break me, and don't fucking hold back."

"Take off your clothes." I turned away from her, heading toward the door of the bar to flip the lock and dim the lights.

Marley was right where I left her, naked and sitting on a barstool with her legs spread open. I watched her breasts as they rose and fell with the deep breaths she'd been taking. Her eyes were closed, her skin flushed with arousal. Her hands explored her body, traveling across her collarbone and down to her breasts as she lifted the round globes in her hands for a moment before taking a hand further south. One hand slid down her rib cage, traveling between her legs. With a flick of her nipple, she slid two fingers through her wetness as she whimpered at the contact.

As I watched the show play out before me, I unhooked my belt as quietly as possible before unbuttoning my jeans and pushing them and my boxers downward. Marley's whimpers turned to moans as the pad of her thumb circled her clit. Reaching behind my neck, I grabbed my shirt and yanked it over my head.

Marley looked sexy as fuck as she played with herself on a barstool in my bar. I'd never had a woman pleasure herself in front of me before. But as I stood in front of Marley, watching as she played her body like a well-known instrument, I knew she was a fucking goddess I'd spend the rest of my life worshipping.

Stepping in between her open legs, I leaned my head down and captured her mouth in mine. She yelped, surprised by the contact, but melted into the kiss as her thumb picked up speed. "It's so fucking sexy watching you get yourself off."

My hand slid between us, grazing her wet pussy with two fingers as she continued to circle her swollen clit. Marley's head fell backward as I slid two fingers inside her, curling them as I stroked her G-spot.

My fingers moved in and out of her, picking up speed as her moans grew loud enough to echo throughout my entire bar.

"Faster," she panted. "I need more."

"You want to come on my fingers or on my cock, baby?"

"Need you inside me," she murmured as her lust-filled eyes found mine. "I want you to bend me over this bar and fuck me as hard as you can." Marley pulled her hand away from her drenched core and climbed on top of the bar before spinning herself around to face me. "Get your ass back behind this bar and take me."

This is a side of Marley I hadn't seen before.

And it was sexy as hell.

Giving in to her request, I went behind the bar and stood behind Marley as she pushed herself up on all fours with her legs parted slightly, her ass on full display for me. I ran my fist up and down the length of my shaft while I rubbed my fingers through her slick heat and circled her clit, teasing her.

Marley pushed her ass back toward me, searching for more friction. "Max." Marley let out a moan as my name left her sweet lips.

"Come here." I tugged her closer, letting her feet hit the floor before bending her over the bar and lining my cock up at her entrance. I rubbed one side of her ass before I brought my hand up and back down in a swift motion, eliciting a yelp from Marley as I drove inside her as she moaned from the sting of the slap.

Grabbing her hips, I pulled her tighter against me as I

picked up my pace. Marley's moans grew louder as I fucked her hard and fast. I raised my hand and brought it down fast on the other side of her ass. She whimpered as I rubbed the redness, soothing the sting.

"I'm almost there," she gasped as I picked up my pace. "Max," she pleaded.

Reaching between her legs, I connected with her swollen clit, and within a moment, Marley was screaming out my name as she detonated beneath me.

What a beautiful sight, to watch her come undone.

With a few more hard thrusts, I buried myself deep and came just as she was coming down from an orgasm-induced haze. Leaning forward, I let my head drop to her shoulder as she pushed herself back up off the bar. With a tilt of her head, her lips found mine in a messy, passionate kiss.

It was a declaration.

She was forever mine, and I, forever hers.

14

MARLEY

Things with Max and I had been better than ever since our hot, passionate night at the bar. And while things had already been pretty great, they were now next-level amazing.

He and the kids moved me into his bedroom the very next day while I was working with my clients in town. When I came home, our lives were even more merged than they already had been. The kids were excited to see how happy their dad was when they revealed the surprise. The munchkins hadn't even batted an eye at us sharing a room. They were just happy.

Things in the bedroom hadn't been dull in the least. I was insatiable when it came to having Max, and he was more than happy to satisfy my needs while I met his stamina and his needs as well. We just clicked.

Things were moving in the right direction in every aspect of our lives. The only downside was that in a few short weeks, our summer vacation would come to an end. And with the end of summer came my inevitable return to my home in New York City.

Except now New York City didn't feel like home anymore.

Feeling unsure of my next steps, I pulled out my phone and checked the time. It was almost midnight, but I knew that if I called Avery for some sisterly love and support, she'd answer.

Avery answered on the first ring. "Hey, bitch. Where the hell have you been? It's been like a month since you called. You know I don't like texting."

My sister was very much so against texting, which was surprising considering everything else about her. She was a firm believer in having face-to-face contact, and if that wasn't an option, she opted for phone calls and letters.

"I know, I know." I rubbed a hand over my face. "Avery, I'm feeling a bit conflicted about returning to New York City in a few weeks."

"Of course you are," she comforted. "Let me guess, you've completely fallen in love with Max, and the kids are happy there." There was sniffling in the background and a pause before she continued. "I'm happy for you. You deserve that life, and so do my niece and nephew."

My heart broke for my sister. "Avery, I want to come home to you. But Max..." The words fell flat, unsure of what to say next.

"I get it, Mar. I do. Hopefully someday I'll have that, too."

"You will have that, Avery. I know you will. You're amazing."

She let out a little laugh before she changed the subject. "But in all seriousness, what is making you second-guess living in Quimby Grove full-time? In fact, I seem to remember telling you to just move there to begin with, not just go to 'visit' for a few months."

Avery was quiet as I filled her in on the incident in the alleyway and my other run-in with the Quimby Grove police. When I laid it all out there, it sounded like a lot of drama. And then when I topped it off with the drama with Jakob, I wasn't sure what Avery's reaction would be.

"Well, there haven't been any incidents with the police since, right? It sounds like you were only questioned the first time because you were a new face in a small town. It sucks but I could understand them wanting to chat with you, just to rule anything out."

"Yeah, true."

"And the big incident in the alley, well, I think that was just someone being a dumb fuck and trying to throw off the investigation by using the new girl in town as a scapegoat. It's a shitty thing to do, for sure."

I sighed into the phone. "Definitely a traumatic event."

"Has Jakob bothered you since?"

"Nope. I think Max punching him in the face really put the nail in the coffin on that. I haven't seen him around town, and I saw photos of him online back in the city. So, I think I'm good there."

Avery groaned. "You're still friends with him on social media?"

"Unintentionally. I deleted him after I saw the photo," I countered. "And you know I suck at managing all those damn apps. I'm almost like you in that regard."

Her laughter sounded through the phone. "Then I think you're safe to stay in Quimby Grove, if you wanted to."

Both of us went silent, and I asked myself if I wanted to stay in Quimby Grove. I thought so. I could see Max and me raising the kids in his beautiful home. I could envision walks through the square and hanging out at Starlight Books and the bar. I could see my business flourishing here. The vision of all the possibilities that could come with staying here were just dangling in front of me, waiting for me to grab on and take control.

The only problem was that Avery wasn't here. I wasn't sure I could leave my twin behind. Not after everything she had done for me and the kids. "Hey, Avery?"

"Yeah?" She yawned into the phone.

"Would you ever consider moving here, too?"

I held my breath as I waited for an answer. I knew deep down that Avery was still trying to navigate who she was and what she wanted her life to look like. Following me on my journey could derail her progress.

I would never want to cause her more harm or to set her back.

"Part of me feels like I'm unsure what I'd do. I know I don't want to be far from you. We're all that each other has. Ever since you went to Pennsylvania, I felt like my heart was out there wandering around without me.

"And that broke me, in a way. You don't know how many times I purchased a train ticket only to return it a few days later. And then the process would repeat. Deep down, I know I have to forge my own path, and I will, but I think I'd rather do it with you close by."

A tear slid down my cheek and onto my chest. "I feel the same way, Av. This is new for both of us."

"It is. Now that you have nothing to worry about on my end, you just need to take a leap of faith and talk to Max about your future." Avery yawned again before continuing. "That's my cue to hit the hay. Good night, Mar."

"Night, Avs."

With one tough conversation out of the way, I felt more confident with my decision to talk to Max about whether he'd want the kids and me to relocate here in the fall permanently so we could start our lives together.

He was my forever.

I just hoped he'd felt the same way.

Max had been a godsend when it came to adjusting his schedule to be with the kids while I met with clients and coordinated various events throughout Quimby Grove and the surrounding towns.

He woke up early each morning, getting ready for the day and making breakfast for all of us before he would usher me out of the house in support of my bustling business. And it worked for us for now. We let go of the babysitter option and just split the kid duty ourselves. I'd make sure to be home by the early afternoon, and then we'd swap positions. Me with the kids, and him at the bar most nights until nine or ten at night. Max no longer closed the bar unless his assistant manager was unable to.

It was seamless.

It was effortless.

It was perfect.

And today was no exception. The work I needed to do was finished early, and I rushed to make it home in time to have lunch with Max and the kids. I turned the handle on the door, pushing it forward, and stepped into the home.

"Hey, guys," I called out as I hung my keys on the key-shaped iron cast hook that hung on the wall next to our door. The smell of turkey wafted throughout the house as I meandered toward the kitchen. "It smells wonderful in here."

Izzy and Jax stood on step stools at the kitchen counter as they watched Max slice the turkey breast. Christmas music played throughout the kitchen, and the three of them were oblivious to my intrusion.

"Don't forget mashed potatoes," Izzy warned him. "I like to beat the potatoes with the big beater thingy."

"And gravy," Jax added.

"How could I ever forget the mashed potatoes?" Max placed the sliced turkey into a pan and slid it into the oven to keep warm. "All right, munchkins." He bent down, grabbing both kids in his arms, and turned toward the table behind them, finally noticing me. "Looks like Mama is home for lunch."

"Mama," the kids said simultaneously.

Max deposited the kids onto the floor. The moment their feet connected to the ground below, they dashed toward me.

"Hi, my babies," I greeted them. "What's going on in here? Christmas music in August?"

"We're celebrating twice this year," Izzy announced. "Because of the missed Christmases with Daddy, we need to catch up."

My heart broke at Izzy's words. It hurt like hell that Max had missed those years with the kids. That they had missed knowing their amazing Dad. I'd beaten myself up about it for years. If only I'd asked his name, where he was from... anything. This all could have been avoided. We may not have been a happy family back then, but it would have been better than them missing out on time together.

I'd never forgive myself that.

A lump formed in my throat. "It's a lovely idea, Izzy."

She beamed up at me, happy with herself for her bright idea, before scurrying back toward Max and handing potatoes to Jax. Lost in concentration, Jax stood on his step stool in front of the sink and rinsed the potatoes his sister had given him.

Stepping in line beside Jax, I got to work peeling the potatoes that he'd pass off to me. Together, as a family of four, we made our first real homecooked meal together while the sun shined through our open windows and Jingle Bell Rock playing in the background.

After lunch, Max went into Remnant Hearts while the kids and I hung back at the house and played in their bedroom until both had passed out from exhaustion on their bean bag chairs. Grabbing a blanket from each of their beds, I covered them up and eased a kiss onto their foreheads.

A nap was exactly what was needed.

I'd just tiptoed out of their room and eased the door closed when I heard something shatter downstairs. I jumped, my hand racing back down to the doorknob of the kids' room. My heartbeat was pounding in my chest as I chuckled.

Max must have come home earlier than anticipated and dropped a glass in the kitchen. Peeking into the kids' room, I made sure they were still sleeping soundly before going heading toward the staircase.

The sound of footsteps downstairs could be heard as I descended the stairs. When I reached the landing, I turned toward the kitchen, expecting to see Max, but I was only met with broken glass shards covering the floor.

Narrowing my gaze, I looked closely at the mess. It wasn't like Max to drop something like that and leave it on the ground untouched. He wouldn't want the kids to stumble upon it and potentially get hurt.

The hair on the back of my neck rose as I realized there could potentially be a stranger in the house. The sound of the front door opening caught my attention, and I ran toward the entrance of the house, hoping to see who was here.

The closer I got to the front of the house, the more the hammering in my chest intensified. The front door was wide open. Before freaking out completely, I quietly pulled my phone out of my pocket, my hands shaking, and shot Max a text, asking if he was at the bar.

His response was instant.

> **MAX**
> Of course.

A chill washed over me, creeping down my spine.

> Call the cops, someone broke into your house.

I responded to Max before shoving my phone into my pocket and making a beeline up the stairs, toward the kids' room. When I reached the second-floor landing, I ran as fast as I could for their door. I yanked it open and locked the three of us inside.

When I whipped myself around to check on them, I was relieved to find my two munchkins fast asleep, right where I had left them. My breathing was coming in fast, shallow spurts as I leaned my back against the door.

Taking a breath, I peeled myself from the sense of safety of the door and tiptoed over to the window that overlooked the front of the house. Peeling the curtain back an inch at a time, I craned my neck, looking for a sign, any sign, that someone was still on Max's property. But all I'm left with is the stillness of an eerily quiet home and the juxtaposition of the police siren coming off the main road as they turned down Max's long driveway, followed by Max himself.

AFTER THE HOUSE being swarmed with police, and a visit from Beckett and Ellawyn, Max and I were finally alone with Officer Barclay, which left us with a lot more questions than answers.

Officer Barclay had been one of the first officers to arrive at the house, with Max hot on his heels. He'd ordered Max to stay outside while I stayed in the room with the twins. The officer had done a sweep of the house, checking each room and nook and cranny for anybody. When he'd been finished, he led Max up to where I was and ordered us both to stay put while him and another deputy did a perimeter sweep of the property.

It felt like hours had passed until he came back and had us join him in the family room so he could tell us that he hadn't found anyone on the property, nor anything out of place beyond the broken glass in the kitchen.

"After examining the glass, I cleaned it up for you, ma'am, so you wouldn't have to worry about it." He adjusted his hat as he eyed me up and down. "You sure you didn't just leave the door open after coming inside?"

My mouth dropped open. "I'm sure," I snapped. "Even if that were the case, I'd sure as hell remember dropping a goddamn glass."

Rolling my eyes, I turned to Max. "I can't deal with this," I whispered before storming off toward the front door, where I pushed it open with more force than necessary. I had tunnel vision as I went down the porch steps and toward the cornfields off to the side of the house. Space. I needed some space from this house and Officer Barclay. How could he even think about asking me if I left the door open and insinuating that I dropped the glass myself?

Max had been the last one to leave, not me, and I knew for a fact that he'd pulled the door closed when he'd left, because he reminded me to lock it behind him.

Which I didn't do.

The toe of my sneaker connected with a rock, and I kicked it across the grass and walked next to the tall field of corn, following it out behind the house and around the other side. When I made my way back to the front porch, the last police car was driving down the long dirt driveway with a trail of dust lingering behind.

Part of me was relieved he had left. The other part wasn't quite ready to be alone in the house again.

The hits just kept on coming.

15

MAX

Ever since the break-in, Marley had been skittish in the house and avoided being alone at all costs. Which meant when she wasn't working, she'd be at Starlight Books or Remnant Hearts with the kids, instead of living her life the way she should be.

While I understood her fear, I wished we could try to move past it.

Izzy and Jax had been confused in the routine change and were beginning to grow restless of visiting the same two places in town. After the break-in, Marley wanted to keep this to ourselves and not let the kids know that something scary had happened. We didn't want to freak them out. But the worst part was, I didn't even know how to talk to them about the changes they were seeing—how their usual routine changed, or how their mama had become so jumpy suddenly—without telling them that something bad had happened at home.

Home is supposed to be a sanctuary, a safe place away from the depths of the world we lived in. We were supposed to be protected, but with a single incident, we'd been stripped of our sense of safety and were left feeling vulnerable and at a loss of what to do to combat that.

While I had readjusted more easily, Marley was struggling. While she was out on the town doing work, I would stay home with the kids and try to get some normalcy back in our lives.

I thought that maybe if Marley saw me staying at home with the kids without incident, then maybe she would give it a try herself.

I'd been wrong.

But during my days at home, the kids and I had a blast. Today was no exception. We had a full day of activities planned, most outdoors and a few inside. We played freeze tag in the yard before having a picnic outside, looked at the cornfield—which they found very intriguing—made homemade popsicles out of some juice and allowed them to freeze during their nap, and then we worked together to clean up their bedroom before Mama came home.

A car door slammed outside, followed by the stomping of high heels coming up the porch steps. When the door opened, a very annoyed Marley was staring me down. "Hey, sweetness," I greeted as I closed the distance between us. "How was your day?"

Dodging my touch, she turned her back to me and pushed the door closed and proceeded to lock it. "Why wasn't the door locked?"

"Because I was down here already, knowing you'd be home soon." Marley's frown deepened. "What's wrong?"

Her shoulder's slumped down, and the attitude she'd had a moment ago had fled. "I'm sorry," she started. "Today was tough. I completely forgot about an event I'm supposed to coordinate tonight…"

Her words lingered between us. If she had to work tonight, and I was due at the bar soon, then who would watch the kids?

I pinched the bridge of my nose while I thought this through. "When do you need to be at your event, and when do you think you'll be done?"

Her gaze darted down to the floor as she shifted her purse higher on her shoulders. "Um, well, I really shouldn't have even left..." Her pleading eyes found mine, tears welling in them. "I'm so sorry, Max."

Fuck, those eyes could break me. I opened my arms, hoping she'd choose to come and let me hold her. She hurriedly threw herself into my embrace. I ran a hand up and down her back before pressing a kiss to her forehead.

"It's okay, Mar. We can navigate this." Unfortunately, there was only one option. "I'll take them to work with me, and you can pick them up when you're finished with your event."

Her arms tightened around my waist as a sigh escaped.

"Does that work?" I asked.

She nodded into my chest before pulling away. "That works. I'm sorry again." She dug her keys out of the front of her purse. "I've got to go, but I'll see you tonight." Her lips touched mine for a moment before she was out the door again.

"Izzy, Jax," I called as I made my way back upstairs to my kids. "Change of plans. You're coming with Daddy to the bar tonight."

I guess it was my turn to feel like a single parent for once.

Normally, I wouldn't have minded bringing the kids to the bar to hang out while I worked, but bringing the kids on a Friday was an entirely different story.

Izzy and Jax were seated at the first booth along the wall and had been occupied with all the toys, books, and coloring pages they had packed for the day. It was easy to watch them when we first arrived—we were so fucking dead this afternoon—but now business was starting to pick up the further into the evening we got. Feeling desperate, I managed to convince Old Man Woodford to sit in the booth directly behind the kids, and stay sober, until I could get someone to pick them up for me. It only cost me a free night of drinking next week and free sodas and a meal tonight.

That was a pretty sweet fucking deal, if you asked me.

I filled up two glasses of water and a root beer for the trio and dropped them off at their tables. When I gave the kids their drinks, I slid into the booth across from them. "Hey, guys. You remember my buddy Beckett and his wife, Ellawyn, right?"

Izzy and Jax both nodded as they continued coloring a picture of a lion and her cubs. "Are they coming to visit?" Jax questioned as he looked up at me.

"Yeah, they're going to come and pick you guys up so you can hang out at their house until Mama gets off work. Does that sound like fun?"

Izzy's eyes lit up. "Yes!" She grabbed some crayons and started shoving them into the box. "Are they here now?" She plucked the yellow crayon from Jax's hand and added it to the box. "Sorry, Jackers, but we need to clean up!"

Jax only nodded before he ducked under the table, likely gathering the fallen crayons.

"They aren't here yet but will be any minute." I ducked my head under the table, checking on Jax. "All okay down there, buddy? Oh—there's a yellow crayon in the corner over there." I pointed to the forgotten crayon.

Jax grabbed it, grinning. "Thanks, Daddy." He pivoted his body and climbed back up onto the booth next to his sister as I stood back up.

I glanced back toward the bar and noticed some new faces had joined and were waiting to be served. "All right, munchkins, I have to go the bar for a few minutes. But my friend Woodford is right behind you if you need anything. I pointed over their shoulders, toward him. They followed my finger and turned to greet him with big smiles and a thousand questions.

That should keep them busy for a few minutes.

"Be right back," I reminded them as I strode past Woodford and went back to the bar.

The crowd around the bar was huge, which was unusual. About thirty people had lingered around, waiting for a barstool or just a drink to take back to their booth. I was used to having all the barstools filled by this time, but the crowd normally wouldn't have appeared until about ten at night. I saddled up behind the bar, apologizing for their wait as I started fulfilling drink orders.

"Where are you all coming from?" I questioned a group of men in jeans, T-shirts, and hats. It was in this moment I realized that I didn't recognize any of them. "Seems unusual for this time of day."

"The fairgrounds just let out," a man with graying hair answered.

"Okay," I drawled. "What was going on at the fairgrounds? And why does that have everyone coming into town?"

The fairgrounds were about a mile away and was the biggest outdoor venue we had here in Quimby Grove. It had over eighty acres of space, a huge grandstand, and plenty of buildings and pavilions. But their biggest moneymaker was their grassy outdoor space that was used all summer for car shows. Then it dawned on me what event just let out.

"Ah, there was a car show this weekend?" Quimby Grove hosted over a dozen weekend-long car events each summer. It brought plenty of tourists to town, and most of those folks would find themselves roaming the square in the evenings after the fairgrounds had closed for the day. "Let me guess, the Corvette show is this weekend?"

I poured them each a beer, as requested, and moved down the bar to begin waiting on the other patrons.

"Yep," the gray man confirmed with a nod of his head. "And the Corvette parade is going to start here in about an hour, so your crowd should thin out here soon for that." He grabbed his beer and took a long drink before smirking. "But then we'll be back. Won't we, boys?"

The group of men surrounding him broke out in cheers and hollered their excitement. Personally, I never really cared for the car show. But I'd been forever grateful for it bringing in extra business during the summer.

"Well, I'm glad to have you all." I grabbed some peanut boats from the counter behind me and placed them in between the men. "Let me know if you want anything to eat while you wait."

The men went back to chatting about their day, and I used the interruption to sneak a peek at Izzy and Jax. When I glanced at their booth, they were gone. My heart started racing as I rushed to get to their table. Rounding the bar, my feet came to a halt as they came into sight. They were sitting in Woodford's booth, directly across from him, giggling as he animatedly told them a story. Izzy threw her head back, her long blonde hair shaking as she laughed harder. Jax sat next to her, laughing at his sister.

Thank God they were safe.

Shaking my head, I went to the little window that looked into the kitchen and yelled at the cooks to get me two orders of fries.

"Got it, boss," one of the cooks yelled back. "Here, take these. They just came out of the fryer."

"Thanks." I snatched up the two baskets, grabbed a handful

of napkins and a bottle of ketchup, and made my way over to my kids. When I saw them this time, their expressions were much more serious as they listened intently to whatever bullshit Woodford was spewing. Both Izzy and Jax were sitting on their knees, their elbows leaning onto the tabletop as they ate up every word he said.

"Hey there, troublemakers," I greeted. "I brought some fries out for you to munch on." It wasn't the greatest dinner, but it was something. I sat a basket in front of the kids to share and one in front of Woodford before placing the napkins and ketchup in the middle.

"I'm no troublemaker," Woodford proclaimed as he plucked a fry from the basket and shoved it into his mouth.

"Woodford, you're the biggest troublemaker I've met."

He chuckled as he picked up his drink and finished it off. "Refill, barkeep." He slapped the table with his hand.

I ignored him as he proceeded to hold up his glass, shaking it in my face, and instead turned my attention to my kids. "You two holding up okay? Beckett should be here soon to get you."

With cheeks full of fries, they nodded excitedly. When Jax swallowed his food, he stretched out his arms, asking for a hug.

My heart swelled. I would never tire of giving them affection. I bent down, taking him into my arms and squeezing gently. "Love you, bud," I whispered.

"Moon and back," he responded with a squeeze of his own.

"Woody was just telling us stories," Izzy interjected. "Some were funny. Others, a bit not funny."

"Stories, huh?" I looked toward Woodford, who just shrugged. "Well, I'm glad you're having a good time." I ruffled her hair as she dipped a fry in ketchup. "You two behave, okay? No leaving this booth."

When they both agreed, I snagged Woodford's glass, refilled it with root beer, and dropped it off again. With one last look out toward the kids, I got back to serving drinks and talking to the tourists while catching up with the locals.

Them being here during a busy night wasn't ideal, but I couldn't help but love how they just melded into my life so easily, as if they'd always been there.

THE RUSH from the car show had dwindled as folks went out to the square to snag the best seats for the Corvette parade. With their arms filled with lawn chairs, coolers, blankets, and food, everyone was ready to watch the nice cars drive down High Street.

When I took in the status of my bar, I had to laugh. It was practically empty. Even my fucking cooks had ditched me for an hour to watch the parade. The only person inside was Woodford, and he was just happy to finally have real beer in his hands instead of a soda.

The spot where my kids had been now sat empty. I was thrown off by just how much I missed them. Beckett and Ellawyn had closed Starlight Books early because of the parade and then came over to pick up the twins, who were beyond thrilled to visit Uncle Beckett and Aunt Ellawyn's house.

Knowing the rush would be back with a vengeance soon enough, I grabbed the bin for dirty dishes, some cleaner, and a rag. The tables were sticky with dried beer that had sloshed over the sides of glasses. Dirty dishes were stacked on tables and tips haphazardly thrown about.

A clear reminder that I needed to hire some extra help in here.

After placing the bin onto the cushion of the booth, I sprayed the table my kids had vacated and wiped it clean. Out of the corner of my eye, I noticed Woodford watching me. I jerked my head in his direction.

"Thanks again for watching Izzy and Jax for me. Marley and I had a scheduling issue."

He nodded. "You're welcome. I quite enjoyed it, surprisingly. They were nice to talk to." He slid out from his booth, grabbing the three glasses and two baskets, and deposited them in my bin for dirty dishes. "Let me help you." He reached down, lifted the bin, and moved on to the next booth.

I stood straighter, caught off guard that he'd offered to help. "You don't have to do that, Woodford."

"I don't have anything better to do, Max. And you could use a little help." He placed a stack of plates into the bin and then moved further down the line. He wasn't wrong. With a sigh, I reluctantly let him continue while I cleaned the tabletops and seats.

We continued like that, working in comfortable silence one booth after another, until we had finished cleaning all the tables, the bar, and barstools. It didn't take near as long as it would have taken me if I'd done it alone.

We sat on the barstools and caught glimpses of the Corvettes that drove past us, but my mind wasn't focused on the cars. Instead, it was forming a plan. "What do you say about a job here?" The statement blurted out of me.

"Me?" He questioned, his eyebrows shooting up.

My eyes narrowed. "Who the fuck else would I be talking to?" I rose from the stool and went back around the bar to pour two beers. I slid one toward him as I took a drink from the other. "You're always here. And I trust you—with my kids and my bar."

He studied me for a moment before a crooked smile spread across his face. "I accept." He grabbed the beer and chugged it down. "You're a good father, Max. I hope you know that." He wiped his mouth with the back of his hand.

The compliment came from left field. "I'm trying to be," I admitted. "I know I probably shouldn't have brought them here today, but it felt like the only option at the last minute."

He waved me off. "They were fine. I was watching them and then you managed to find them a babysitter. No harm done. They had fun."

A sense of pride formed within me as I caught myself staring down at my beer. Maybe I could be a good dad after all. Maybe I wouldn't completely fuck this up. "Thanks, Woodford."

"Call me Woody." He grabbed his beer and drained what was remaining. "There are a lot of shitty parents in the world, Max. A lot of kids aren't lucky to be born into a family that loves them." He looked away longingly. "I don't know a lot about your situation, but even if you missed four years of their lives, they're lucky to have you. You're here now, and that makes all the difference."

We remained quiet as his words sank in and took over my thoughts. He was right. While those four lost years hurt, I had to move on from questioning the what-ifs and made sure our future was together.

"Thanks, Woody—"

A crash came from the kitchen, interrupting our conversation. Woody's gaze narrowed on me as he rose to his feet, hesitating. "I thought everyone was at the car parade?"

"They are..." Vacating my barstool, I grabbed a bat that had been displayed on the wall and pushed my way through the door that led into the kitchen. I could barely see as smoke filled the room, invading my lungs, making it harder and harder to breathe. Turning around, I ran back out into the bar. "Call 911 and then get out," I barked to Woodford.

I didn't hang around waiting for his response. Instead, I grabbed one of the fire extinguishers that hung near the entrance of the kitchen. Pulling my T-shirt up over my nose and mouth, I stormed back into the kitchen in search of the flames.

It might have been a fucking reckless decision, but I refused to let this bar go up in flames without a fight; it was far too important to me.

And I'd fight like hell to save it.

16

MAX

It had been a few hours since the fire had started, and my ass had gone numb from the curb I'd been sitting on ever since the firefighters ushered me out of my own goddamn bar so they could put out the fire before it spread.

I understood it but I didn't fucking like it. Not one bit.

It may have been just a few hours, but it felt like an eternity. Old Man Woodford had been by my side almost the entire time. He'd helped answer questions the police had, given a written statement, and had texted Marley from my phone for me. I just was not in the right headspace to be around other people right now. I didn't want to snap at Marley, or even worse, the twins. Not that I thought I would, but my level of fury was through the fucking roof.

After I'd been escorted out of my bar, I marched down the square in search of my kitchen staff and relentlessly questioned them on whether they had turned off the stove and fryers. My main cook was adamant that everything had been turned off, that he had checked it three times with the fry cooks, just to be sure. He'd been shocked at the news of the fire and seemed as devastated as I was. With a heavy heart, I told them to enjoy the rest of the evening and to just head home tonight.

Obviously, nobody could work now.

It was a fucking punch to the gut.

And now, here I was, sitting outside my most prized possession in the dark, completely heart broken. My father's bar had caught fire. My bar, that my dad had passed down to me, had caught fire.

A lump formed in my throat as tears threatened to come. Refusing to give in, I stood from the ground and watched as firefighters went in and out of the bar. Most of them avoided my gaze, and the ones that did look at me, their eyes were filled with pity as they passed me by.

The joys of small-town living.

Everyone knew your name and your story. I could see the headlines on the *Quimby Grove Gazette* already. The story of a high school graduate losing his only living relative since his mother had died during childbirth. Orphaned at eighteen and alone, he now dealt with the flames of destruction of his late father's bar.

An agitated growl flew out of my mouth as someone tapped on my shoulder not once, but three times.

"What?" I barked. When I turned around, I was face to face with Beckett and his co-worker, Kennon. "Sorry," I muttered. "I thought you were someone else."

Beckett focused beyond my shoulder, clearly looking at the bar and assessing it from the front. "The front looks like it always has. I take it the fire broke out in the back near the kitchen?" His body was rigid, his hands forming fists at his side.

Beckett was as upset as I was. This bar had been a huge part of both of our lives, not just mine. "Yeah," I mumbled. "In the kitchen."

Kennon was stoic as he took in the scene. "I'm sorry to hear about your bar." His eyes found mine, and while I couldn't read the emotion behind them, I knew he meant it.

Kennon was Beckett's VP for his company back in Boston. He was older than us, roughly ten years, if I had to guess. He was the quiet type, mostly unemotional and rather detached to those who didn't know him well.

From what I've learned, he was a good guy.

"Thanks, man." Refusing to turn back around to the wreckage, I was left standing in front of these two, either waiting for them to say more or to leave me alone so I could continue sulking.

Beckett broke the silence. "Let's go back to Starlight Books for a bit. We can make some coffee, and we have all sorts of food if you're hungry."

Kennon nodded his head. "I think that's a good idea." He looked around me, his eyes flitting between the folks on the scene until his gaze settled on the fire chief. "You guys go ahead. I'll hang back for a few and get some more intel."

Reluctantly, I agreed. I hadn't eaten since lunch, and my stomach was finally clueing me into how fucking hungry I was.

"All right," I responded and within a moment, Beckett and I were crossing the street and stepping inside a warm, inviting place of business that didn't just get fucking torched with a kitchen fire.

Although, I guess my bar was also literally warm right now.

And I can't help but feel fucking bitter about it.

Bypassing the tables, I opted to take up residence on the couch that was placed right in front of the front window, with a view of my bar. I hadn't even realized Beckett hadn't joined me right away, until he held a coffee mug right in front of my face.

"Thanks." I turned away from the window and accepted

the warm beverage. "I just can't wrap my head around what caused the fire."

Beckett sat down in the chair across from me. "Hopefully we'll know more soon. I'm just glad you're safe."

My eyes rolled involuntarily. "I'd rather have my bar and my dad's legacy intact." On some level, I knew it was a dumb thing to say. But I couldn't help feeling some sort of way about it.

Beckett stared at me, the pain written all over his face.

"Fuck, Beck." I ran a hand over my jaw. "I'm sorry. I don't mean that."

Beckett went to respond but was silenced by the sound of the bells chiming over the entrance to the bookshop. Kennon strode toward us, an unreadable expression on his face. It wasn't until he sat down in the chair next to Beckett that he broke his silence.

"They're thinking it was arson."

"That can't be," Beckett reasoned.

"Are you fucking kidding me right now?" I bellowed. "Arson? Somebody did this to my bar on purpose?"

"It's looking that way." He leaned forward, snagging his cup of coffee and bringing it to his lips. "The kitchen door in the alleyway had been smashed, and the sprinkler system was damaged severely."

My feelings had moved from simply being upset to being fucking enraged. I dropped my head into my hands as I tried to make sense of this mess. When that didn't help, I jumped to my feet and paced the length of the bookshop. Back and forth, back and forth repeatedly until I was pretty sure I'd left a lasting impression of my trail on the floor. When my legs grew tired, I retreated to my spot on the couch and looked at my bar.

"I just don't know what to do," I admitted.

"I don't think there's much to do until they're able to give you a full report," Kennon offered.

I needed something to distract me from this mess. Grabbing my now cold coffee, I turned back toward them. "What are you doing in town anyway?"

"Beckett and I discussed my relocating to Quimby Grove to help with the remote business while he tends to Starlight Books more and so I could provide a change of scenery for my kid."

I hadn't even known Kennon had a kid. Hell, I guess I didn't know much about him beyond what he did for a living. "Well, just beware of the arsonist we have running around here, apparently," I muttered.

"Noted," he said with a straight face, void of any emotion.

When he said nothing else, I looked across the street just in time to see one of the fire trucks drive off. "I'm heading out. I'll see you guys later."

Maybe I could finally get some fucking answers about what the hell happened in my bar. And just maybe, it wouldn't be left in ruins like me.

WITH NO INFORMATION from the fire chief tonight, I was left standing alone outside my bar, an empty town surrounding me with its deserted streets.

As I stepped toward the door, I took notice of the dark interior inside. I'd never seen it this dark before. Usually, I had some semblance of light on inside, even when closed. I pushed the door open, crossed the threshold, and flicked on the lights. Residual smoke lingered throughout the space, the smell invading my nose as I moved further inside, coughing the further into the building I went.

The front of the house had made it through the fire unscathed, except for the residual stench. I sighed as I made my way behind the bar—where I belonged—and poured myself two beers before I retreated to where my kids had sat just hours ago. Slumping into the booth, I slid toward the back and leaned my back on the wall.

My eyes focused on the doorway into the kitchen, unable to look away. I couldn't imagine what the damage was like. I knew how bad it had been before the fire department showed up, and it took them a decent amount of time to get everything under control.

If I had to guess, I'd bet it was completely wrecked.

The icy glass sent a chill running through my body as I latched onto my first beer. I downed it and then immediately went for my second. As my gaze stayed focused on the entryway into the kitchen, a knot in my chest formed as the reality of what occurred started to sink in. My bar—*my dad's bar* caught on fire. Someone did this. Someone was out to ruin something that meant everything to me.

Someone could have been trying to ruin me, too.

I stalked over to the bar and grabbed a couple of bottles of beer before returning to my booth. Racking my brain, I tried to think of anyone who would have the motive to do this. But I came up empty-handed. I kept to myself—mostly—and when I did frequent local shops or town events, everything had always been pleasant. Everyone knew me here. Quimby Grove's residents were like family—not just to me, but to everyone. Sure, we had some higher crime rates within the last year or so, but overall, our crime was low, and our town banded together to protect our own.

Popping the top of my next bottle, I leaned my head against the wall and let the liquid momentarily soothe my soul. A temporary Band-Aid for the shitty hand I'd been dealt tonight.

After grabbing my phone, I finally sent a text to Marley—admittedly something I should have done hours ago—filling her in on the fire and that I wasn't sure when I'd be home and gave her a warning that my phone was going to die soon. With the battery at five percent, I put the phone on airplane mode and abandoned it on the table.

While my buzz started to set in, my mind wandered back in time to whenever I was reopening my dad's bar as Remnant Hearts. The headline on the front page of the *Quimby Grove Gazette* had been dedicated to the grand opening. The town had been so supportive. Everyone showed up on the opening night—high school friends, fellow local business owners, friends of my dad's, Beckett, and so many others. It felt like the whole town was in attendance.

We held a ribbon-cutting ceremony with the giant scissors and everything, along with a lighting of a neon sign I'd proudly hung in the window ever since. The neon sign proudly displayed the bar's name and was accompanied by a deep red broken heart that would intentionally flicker every so often. It looked fucking amazing.

I'd never been much of a believer in the afterlife. I'd never given it much thought, though either. But I could have sworn I felt my dad alongside me that day. His presence was there, enveloping me like a warm hug I'd missed for far too long.

That moment had gotten me through many bad times over the years. My dad was my best friend. When he passed, I was alone and terrified of knowing a life without him. I wasn't sure I could even survive life without him, but when I decided to reopen the bar, to continue his legacy, I'd found purpose. I'd found my dad again. I felt it the strongest back then, but as I sat in the smoke-filled bar tonight, the feeling returned. The feeling that, while this fucking sucked, everything would be okay. It was a setback, not a complete loss.

I could rebuild.

I *would* rebuild.

But if I ever found out who fucked with my bar, there'd be hell to pay, and I was as determined as ever to find out who did this.

17

MARLEY

It was early morning, and the inside of Remnant Hearts was dark, with not a single light on in the joint. Not that it was needed, but whenever Max was inside, he'd always flip a light on to show he was there.

Pressing my face to the storefront window, I cupped my hands around my eyes and searched for any sign of him. I'd almost given up when I saw a pair of jean-clad legs coming out of a booth. I twisted the doorknob as quietly as possible, then pushed the door open and stepped inside before gently letting the door shut behind me.

The bar reeked of smoke from last night's fire. The space had a heaviness about it that was almost suffocating. After grabbing a barstool, I went back to the door and propped it open, hoping we could air out some of the smoke and make it a bit easier to breathe.

Max never made it home last night, and I hadn't heard from him after he sent me a text letting me know what had happened to the bar. I knew before he told me, of course. Beckett had filled Ellawyn in and then she'd called me. I had a feeling he'd need his space for this, so I decided it was best if I stayed put until he reached out. Beckett had agreed, knowing Max was in a bad place, and offered to keep the munchkins overnight in case Max needed me.

My heart broke last night when he didn't reach out to me. I'd desperately wanted to be there for him through this. To be his rock, a safe place for him to land. I wanted to give everything I had to this man. But he didn't give me the chance. Instead, he stayed inside his bar and drank himself to sleep.

I strode over to him and nudged his foot with mine. "Max," I called out. "It's time to wake up, babe."

He was lying down in a booth, hunched up with his head lying on a makeshift pillow made from a rolled-up hoodie. On top of the table were six empty beer bottles and four empty bottles of water.

His black Remnant Hearts T-shirt was dirty with debris from the fire. His jeans were just as bad. His face and arms were also tainted with a reminder of what had happened last night.

My heart broke for this man.

Leaning down, I gently shook his shoulder and called his name again. His eyes fluttered open, and his hands curled up into fists as he wiped the sleep out of his eyes. It was the cutest thing I'd ever seen.

"Hey, sleepy head," I greeted as I extended a hand to help him up. He placed his hand in mine, and I tugged him upward until he was seated. I slid in on the opposite side of the booth, sitting across from him. "Are you okay?"

He dropped his head and sighed. "I've been better." When he met my gaze, his eyes were swimming with tears. One tear escaped before he looked to the ceiling, blinking his eyes to stop the floodgates from breaking.

"I'm sorry this happened, Max. I'm so fucking sorry." I reached out, taking his hands in mine, and held them on the table. "What can I do?"

I'd do just about anything to remove the frown from his face. To make his sadness a little bit lighter.

He laced his fingers with mine. "You're doing it. You being here is exactly what I need right now. I'm sorry I didn't come home last night. I just needed to be here by myself for a bit."

Any hurt I'd felt last night had vanished once he said those words. I could understand Max needing that space. After all, this bar was everything to him. It was a connection between him and his father.

"It's okay." I gave a squeeze before rubbing my thumb over his hand. "How's the damage?" I lifted my head toward the kitchen.

"I haven't had the balls to go back and look." He lowered his head. "I wanted to check it out last night, but I just needed one night to mourn what happened. One night to let my feelings out. To shout my frustration and to cry out the sadness." He ran a hand over his beard, chuckling. "Apparently, I needed to have a fucking pity party where I drank my damn sorrow away and drowned in my own tears."

My lips curved. "I'd say it was quite the party," I teased as I gestured to the empty bottles. "Do the police know what happened?" It didn't make sense. A fire wouldn't just erupt out of nowhere. Not here. Not whenever Max took impeccable care of his business.

Max's jaw ticked. "They're thinking it was arson."

My mouth dropped open. "Who would have done that?" In the couple of months I've been here, I knew Quimby Grove wasn't a sinister place. Everyone knew everybody here. Everyone was friendly and looked out for one another.

Except whoever vandalized that business when I had first visited.

Or whoever had stabbed that man in the stomach in the alleyway.

A chill crept through my body, causing a shiver. All those incidents happened after I'd arrived in Quimby Grove. The vandalism could have been an isolated incident, just similar timing. But the stabbing had been linked to me—my business cards were found on the scene. Then someone entered Max's house when I was alone.

And now this.

The realization hit me like a ton of bricks. How could I have been at the center of all this? What could I have possibly done? I'd only known Ellawyn and Beckett when I first came to town. And Max, of course. But Max wasn't behind any of this.

Jakob.

Could it have been him? He'd only been in town those two times, when Max had swung at him whenever Jakob had been a dick outside of Starlight Books. I pulled out my phone and sent a text to Avery.

> Have you seen Jakob lately?

Sliding my phone back into my purse, I turned my attention back to Max as he answered my question. "I've been thinking about it all night, and I can't come up with anyone." He stood from the booth, stretching his arms over his head before gathering his empty beer bottles. "Probably some punk-ass teenager thinking they're hot shit. Fuck if I know." He rounded the bar and placed the bottles inside a bin for recycling. "I just don't know."

I pushed off the table, then went over to the kitchen door. "Shall we?"

Max and I were covered in dust and dirt as we worked our way through the aftermath of the fire. We were sweaty, disgusting, and downright exhausted.

After Max had called his insurance company to file a claim, we ended up having to take photos and videos documenting the damage. The rest of the day was spent rummaging through everything and filling the trash bins in the alley behind his bar. While there were a lot of debris, the damage wasn't as bad as we'd imagined.

That didn't mean it wasn't horrible, but Max would bounce back from this hit. He'd need some new appliances, and the entire kitchen would need a deep cleaning, but we could handle that.

I grabbed a brick that had been on the floor near the fryer and examined it. "How the hell did a brick get in here?" I looked around the space, searching for where it could have come from. "Uh, Max?" I called out. "There's a note attached to it." The piece of paper had been secured by a rubber band, unmarred by the fire.

Max strode over. He grabbed the brick and ripped off the band. His brow furrowed as he unfolded the paper, carefully inspecting every detail. While he read the note, a deep growl escaped from his throat as he crunched up the paper in his fist, angrily squeezing it in his hand.

"What did it say?"

"It doesn't matter," he muttered before tossing it carelessly aside on the prep table he had. "I'm going to walk to the police station and let them know about this. You okay here for a few minutes?" He raked a hand through his hair. "I just need some air."

"Yeah, of course," I assured him. "I'll clean up the front of the bar while you're gone. I tried my best to give him a reassuring smile, but I'm sure it was clear that shit was forced.

After Max left, I deposited myself into the very booth he'd slept in last night and pulled out my phone to see if Avery had responded to my text yet. It took all I had not to peek at my phone all day. When I saw her name on my notification screen, I wasn't sure if I should feel relieved or terrified.

Taking a deep breath, I opened our text chain and read her message.

> **AVERY**
> Ugh. Yes, unfortunately. I've seen him more times in the last seventy-two hours than I'd care to. Last night, that douchebag was at a bar I visited, and this morning I saw him on the subway. Bleh.

If my sister had seen Jakob both last night and this morning, then he couldn't have been responsible for the fire. I typed out a quick thank-you to Avery and put my phone away. An unsettling feeling took over. If it wasn't Jakob, then who could have done this? I didn't want him to be responsible, but I was hoping for some answers at least.

Now more than ever, I needed to know what was written on that paper. Not wanting Max to walk in, I rushed to the kitchen and grabbed the balled-up paper. The air in the bar felt heavy as I smoothed it out on the table. The words, written in thick black marker in an angry scrawl, made my heart drop.

If she doesn't leave town, next time it'll be her caught in the crossfire.

The air vanished from my lungs like I'd been sucker punched. I was the 'her' from the note. I was the one they were pissed at. I snapped a photo of the note before crumbling it back up and calling Avery.

She answered after one ring. "Hey, sister," she greeted. "Are you calling to talk about how fucking unlucky I am to have run into Jakob so much these past few days? Because he is such a—"

"Avery." I left the kitchen and returned to the booth out front. "Are you absolutely sure you saw Jakob last night and again this morning?"

She groaned. If there was one pet peeve of Avery's, it was that she hated being interrupted when she was talking. "Marley, I think I know who Jakob is, so yes, I'm sure."

"I need you to be a thousand percent sure, Avs."

"I am. Last night he and I talked. He thought I was you, and I had to set him straight. We were in the club around eight o'clock last night, and I saw him there at last call, too. This morning he was on the subway with me at about eight or so."

If Jakob wasn't behind all this, then who was? He couldn't have been in Quimby Grove and at the same club as my sister. "Avery, someone is threatening me, and I'm scared."

I told her everything. She knew about most of it, but I hadn't had a chance to fill her in on the break-in, and now I had to spill on the bar fire and the note. When I was finished talking, she was livid and threatening to hop on the train and haul my ass home.

I wasn't going to lie, heading home was on my mind, too. It was the only option that made the most sense. Someone in Quimby Grove didn't want me here, and I wasn't about to be a sitting target with my children close by.

But fuck that. My fear had morphed into anger the more I thought about what had happened this summer.

I was done.

I wanted out of Quimby Grove and on the next train out of here.

Fuck this town, the psychopaths in it, and fuck Max for luring us here. I threw my purse over my shoulder and turned the doorknob to leave. But when the door swung open, I knew I wasn't going anywhere anytime soon.

18

MAX

"Where are you going?"

I'd just returned from the police station and opened the door to the bar when Marley appeared, looking like she was ready to leave, with pursed lips and a challenging stare. I'd never seen her so pissed. Granted, I hadn't known her long but still. "What's wrong?" I questioned when she didn't answer me.

She turned away from me in a huff and sat on a barstool. "I was just about to leave."

"I know. Where were you going, though?" I eyed her up and down. Nothing seemed wrong physically. Had something happened when I was gone? My eyes scanned the front half of the bar before landing on the kitchen door. When I looked back at her, she was glaring in the direction of the kitchen. "What's wrong?"

"I read the note that you carelessly crumpled up and discarded like yesterday's trash." She dropped her head, her shoulders shaking. "Someone doesn't want me here, Max."

I moved into her space, taking the barstool next to her. "I didn't mean to imply that the note was trash. I was angry and about ready to fucking snap, so I tossed it aside and marched down to the police station to let them know about it." I rubbed a hand over my face. "I should have taken it with me since they need it. But more importantly, I should have told you what it said instead of just leaving."

Her hands reached out, latching onto mine for dear life. "I was going to go home," she whispered. "To New York, I mean..."

"You can't run away, Marley. That won't—"

The door to the bar opened, interrupting our conversation, and in walked Officer Barclay, whom I had just spoken with down at the station.

"Hey, what's up?" I asked.

"Just thought I'd walk down and grab the note from you." He glanced around the bar, his eyes landing on Marley for a split second before he brought his attention back to me. "Just thought I'd save you the trip. I didn't get to tell you last night, but I'm sorry about what happened." He jerked his head toward the kitchen.

"Thanks. Let me grab it." Leaving the two of them alone, I went into the kitchen and grabbed the note. When I returned, Marley had moved behind the bar and was getting herself a bottle of water, and Officer Barclay had taken a seat on a stool and had a pair of blue gloves on. "Here you go." I handed him the note and watched him smooth it out on the bar's surface.

His eyes lingered on it briefly before snapping up at Marley. "I take it this threat is directed at you?" He folded up the note and deposited it into an evidence bag he had brought with him. "Do you have any idea who would be targeting you?"

Marley's expression turned cold as she stared at Officer Barclay and answered his second question. "I thought it could have been my ex-boyfriend from New York, but I confirmed he was in town last night and this morning. His name is Jakob Anderson, though, if you want to confirm his story."

Officer Barclay nodded, taking note in a small notepad he kept in his jacket pocket. "I think I will check in with him," he said. "And when do you go back to New York?"

"It hasn't been decided yet," I cut in. "When will we know more about the fire and this note that was attached to a fucking brick?"

"Mr. Quinn, we're doing everything we can."

"It's Max, not Mr. Quinn," I interjected. I'd known Allen Barclay since elementary school, and we'd never been friends. More like acquaintances that tolerated each other. We didn't run in the same circles. His crew hated mine and vice versa. I wasn't at all surprised he'd ended up becoming a cop. He loved being in charge; his superiority complex thrived off it.

"Okay, Max," he muttered as he stood from his stool. "You didn't mention the brick when you came down to the station. That brick hadn't been inside the kitchen last night when we investigated the fire. That had to have happened after."

Son of a bitch. Had someone come into the kitchen when I'd been inside last night? How had I not heard anything?

Oh, I was drunk.

Officer Barclay looked up at the ceiling, debating something. "Can I take a look at the kitchen?" Without waiting for an answer, he charged toward the door, with Marley and me on his heels. He looked around the space, taking it all in before pointing toward the back entrance. "Looks like the brick was thrown through the window."

How had I not noticed the broken window earlier today? Perhaps I'd just assumed it happened with the fire. "Son of a bitch," I mumbled. "If one more thing goes wrong in this damn bar..."

Marley stepped up, rubbing a hand up and down my back. "We'll get it fixed," she reassured. "It'll be fine."

With his phone, Officer Barclay snapped a photo of the door with the broken glass, along with the brick. "I'm going to head back to the station and get this note processed and add the photos of the brick and broken glass and modify the incident report. I'll see myself out. Thanks."

After he was gone, all I was left with was a broken bar and the terrified look of the mother of my children, who desperately wanted to leave town.

THE TENSION from the incident at the bar had crept into our lives more and more as time went by. A few weeks had passed since the fire and the threatening note, and we were no closer to any real answers than we were back then.

We knew it was arson, but that was about it. Whoever was responsible had just dumped some gasoline in the kitchen—on top of the grills, the fryers, on the floor, and anywhere they could—then basically lit a fucking match and bolted.

Thankfully, they hadn't completely doused the place, and it was caught quickly. The police had zero leads for me for the fire, and they were working under the assumption that the brick was thrown through the window by the same sick fuck who had started the fire to begin with. The note was also a dead end. There were no fingerprints to be found except for my own and Marley's.

The only plus side was that Office Barclay was able to confirm an alibi for Marley's ex-boyfriend for the night of the fire and the day that my house was broken into, so we knew he wasn't the culprit. While it would have been nice to have an answer, it was also a relief to Marley to know he wasn't responsible.

It was bittersweet.

With zero answers, we were stuck in limbo. I'd managed to convince Marley to stay in Quimby Grove with the kids instead of returning to New York early. With the summer coming to an end, everything was unresolved. Would they want to stay and move in? Would Marley want to continue building a relationship with me? The closer the end of summer got, the further she'd been pulling away.

Marley had taken to sleeping in the guest bedroom ever since the fire, saying that she just needed some space to process everything. Often, though, I found her asleep in a bean bag chair in Izzy and Jax's room.

She was afraid. I couldn't fault her for that. Fuck, I was afraid too.

I'd been on high alert ever since. We kept the doors locked at the house at all times, and whenever I was at the bar working on repairs, Marley took the kids to Starlight Books to hang out with Ellawyn and Beckett so she wouldn't be home alone.

This was our new normal.

Living in fear, constantly looking over our shoulders and waiting for the other shoe to drop. Only, it never came. We'd been left alone ever since, which somehow was almost worse than something happening.

We'd put on a brave face for the kids, trying to keep things as light as possible. But Izzy and Jax weren't dense; they knew something was up. We did our best to occupy their time and keep them entertained as best we could. They were safe and happy—that was all that mattered to me. Them and their mother were my top priority.

The sounds of little feet running on the second floor had my spirits lifting. While Marley was out working today, I'd taken a day off from repairs at the bar and was on kid duty instead.

"Daddy!" Their voices carried as they rushed down the stairs and grew louder until they found me in the kitchen. "We have an idea," Jax said as Izzy nodded eagerly at his side.

I crouched down to their level and opened my arms toward them. "Oh yeah?" They stepped into my embrace, and I hugged them tightly. "Tell me about it."

Their arms went wild as they animatedly told me about their plans for the day. Their smiles were contagious. I found myself growing excited with them

"So let me get this straight—you want to have lunch at the hotdog house, go to the flower shop to get flowers for Mama, and then hit up the new bakery for some after-dinner sweets. Did I get all of that?"

"Yep," Jax said with a loud p sound at the end.

"It was Jax's idea," Izzy encouraged. "We're so tired of staying home all day." Her shoulders slumped.

They had a point. They'd been kept at home for far too long. It was time for a little adventure. "I'm in. Let's get our shoes on and head out." I started to head toward the front door to grab our shoes, but Izzy stopped me.

"Uh, Daddy," Izzy called.

"What's up, munchkin?"

"We're in our jammies," Jax said.

I looked at their outfits and laughed. It seemed that they were in pajamas. Izzy had on a light pink two-piece sleep set that was covered in dark pink hearts. Jax wore a dark blue pair of pajamas with dinosaurs on them.

"First one upstairs gets to give Mama the flowers this evening."

They both ran up the stairs, each fighting to take the lead.

"Wait for me," I called, chasing after them while they giggled in the next room.

It was my first day taking the kids around Quimby Grove on my own, and we melded into the town as if the three of us had always been here together. The two of them were home. I'd always lived here, but now, with the kids here, it felt like home. *They* were home.

Lunch at the Hamilton was entertaining. Izzy was game to try the infamous hot dog, while Jax ordered a grilled cheese sandwich and the three of us shared an order of fries. Izzy was a lover of ketchup, while Jax liked to dip his in gravy. Both were in awe over the tiny crushed ice cubes that came in the water glasses. Izzy insisted on refills of not only the water but fresh ice as well.

An ordinary meal taught me a lot about my kids.

The three of us poured out onto the sidewalk, hand in hand in hand, and headed in the direction of our local flower shop, Fairytale Blooms. When we finally stumbled upon it, the three of us stopped out front, staring in awe. The shop was beautiful. The exterior was a deep, dark green with bright red flowers intertwined with vines that lined the doorway and trailed up toward the second floor of the building.

How had I not appreciated this building before?

Izzy pulled on my hand, tugging me toward the entrance. "Daddy, come on."

I fell in line behind her, and Jax and opened the door for them.

"Jax!" she said. "Do you smell all of this?" She stepped inside, twirling around in circles as she took in the space.

Jax sniffed the air, nodding. "It smells like Mama."

Izzy smiled at her brother. "It does."

We made our way through the store, admiring all the floral arrangements and plants. The walls had been lined with flowers in galvanized planters and arranged by color.

"Good afternoon," a voice carried toward us from across the shop. "Welcome to Fairytale Blooms, my dream come true."

We moved to the middle of the store, where the cash register was.

"Hey, Miranda," I said. She rounded the counter, and I pulled her in for a hug. "How have you been?"

Miranda and I had gone to high school together. She had been the shy new girl in town who was nice to everyone she'd come across. She had a love of flowers back then, too. And love for fairy tales and the happily ever after that came with them.

She smiled warmly, brushing me off with a wave of her hand before she crouched down to greet the kids. "I want to hear all about these two lovely children." She held out her hand. "Hi there, I'm Miranda. I own this shop."

Jax stepped back toward my legs, while Izzy shot her hand out. "I'm Izzy and we're here to buy flowers for Mama."

Miranda shook Izzy's hand and gave a small wave to Jax before rising. "Your Mama is a lucky lady. What kind of flowers does she like?"

Jax stepped forward. "She likes lily flowers."

Miranda beamed. "I've got the perfect thing for you."

With two fresh bouquets of tiger lilies wrapped up and held in little hands, the three of us meandered a few blocks from my bar toward the newest bakery, Erin's Sugar Shack. I knew just from looking at the exterior that I would hate this goddamn place.

It was pink.

Fucking pink. It was like that damn Strawberry Shortcake girl had thrown up all over the place, leaving specks of sprinkles and frosting everywhere. Everything was covered in pink except for the awning above the windows—which was white and resembled frosting. With a groan, I pulled open the door, following my munchkins inside.

As predicted, it was insane. The walls were lined with alternating shades of pink stripes, the floor was checkered black-and-white. Along one side of the wall, a pink vertical booth ran down the length entirely, and the back of the booth was decorated like an actual fucking cupcake, with a wrapper, frosting, and a cherry. The chairs across the table even had rainbow upholstery on the seats.

Izzy's and Jax's mouths dropped open, their eyes as wide as saucers. "Wow," they said at the same time.

Placing my hands on their backs, I nudged them forward toward the display case. "Come on, we've got to head home soon if we want to beat Mama." That and the sooner we ordered, the sooner we could get the fuck out of there.

The swinging doors leading into the back of the shop opened, and a petite brunette appeared behind the counter. "Hello there, I'm Erin," she greeted. "I'm the new owner of this bakery since Miss Charlotte decided to retire." She shimmied behind the counter. "I spruced it up a bit. What do you think?"

"Was it always this pink?" I deadpanned.

The woman giggled as she slid on some clear gloves. "No, the décor used to be all brown." She shuddered. "Which didn't fit the vibe I was going for."

"Was your vibe pink?"

She paused for a moment, considering my question before she broke out into laughter. "Goodness, you're a funny one. You're Max, right? And these are your kids?"

"Yep." I'd never met this woman before, but I guess I could thank small-town living for information traveling fast. She must have read my mind, because she quickly explained herself.

"Sorry." She put her hands in the air. "I heard about the fire in the bar and then saw your picture in the following *Quimby Grove Gazette*."

Now that made more sense.

"As I said, I'm Erin." She held out a hand. "I just moved here from out of state. It's always been my dream to open a bakery. When I saw this space for sale, I had to snag it up for my Sweet Dreams Bakery."

I shook her hand and pulled away before continuing to eye the display case. "That's great. Welcome to town." Izzy and Jax were pointing to the display case, practically drooling over the cupcake selection. "We're here for some after-dinner desserts."

Erin was patient as the three of us took our time selecting our desserts and picking out two for Marley to choose from. Izzy picked out a unicorn cupcake, Jax selected a giant iced sugar cookie, and the munchkins picked me out a tie-dye cupcake and donut. For their Mama, we went with peanut butter cookies and an iced donut. The kids were so excited about picking out a dessert that Erin offered both kids a chocolate chip cookie for the road.

With the kids on a sugar high, we grabbed our selections and made our way back to the car with our hands full so we could start dinner before Marley got home. Both kids fell asleep as soon as they were buckled into the car. As the silence seeped in, I couldn't help but notice that this whole experience today taught me how much I didn't know about Marley yet.

But I hoped I had a lifetime to learn.

19

MARLEY

The aroma of garlic, sauce, and cheese wafted through the house as soon as I opened the door and stepped inside. My mouth began to water, and my stomach suddenly growled because I had missed lunch. Dropping my purse to the floor, I followed my nose down the hallway and into the kitchen, the smell growing stronger with each step.

    Classical music played in the background while Max stood at the stove, slipping on oven mitts and pulling down the door to the oven. Izzy sat at the kitchen table with her knees on the chair as she placed garlic bread into a cloth-lined serving dish. Jax mimicked her pose and strategically placed desserts onto the table. He'd rearrange the desserts, trying to find the arrangement that looked best. In the middle of the table were tiger lilies—my favorite—placed in a beautiful water-filled vase.

    Tears pricked my eyes as I stood in the doorway, watching them work while I committed this image to memory. They were oblivious to me witnessing their private moment. I felt like an intruder in their day.

    It was Izzy and Jax's first full day alone with Max. My fears from earlier this morning had been for nothing. I'd been worried, thinking that maybe Max couldn't handle the munchkins, which he wasn't used to. It was silly for me to worry; I knew that now, and deep down, I knew it then too.

Summer had flown by. We'd all been busy and fully immersed in one another's lives. This summer was about getting to know one another and seeing how we fit together. And while we still had a lot to learn, Max got a glimpse into my life as an event planner while the kids and I watched him pour his heart into his bar day in and day out.

Until someone had tried to burn it down.

Because of us.

Because of *me*.

It was a reality I couldn't shake just yet. Ever since the fire, I'd been haunted by the thought that this was all because of my being in Quimby Grove. It was a nightmare turned reality, each night a sleepless one as I tried to put the pieces of the puzzle together.

I had nothing—no idea who would want me out of town or why. I didn't really have enemies. Alison and Jerin were on the other side of the country, settled in California. My ex-boyfriend Jakob had stayed in New York since Max had punched him outside of Starlight Books. Based on what Avery had told me, he'd even started a new relationship a month or two ago.

There wasn't anyone left for me to consider.

After my hookup with Max on the beach all those years ago, I'd been celibate even when I was with Jakob. I was a pregnant young woman and then a single mother to twins. There was no time for men, not until I'd met Jakob when the twins were three, and by the time Max stumbled back into our lives, things with him were fizzling out naturally.

I had no ill feelings toward him, which I made sure he

knew. There was just no spark. The last spark I'd felt had been all those years ago on the beach, drunk off champagne. Once Max reentered my life, the spark returned, even if he was a pain in the ass at the beginning of summer.

Smiling at the memory, I leaned back against the doorway, crossing my arms and taking in my family. The corners of my mouth turned up—Max was family now. No matter what happened, we'd forever be linked. Even if the kids and I went back to New York soon, we'd forever be tethered.

Izzy slid down from her chair and turned toward me, her little mouth dropping open when she noticed me standing there watching. "Mama!" she shouted as she ran toward me.

I crouched down just as she barreled into my arms. Jax turned when he realized what his sister said, grabbed a handful of flowers that were lying on the windowsill, and took off after Izzy.

"Hi, baby." I kissed her hair and hugged her tight before opening my arms for Jax to join in our favorite group hug. Jax squeezed in, flowers going behind my back as he kissed my cheek. "Hi, Jax. I missed you, buddy." I kissed his cheek in return before standing and glancing toward Max.

He was leaning against the counter with his arms crossed over his broad chest, watching us with a grin. "Welcome home, beautiful." He moved toward us, crouched down like we just were, and opened his arms wide. "How do we make the awesome-looking hug into one for four people?" He questioned with a tilt of his head. "Is there room for me?"

Jax stepped into Max's outstretched arms and wrapped his arms around his neck. Izzy was next, adding her arms to his neck too.

"There's always room for you, Daddy," she murmured. Max looked up at me, waiting. "Come on, Mama," he said.

Blinking the happy tears away, I stepped into the group

hug, wrapping my arms around the kids as Max held me firmly in place.

"I never want to let go," Max said into the kids' hair as his eyes found mine.

"Me neither," I whispered. "Me neither."

OUR DINNER WAS AMAZING. The lasagna was perfect, even more so because the kids had helped make it, and the garlic bread hit the spot. Izzy and Jax were proud of their contributions to the meal but were even more excited for dessert when they placed two options in front of me: peanut butter cookies and a donut with white icing.

We ate our desserts together, chatting away about our day and what we liked most about it. The kids agreed that their favorite part about today was spending the whole day with their daddy. Mine had been coming home to a lovely surprise dinner, and Max's had been spending time with the kids and seeing my face when I came home.

While my heart was full tonight, it was also cracking a little each time I thought about the fire and what that could mean for me.

For us.

But now wasn't the time to bring down the mood, as I was meeting Ellawyn at the wine bar, Illusion, in town tonight.

Max had surprised me with a girls' night. After we finished eating, he pushed me up the stairs, insisting I change into something comfortable, and dropped the bomb that I'd be going out for a little fun this evening.

My heart cracked a little more at that moment.

Maybe a night with Ellawyn was what I needed the most? Maybe I could talk this out with her, get some perspective and go from there. If I didn't have Avery with me, this was probably the next best thing.

The drive into town was quick, the streets were bare for a Thursday evening, and I even managed to snag a parking spot right outside of Illusion. The building was huge—three stories high—and had beautiful windows on the lower level. The exterior accents of the building were painted in a plum color in contrast to the lighter color surrounding it.

Someone waving from inside caught my attention. I smiled as I watched Ellawyn stand from her chair by the window so she could hurry to open the door for me.

"Marley," she greeted me. "You're going to love this place." She led us back to the table she'd just vacated and held out a hand for me to sit down. "This is my favorite seat in the whole place. I just love it."

The table she had picked was a smaller one with two purple velvet seats on each side. It was comfortable. I sank further into the cushion of the chair and let out a sigh.

"They are beyond comfortable." I looked around the space, soaking everything about it in. "I think I could live here."

"You and me both," she said with a laugh.

Over the next two hours, we tasted Illusion's ciders and wines and enjoyed their delicious food. We talked about anything and everything. From Ellawyn telling me about what her life was like before finding Quimby Grove to giving me the scoop on the locals, we never ran out of topics to chat about.

But now our time together was running out, and I hadn't brought up my dilemma.

Sweat beaded on my forehead, and my palms were clammy. I felt like I was going to be sick. "I think I may need to go back to New York before summer ends," I blurted.

Ellawyn's eyes went wide at my outburst. "Wait, what?" Her brow furrowed. "Why, though?"

"Ellawyn, someone is doing shit in this town because I'm here. There was that vandalism, that poor man in the alleyway, that break-in at Max's house, and the big kahuna was Max's bar being lit on fire and a brick thrown through the window on the back door." Feeling defeated, I sunk back into the purple velvet chair and took comfort in the softness. "I don't want to leave early, but I want to keep everyone safe. Mostly my kids and Max, of course." I cradled my head in my hands as I thought about everything all over again.

Ellawyn listened, remaining quiet until I was finished. "Before I say anything, did you say all of that purely for me to listen and support, or did you want advice?"

Lowering my hands from my face, I looked at her. She was calm and unbothered by what I'd just told her. She had a small half-smile, full of support and kindness. She truly wanted to offer what I was looking for in this situation instead of just butting in as most people do.

"I want advice." I leaned forward and took a drink from my water glass. "I'm just lost, Ellie."

"I'd be lost, too, Mar. You're in an incredibly difficult position in general, and tack on all the scary things that have been happening, and it just elevates everything."

She was right. My life was complicated enough before we decided to spend our summer here. Max and I had just reunited after many years apart. We'd found each other again and had collided as we tried to navigate the path we were on. We'd added sex into the mix sooner than I would have expected.

But at the same time, connecting on that level felt like a long time coming. Max and I were a force. We ran hot for each other that first day on the beach. I'd never felt more alive. And then we had Izzy and Jax, and Max was on a mission to make up for lost time with his children. He'd missed out on precious moments I'd never be able to give him back.

We were thrust into chaos just a few months ago, and we had accepted it. We'd made the decision for us to spend the summer here in Quimby Grove instead of driving back and forth between two states.

And now, here we were, nearing the end of the summer and I was debating on leaving early to keep my kids safe. But going back to New York meant leaving Max behind, at least for now.

"I just don't know what to do," I admitted. I felt selfish for wanting to stay when I'd be putting people's lives in jeopardy. What if the police never found out who was responsible for all these incidents? My family and I would forever live in fear. We'd be together but fearful for the next big thing to happen. But if I left town, then maybe everyone could be safe.

Ellawyn pursed her lips, probably thinking of what to say. "I think that only you know what's right for you and what you'd be comfortable with. I can understand wanting to leave town and keep your babies safe and put an end to all this. But..." She leaned forward, taking my hand in hers. "But is that really the right decision for all of you?"

It wasn't the right thing to do when it came to Max.

Either way you spun it, someone would get hurt. Either by me or a faceless stranger with a fucking vendetta against me.

Deep down, I knew what I had to do, and Max wasn't going to like it. But frankly, neither would I.

20

MAX

"The bar is just about ready for reopening." I poked my fork into my steak and lifted a bite to my mouth as I waited for Marley to answer.

"Hm?" She shook her head, refocusing her gaze on my face. "Oh, the bar. That's wonderful."

"I was thinking of throwing a grand reopening event to celebrate. What do you think?"

Marley pushed her salad around her plate, not even eating it, before reaching for her wineglass. "Sounds like a plan."

Ever since that night out with Ellawyn two weeks ago, something had shifted in Marley, even more than it had before her night out. She'd been more withdrawn lately, keeping quiet and busy when we were home together. I couldn't remember the last time we'd had a real conversation just the two of us—before the fire, if I had to guess—but the absence of it was prominent. The distance had been the whole reason I'd orchestrated a night out in the next town over, just the two of us. We needed to reconnect. I just wished she would talk to me so we could work through it. I missed my spark—my Marley

"How'd you like to plan it?"

"Me?" She tilted her head, gazing at me. "I mean, I guess. When is it?" She shifted in her seat, crossing her legs just to uncross them. She folded the napkin in her lap before going back to moving her food around her plate.

"How about a week from today?" Sure, it was short notice, but we didn't need a big extravagant event. I just wanted to mark the occasion with those I cared about. The arsonist may still be at large, but I wasn't about to cower and go into hiding. Not to mention, I had a feeling that whoever was responsible was long gone. They could have set the whole building on fire since it'd been closed ever since.

"That sounds good. We can plan something." She gave me a small smile, reaching her hand across the table and lacing her fingers with mine. "I'm sorry I've been such shitty company lately. I just have a lot on my mind."

My first instinct was to tell her that it was okay and that it wasn't a big deal. But it wasn't okay, and while it wasn't a huge deal, it was unsettling nonetheless.

"I appreciate the apology," I started. "You've been distant and pulling further away each day. What can I do?" I rubbed my thumb along her hand, making tiny circles on her skin—a silent plea to come back to me emotionally.

She sighed and lowered her gaze to our joined hands. "Where do we go from here?" She lifted the hand I wasn't holding and gestured between us. Her tear-filled eyes were about to spill over. "Summer is about to end and then what?"

Her words shocked the hell out of me. I wasn't expecting her to dive into this right here in a restaurant. "Why don't we get the check and finish this out—"

The dam that held Marley's tears back broke. Tears slid down her cheeks one by one. "With everything that's happened in Quimby Grove since I've arrived... It's a warning. I can feel it. I can feel it in the way I can't sleep at night anymore. It's how I feel when I walk down High Street and the hair on the back of my neck stands up. It's in the way I'm constantly looking over my shoulder, even at your house. It's in the way I memorize exactly what Izzy and Jax wear each day—just in case they go missing." She let go of my hand and frantically wiped the tears away. "I'm terrified," she whispered. "I'll meet you in the truck." She slid from her side of the booth and rushed toward the exit.

Fuck. I'd known she'd been afraid, but I hadn't realized how deep that fear ran. I pulled my wallet from my back pocket just as our waitress stopped by.

"Here." I handed my card over without looking at the bill. "We're ready to pay now," I added so I wouldn't sound like a total dick. After I signed the receipt and tipped, I headed to the parking lot to join Marley. She'd pulled the hatch down on the back of my truck and sat on the edge, letting her legs dangle as she looked up at the sunset.

It was a picture-perfect moment. She looked gorgeous, with her long blonde hair hanging down her back in luscious waves while her skin was on display in a summer dress that captured her curves in all the right places.

"Sorry for the wait. I had to pay," I said as I planted my hands on the edge of the truck and boosted myself up. She reached over, brushing my fingers slightly before lacing them with hers. "I know it's scary, Marley, I do."

"I just don't know what to do, that's all." She turned her head, tears tracking down her cheeks as she looked at me. "Remember our time back on the beach all those years ago?"

"Couldn't forget it even if I wanted to, love."

She sniffled, glancing once more at the sky before continuing. "It was the best night of my life, you know. We found each other in a moment that probably wasn't my finest, but you cherished me like I was a gift you'd been asking for." She hopped off the back of the truck and straightened her dress. "In a moment I felt unworthy, you made me feel like the most important thing in the world. I'll never forget that."

She gave me a sad smile before turning on her heel and making her way back to the passenger side of the truck and getting inside.

"It was the best night of my life too," I whispered to myself.

THE DRIVE back to Quimby Grove was a quiet one. Marley pressed her head against the cool glass of the window, looking up at the sky while the tears continued to fall. I kept my focus straight ahead on the road, hoping she would use this moment to collect herself before we reached Beckett's house.

"I'll go get them," she said as I pulled onto the street where Beckett lived.

"Do you want help?" I questioned, flicking my gaze to her as I pulled into Beckett and Ellawyn's driveway.

"It's all right, busker." She hopped out of the truck, going straight to the front door.

The use of the nickname helped relieve the uneasiness that had been building. My hope was that this was just a bad night, a moment of overthinking, and that tomorrow we'd start over and feel a bit better about the situation here in Quimby Grove.

A headache started to form as I watched as Ellawyn gave me a concerned look after she let Marley inside to pick up the kids. I shrugged, not sure how to convey what was going on with a single facial expression.

A moment later, both Izzy and Jax ran out of the house with their backpacks settled on their shoulders, full smiles as they barreled toward the truck. I turned off the engine and got out of the car to meet them.

"Hey, munchkins." I gave them high fives and reached to collect their backpacks from them. "How was staying with Uncle Beckett and Auntie Ellawyn?"

They giggled as they started recounting their evening to me, giving me a minute-by-minute playback of all the activities they did. Grabbing Izzy by the waist, I lifted her into the back of the truck while Marley did the same with Jax. After we buckled in the kids, Marley and I were back in our seats, silence filling the front of the truck once more.

"We had cupcakes, too," Izzy said from the back as she kicked the back of my seat.

"Oh yeah?" I asked. "What flavor?"

"Pink and blue." She shrugged. "I had blue. Jax had pink."

"They were yummy," Jax added.

A forced laugh came from the passenger seat as Marley tried to engage with the kids. "That sounds like a good time," she offered.

"It was, Mama," Jax responded before turning to chat with his sister.

The rest of the drive home was excruciatingly long. My shoulders unhunched a tad when I turned onto my long driveway. "Home sweet home," I said, throwing the truck into park and turning the ignition. "I've got bath time tonight. Who wants to go first?"

"Me!" Izzy shouted. "With bath crayons! And extra bubbles! I want a bubble beard tonight," she said with a giggle.

"Me too." Jax threw his fist in the air excitedly. "Bubble beards like Daddy!"

Marley and I went through the motions of getting the kids out of the car and into the house.

"Princess," I called out to Marley before she could head up

the stairs. "How about you have some alone time and hang down here with a glass of wine and read?"

"That sounds nice. Thank you." She stood on her tiptoes, her lips lingering on my cheek as she kissed me. "I appreciate it."

AFTER TWO BATHS, toothbrushing, two bedtime stories, and three drinks of water, the kids were finally ready to be tucked into bed for the night. Of course, that hadn't stopped them from asking all the questions they could get in before lights out.

"I like it here," Izzy murmured as I pulled the comforter up to her chest.

"Me too," Jax said from the bottom bunk.

Bending down, I snuck my head underneath the top bunk and gave him a hug and a kiss on the forehead. "I like you both here, too." I grabbed the comforter, pulling it up over him.

"Daddy," Izzy called from the top bunk. "Can you get me Effie? I don't got her up here."

"Sure." I turned, moving toward the bean bag chairs where I last saw Effie, and found Marley standing in the doorway, watching the nighttime routine. "Hey there," I whispered to her as I passed by to get the stuffed elephant.

She smiled before moving toward the bunk beds to say goodnight to the kids. "Good night, Izzy-bug." She tucked the blankets in more by Izzy's sides. "Snug as a bug."

"I want to be a snug bug," Jax called.

Marley laughed, a real melodic laugh, as she ducked under the bed, tickling his sides before she tucked him in as much as possible. "There ya go, Jackers. Now you've both had your lovins from Daddy and me. You know what time it is. Sweet dreams."

"Sweeter dreams," Izzy chimed in with her part.

"Sweetest dreams," Jax said with a yawn.

"Daddy, your turn," Izzy called out. "You need a part."

"Hm... sweetester dreams?" I placed Effie down next to Izzy and brushed her hair out of her eyes.

"Perfect," Jax whispered before rolling onto his stomach and closing his eyes. Izzy was almost asleep a moment later.

Marley led the way out of their bedroom, and she quietly shut the door behind us after I exited. She walked down the hall toward her room and placed her hand on the doorknob, hesitating. "They really are happy here, you know."

Going to the door to my room, I leaned against the frame, crossing my arms over my chest. "I'm glad. You promise to attend the grand reopening at the bar?" A part of me didn't think I should have to even ask, but right now, I wasn't sure where we stood.

"Yes, of course." She turned the handle on the door and stepped inside.

"Hey, Marley?" I called after her, hoping she'd stop before closing the door.

"Yeah?"

"I hope you're happy here, too."

"Yeah, me too." She gave me a sad smile before stepping further into her room and closing the door.

Once again, I was alone in my bed without my arms wrapped around her.

21

MARLEY

The laundry room was filled with piles of dirty clothes that I'd been washing and drying all morning. My goal had been to get it all completed by dinnertime. If I kept on track, I'd meet that without any issues. But if the guilt kept creeping in, settling in the pit of the stomach and working its way into my heart, then I'd be doomed.

Today was the day of the grand reopening of Remnant Hearts, and Max had been at the bar since early this morning in preparation for the event this evening. He was so excited, so eager to get back to his life before the fire.

Maybe before us?

Shaking those negative thoughts away, I threw a load of whites into the washer before moving on to fold the clothes that were dry. Folding laundry was a mindless task that allowed my head to wander and daydream. Only this time, the thoughts in my mind were that of a nightmare instead of a dream.

I hoped I was doing the right thing.

I'd just finished this round of laundry when the doorbell

rang and echoed throughout the house. A smile inched its way onto my face as I rushed for the front door, whipping it open as soon as I had the lock flipped. "Avery!"

My sister beamed at me, dropping her bag onto the porch and charging into my arms, squeezing me tightly. "I missed you, Marley."

We stood there, locked in each other's embrace, unmoving. I knew I missed my sister this summer. I just hadn't realized I'd missed her this much. She was like coming home. The nerves that had taken up residence within me these past few weeks vanished as soon as I saw her.

She calmed me.

She pulled back, laughing. "Are you going to invite me into this gorgeous house or make me stand outside in the heat?"

I grabbed her bag and dragged her inside. "How was the train?"

"It was awesome," she said as she moved through the foyer and into the family room. "You know I love a good train ride."

"That I do."

My sister loved anything and everything that gave her a sense of adventure. She lived for the small things and had a childlike ability to be excited about anything.

Something I envied about her.

"Totally love this couch." She slid her hand over the top of the velvet, soaking it all in. "What time do we have to be at the party at the bar?" She rounded the couch and plopped down onto the smooth, soft seat, and sighed. "I could live here." She chuckled.

"Um, about the party tonight..."

I'd invited Avery to Quimby Grove under the pretense of attending the party with us and getting to know Max more. But really, I brought her here to confess my plan of returning to the city tonight.

The smile slipped from Avery's face as I sat down beside her, grabbing her hand. "I'm thinking of leaving Quimby Grove tonight... instead of going to the party."

"What?" She pivoted on the couch, facing me directly. "You can't just do that, Marley. That's not right."

Avery never sugarcoated her opinion. I loved my sister, but she couldn't possibly understand the constant stress I was under. How I lived in fear, not just for my life but for Izzy's and Jax's life, too. "It's not safe here. I've told you what happened throughout the summer."

Her frown deepened. "Yeah, I know all of that. But you can't run from this, Mar. That will make everything so much worse between you and Max." She stood from the couch and began pacing in front of me. "There has to be another way."

Her pacing was giving me a goddamn headache. "There is. I stay in town and get killed, or I leave Quimby Grove and keep myself and my babies safe. Which do you prefer I do?" I huffed my annoyance, crossing my arms over my chest.

I shouldn't have said it like that, but there was no going back now. It was the truth.

She cut a glare in my direction, looking as if I'd just slapped her. "Don't," she snapped. "Don't you dare think that I want you and the kids to be in danger. How could you? You three are my entire fucking family, Marley. I'd do anything for you guys."

"Good." I moved to face her head-on, just inches away from her. "Because there's something you need to do for me tonight. And you won't like it."

"I probably won't. But I guarantee you'll regret whatever the fuck it is you're about to do."

Little did she know, the regret was already there.

WHILE I LEFT Avery back at Max's house to pack up Izzy's and Jax's suitcases and get them ready once they woke up from their nap, I went into town to visit Remnant Hearts.

And Max.

When I stepped inside, my mouth dropped at the sight before me. Max and Woody had decorated the space with streamers and twirling decorations that hung and sparkled from the ceiling. There was a crescent moon-shaped pinata hanging right in front of the door to the kitchen. The suit of armor wore a blindfold, and the telephone booth had been filled with multicolored balloons.

It looked fucking amazing.

"Hello," I called out as I meandered through the space. "Anybody here?"

"Hey, princess." Max stepped through the swinging door to the kitchen, carefully sliding the pinata out of the way, and walked right into my space. My breath hitched when his hands settled onto my waist. "You look beautiful today, dear." He pressed a kiss on my cheek as he pulled me closer.

Being like this, with him, took me back to how I felt at the beginning of summer. This was the man I'd been drawn to years ago, and at this moment, I was the woman on the boardwalk, not taking any shit.

To be fair, Max had always been the man I wanted, even throughout this summer. It was me who'd been different after everything that had happened. But right now, I felt like my old self.

I lifted my arms up, snaking them up his chest and settling on his nape. "Thank you. But I'm not wearing anything special, and I don't have makeup on." My fingers traveled up the back of his head, running my fingers through his hair that had gotten longer in the back throughout summer.

Max's fingers gently traced one side of my face, leaving little traces of appreciation as he touched my soft skin. "You're always beautiful. You don't need fancy clothing or a made-up face. You're beautiful just as you are. I'd devour you right here, right now, if you'd let me."

"You're too sweet." I swallowed past the dryness in my throat and stepped out of his embrace. "I like what you've done to the place." I changed the subject, hoping he didn't notice, as I spun in a circle to take everything in. "It's going to be a hell of a party."

Guilt consumed me. Flirting with him right now wasn't fair. But damn, I missed the ease with which we used to connect prior to all this bullshit happening. Deep down, though, I knew I was the one who kept pulling away. I had every reason to be afraid, but instead of shutting Max out, I should have leaned into him. We should have grown stronger.

But I only tore us further apart.

I was wrecking everything.

"It is." He moved behind the bar, grabbing two glasses from underneath. "Want a drink?"

"No, I'm good." I took a seat at the bar as he poured himself a glass of water. "I was just checking to see if you needed anything before I head home and change for tonight."

Change... Pack up Avery's rental car... Flee town.

His eyes warmed as he smiled at me. "That's sweet of you, but it's all settled. I'm just going to tidy up and shower at the upstairs apartment quickly before everyone arrives."

I nodded. "Okay, cool. Well, I'll see you in a couple of hours, yeah?" I took a few steps backward before turning to head for the door.

"Hey," he called out, pausing me. "Kiss."

He was killing me with how he was being tonight. The bar

reopening had really put Max back into his element. His confidence was blinding tonight. I couldn't help but smile at him as my feet gravitated back toward him. I leaned over the bar, capturing his lips in mine for a long, passionate kiss as his tongue slipped into my mouth, dueling for control with mine. Heat filled my cheeks as I pulled away, unable to hide how turned on I was.

"Goodbye, Max."

"Goodbye, princess. See you soon."

He wouldn't.

WHEN I GOT HOME, I heard my kids crying upstairs. I took the stairs two at a time until I made it to the doorway and heard what Avery was saying. She was reassuring them that they'd be seeing their daddy again soon. I stepped forward, trying to sneak a peek at what they were doing.

My heart dropped at the sight. Shame filled me as I took in my sister hugging both of my children in her arms as they cried.

"Did Mommy say when we'd be back?" Izzy questioned through sobs.

"I don't want to leave Daddy," Jax added as tears trekked down his chubby cheeks.

"Hey now," Avery started. "Your mama would never do anything to hurt you both. Or your daddy. She just wants us all to be together in New York City for a few days, that's all. It's been so long since we had a fun date in the city, just the four of us."

"Promise?" Izzy asked.

Avery hesitated. She didn't lie to my children, and she never made promises she couldn't keep. We knew of false promises from our own childhood, and we didn't want that for these kids. I squared my shoulders, preparing for the battle and performance of a lifetime, and entered the room so that Avery wouldn't have to promise.

"There are my favorite munchkins," I said as I walked into the room, pretending I hadn't just heard them moments ago. "What's with the sad faces?" I dropped down onto the bean bag next to them.

Avery avoided my gaze. Instead, she leaned down, kissing my children's foreheads before shifting them off her lap. "I'll let you talk to your mama while I pack up the rental car."

The energy in the room was thick, almost debilitating. "We're just going back home for a while," I reassured them, hoping to diffuse the situation. "We'll be back to see your dad soon."

"Promise?" They asked in unison.

I swallowed hard. "Of course. I'll try to get us back as soon as we can."

I'd always taught my kids that lying was wrong. Even those little white fibs we'd always talked about. Tonight, I knew I was playing dirty, and I didn't like this about myself. But if it came down to a little fib to keep them safe or putting them in danger, I'd lie every damn time. But honestly, while I didn't know when we'd return to Quimby Grove, I knew Max would come into the city to visit as much as he could. They wouldn't lose Max, not ever. Even with us not really talking right now, I knew that.

With a heavy heart, I took my time leaving Max's house, soaking in his woodsy scent and his presence that was embedded within these walls. Deep down, I knew we belonged here with him. I felt it in the very depths of my soul. It killed me to leave. My fingertips grazed the railing of the staircase as I transcended one last time and made my way into the kitchen.

Reaching into my purse, I grabbed the mint green envelope and hugged it to my chest before placing it on the kitchen table.

With the trunk of the rental car packed up, I loaded the kids into the car with their favorite blankets and Effie riding in between them. With one last look, I glanced back toward the front of the house, wishing things could somehow be different.

22

MAX

The music was blaring, and the drinks kept on coming as the night went on. The bar was packed with what felt like the entire town of Quimby Grove, including Ellawyn and Beckett. All I was missing was Marley. She'd gone home to shower and change a couple of hours ago; she should've been back by now.

Tonight was a big night for Remnant Hearts. Not only were we reopening after the fire, but Woody was getting his first real taste of the bartending life. He stood behind the bar, looking like he owned the fucking place and taking drink orders like a damn pro.

He'd proven himself in just one night, not that he had to. He would be a huge asset to the bar and to me. For the first time in a few months, I felt like I could breathe a little easier. I'd been able to have more consistent hours and would be home more with Marley and the twins.

This was just the beginning for us.

"Barkeep," a sweet voice sang from the end of the bar, followed by a silly giggle.

When I turned my head to see who it was, I found a drunken Ellawyn with her cheeks tinged pink from drinking.

"Hit me with another!" she shouted as Beckett stood behind his wife, laughing. He dipped his head, dropping a kiss on her bare shoulder.

"What do you fuckers want?" I teased before sliding two more beers down toward them.

Ellawyn frowned as she picked up the drink and inhaled the scent. "I wanted something fruity," she whined. "And stronger." She waggled her eyebrows at me.

I snagged a bottle of water for her and placed it in front of her. "Sorry, Ellie, you're drunk enough. This is your last drink tonight, okay?"

"Ugh," she huffed, rolling her eyes. "Just kidding." She laughed. "You know my limits better than I do. Hey!" She paused, looking around the bar. "Where's Marley?"

I shrugged. "Probably got held up by the kids." My eyes darted to the entrance when I saw a flash of blonde hair. "Woody, cover me."

He jerked his head in response and kept serving drinks as I made my way through the crowd of people that were standing in the walkway.

"Hey, Mar—" My words halted as I took in the woman standing in front of me, who looked a lot like Marley.

Except it wasn't Marley. It was Avery.

They seemingly had the same face, but there were differences too. This woman had the same blonde hair but cut near her shoulders. She was slightly shorter than Marley and the shape of her eyes was different just a bit.

"Avery," I corrected myself. "I didn't know you were coming to town."

She gave me a shy smile and extended her hand. "Hey,

Max." She nodded as she glanced around the bar. "This place looks awesome."

Marley hadn't mentioned that Avery was coming to town at all. Why would she be here without Marley? Wouldn't they have come together? I peered over her shoulder, hoping to see her walk in the door.

"She's not coming," Avery said, snapping my attention back to her. "I'm sorry."

Grabbing her elbow, I pulled her outside. "What do you mean? Where is she? Is she okay?"

"She's fine. Um, but listen..." She sighed. "She's not coming. She's going back to New York City tonight, with the kids." Avery glanced down at the ground before peering back at me through her eyelashes.

My jaw tensed, anger pulsing through my veins. "Why?" I snapped.

"You need to talk to her about that. I didn't want to be the messenger," Avery said, taking a step backward. "For what it's worth, I don't agree with her." She gave me a sad wave before turning her back to me and walking down the block.

How could she leave town like this? I'd known she was scared and had been considering going back into the city, but I didn't see this coming. She up and left without so much as a goodbye. Without even letting me talk to my kids. Without any sort of plan.

I rubbed the back of my neck as I kept looking down the block where Avery had disappeared, half expecting Marley to jump out and tell me that this was some silly prank.

My feet stayed rooted on the sidewalk, unable to go inside and face everyone who had expected Marley. I was hurt and betrayed and just wanted to go the fuck home. I grabbed my phone from my back pocket and sent a text to Woody, asking him to close the bar when the party was over. When he asked if everything was okay, I lied and told him I didn't feel well. I doubted that he bought it. But I didn't have it in me to care.

My feet were on autopilot as they led me through the dark alley that ended right behind my bar. I climbed into my truck and drove home. When I parked in front of the house, I noticed that all the lights were off.

The lights hadn't been off when I'd gotten home at night since before Marley had moved in. It was a haunting reminder that I was alone once again.

I was beginning to think that was how my life was supposed to be. Maybe I was destined to wind up growing old and dedicated to my bar instead of some woman. But Marley wasn't just some woman. She was the woman for me.

Swallowing my pride, I pulled on the door handle in the truck and trudged up the front stairs and into my home. My dark, empty home. I flicked on the lights in the entryway and was greeted with an empty space and silence, the harsh reminder that they truly were gone.

It felt like a punch to the gut as I made my way down the hall and into the kitchen in search of a drink. Something strong, I decided. I opened the freezer and grabbed a bottle of vodka before reaching above the fridge for a shot glass.

The kitchen table was clean and free of any stickiness or accidental crayon markings. I sat down in my normal seat and stared at the other three empty spots. Closing my eyes, I pictured the three of them sitting there. Marley would be watching her kids with adoration as they talked about their day. Izzy would be holding Effie in her hands or tucked underneath her arm as she bounced in her seat with excitement. And Jax would be all smiles while he quietly played with toys or chatted with us. The ache in my chest intensified. I didn't know I could feel this way. They'd only been gone about an hour or so, and I felt like two pieces of my heart were lost.

My gaze landed on an envelope that sat in the middle of the table, addressed to *Busker*. I grabbed it and wasted no time ripping open the paper and yanking out the card. The message was short and simple: *I'm sorry. XO, M.*

Sadness fused with anger as I removed the cap of the vodka bottle and poured a shot. I downed the shot and poured another. And another. And another. Eventually, I ditched the shot glass and swapped it out for the actual bottle itself before dragging myself up the stairs and into my room.

Hours ago, I'd said it was the beginning for us. Turns out, it was actually the end.

A BRIGHT LIGHT illuminated from outside, shining through my curtains and into my room. The luminance hit my face, heating my skin. A pounding radiated throughout the room so loudly it hurt. I squeezed my eyes shut, hoping the noise would stop and I'd be at peace again.

My eyelids fluttered as I forced them open, the sun blinding me temporarily. I shifted in my bed, attempting to get comfortable and maybe pass back out. But suddenly I realized this wasn't my bed. My eyes snapped open, and I was met with two pairs of eyes staring back at me.

"What the fuck," I cursed as I sat up straight, realizing I was in the children's room sitting on one of the bean bag chairs, with Beckett and Ellawyn staring down at me, concern etched on their faces. "What are you two doing here?"

Beckett held out a hand to help me up, which I gratefully accepted. "We were worried about you whenever you didn't come back inside last night," Beckett said as he looked around Izzy and Jax's room. "Where are the kids, and why did you sleep on a bean bag chair?"

"You smell of alcohol, Max. What's going on?" Ellawyn ran a hand up and down my back. "Hold that thought. Let's go downstairs and I'll start a pot of coffee."

Coffee sounded fucking amazing, but I needed to cleanse myself of the remaining stench of vodka. Or at least attempt to. "Do you mind starting without me? I'm going to hop in the shower, and then I'll be right down."

"Of course," Ellawyn said.

"See you down there, man." Beckett placed his hand on the small of Ellawyn's back, guiding her out of the room. The gesture was innocent enough, but the ache in my heart multiplied at their affection.

As I stood in my bathroom, facing the mirror at the sink, I took in my hungover state. My eyes were puffy, the dark circles visible, my hair disheveled, and my T-shirt stained. My mouth was turned down, unable to be lifted into a smile. The pain was palpable. The heartbreak was clear as day. I was fucking destroyed.

"Have a seat." Ellawyn pulled out the chair that had once been Marley's. But I didn't have it in me to care, so I did as I was told and sat down as Beckett placed a cup of coffee in front of me and two slices of toast. "Eat this, too." He said, taking the seat across from me while Ellawyn settled in at my side.

Despite not really wanting to eat, I grabbed the toast, slathered it in butter, and took a bite before devouring my coffee. "They left," I confessed in between another bite of toast. "They're gone."

Ellawyn's mouth pursed. "I didn't think she'd actually do it." She runs her hands through her hair, pulling it to the back of her head before tying it into a bun. "A few weeks ago, when we went out to Illusion, she confided in me that she was considering leaving."

"What did she say?"

Ellawyn sighed. "She told me how afraid she was. Not only for herself but for the kids and you. With everything that had happened since she arrived, she didn't know what to do. She was distraught by it, Max. I can't say that I blame her for weighing the option of leaving, though."

"How could you say that?" I snapped. "I'd protect her. Protect them."

She reached out, grabbing my hands and holding on for dear life. "Of course you'd protect them, but you can't be everywhere. Look at what happened to your bar. That was a clear threat, and it was dangerous."

I pinched the bridge of my nose. "What am I supposed to do?" I left the table and poured myself another cup of coffee. "It's not like I know who is fucking with us. I can't make that go away yet."

"That's true." This time, it was Beckett who spoke up. "But the woman you love just fucking left, man. With your kids. You need to square up and go fight for what you want. Don't let Marley get away and think that you don't want her and the kids."

"She knew I wanted her, and she still fucking left," I growled. "I was clear with my intentions."

"Then don't let her think she's not worth fighting for," Beckett countered. "You lost her once all those years ago. Don't let it happen again."

My bruised ego and broken heart wanted to dismiss the idea of running after her. She was the one who left me, after all, and hadn't been clear with me where her head was at when it came to us.

But Beckett was right.

I'd lost too many years with her already. Too many days where she could have been mine and too many memories lost. Precious moments had passed by, and I'd never get that back. I'd spent years searching for the mysterious woman from the best fucking night of my life. Countless times I'd gone back to that boardwalk, replaying the way she'd come apart against me and how her smart mouth had tasted of champagne and lust. There were an endless number of dreams where she'd starred as the main character. My beautiful, treasured leading lady in an elegant emerald gown.

I'd spent years regretting not chasing after her that day on the beach. I'd craved redemption and I chased it all these years, daydreaming of ways to make it up to her, and now, my kids.

The next step was clear—I'd follow her to New York today and hope like hell that she'd feel the same way about me, and we'd figure out our next steps together. Either way, I refused to let her go without one hell of a fight.

23

MARLEY

It was our first full day back in the city, and it felt so fucking foreign. The busy streets I'd once loved had turned bitter in the light of the small-town charm that Quimby Grove offered. One day away and I'd found myself longing for the slow-paced stroll through the square. Where faces were friendly and everyone smiled, waved, or said hello. The walk through New York City on my way to drop Izzy and Jax off at Avery's for the day was less welcoming. Instead of walking back home, I'd opted for a cab ride. I just didn't have it in me to walk the five blocks back to my apartment, with my heavy heart dragging behind me.

Once I returned home, I looked at it with different eyes. I thought it'd feel like what it was like going on a long trip away from home. How you returned home and would be relieved to be back in your own space. But now, for me, my apartment didn't quite feel like home anymore.

I'd become a visitor in my own space. A spectator looking in on something that once was but now... wasn't.

A knocking on the door pulled me from my assessment, the haze lifting as I made my way to the door. I could feel myself starting to sweat, unsure of who was on the other side, as I placed my hand around the doorknob and quietly turned my wrist to open the door. It could be whoever was fucking with us in Quimby Grove. Or it could be a neighbor with my mail. I gave the door one last push, and all the breath in my lungs evaporated as I took in the person standing in front of me.

"W-what're you doing here?" The words stumbled out of my mouth, as my heart started beating faster.

Max stood tall in my doorway, arms crossed over his chest, his muscles pulling his T-shirt tight across his broad shoulders. He stepped into my space, backing me further into my apartment, and kicked the door shut. He continued to stalk toward me, moving me further through my apartment.

My gaze stayed locked on his, unwilling to break the contact we had. Words were unable to form on my lips. Nothing was said between us as I let him lead me to wherever he wanted. At that moment, I would have followed him anywhere. We didn't stop until we were in my bedroom and the back of my legs were up against the mattress.

His breathing intensified, his eyes zeroing in on mine as if searching for something.

"What are you waiting for, Max?" I questioned, wanting him to say something.

"What am I waiting for?" he bellowed, stepping closer to me until we were chest to chest. "I've spent my days, long before you left, waiting for you to give me a fucking sign or just... anything. For you to tell me how you felt and if you wanted to stay with me in Quimby Grove or come back here. I waited weeks for you to admit whether you're all in when it comes to us."

His chest rose and fell, brushing against mine. My nipples pebbled at the contact. Fuck, I'd missed him.

"You may have physically left yesterday," he said, "but you've been gone for fucking weeks, Marley."

Frustration roared within me as I pressed a finger into his hard chest. "I've given you everything!" My hands came to his chest, wanting to push him back but refusing to put distance between us. My chest heaved against him, and desire pooled between my thighs. "I want you to want me and everything this is." I glanced around my room. "To want this life with me—with us—for the rest of our days."

"I've wanted you from the moment you stepped foot on that goddamn beach five years ago. And I've spent every fucking day since either trying to find you or forget you." He reached out, brushing my hair over my shoulder. "Turns out you're really fucking hard to forget."

His hands traveled to my waist, gripping my skin before pushing me down onto the bed. "Every fucking day was spent thinking of you." He reached under my dress and pulled my panties down my legs and then dropped them to the floor. He stepped between my legs and raised my dress to my waist. "And now I'm going to make sure you never fucking forget me either." His fingers trailed over my thigh, traveling further up my body as his exploration continued. "Sit up."

I sat up on the bed and lifted my arms as Max raised my dress over my head, leaving me completely uncovered before him.

His gaze raked over my body, appreciating every dip and curve. Every flaw and imperfection. His admiration caused my skin to heat.

Max rolled on top of me, the tip of his cock hitting my entrance as his lips hovered over mine. Just as our lips brushed, he slammed into me with a deep thrust. The intensity continued, the rhythm set, and I met him with a force.

I wrapped my legs around his waist, the sensation building

quickly as I dug my nails into his back. "More," I pleaded. He gave me what I wanted—hard, fast thrusts, with my hips meeting his every step of the way.

"Never forget," he said, growling into my ear. "Mine."

"Never." I gasped as he reached down, circling my clit with his thumb. "Yours."

As we claimed each other, we came together and let go of our fears and anxieties and instead chose to focus on what we wanted, on what we deserved.

Max was my everything and I was his.

Neither of us would ever forget it.

Being intimate with Max again was incredible. I snuggled into him, draping my arm across his chest as he ran his fingers over my bare back. "You came back for me," I whispered. "I never thought I'd be worth coming back for."

The hand on my back stilled as his other hand tipped my chin up until we were eye to eye. "Did I ever tell you how I came back for you all those years ago, too?"

What? I hadn't known that. "What do you mean?"

"After I let you leave the beach that night, I knew I'd made the worst mistake of my life. I ran after you, hoping to catch up, but you'd disappeared on me. I went back to that beach every night for the rest of my stay until I had to return to Quimby Grove." The movements started on my back again, soft little caresses left pinpricks on my skin. "But every year after that, I returned to the exact spot on the anniversary of the day we met, just hoping to find you again."

Chills cascaded over my body. I shivered, and goose bumps covered my arms. "Max..." Leaning up, my lips found his. "Max..." My words came out as a whisper. "I'll come back to

Quimby Grove with you." His mouth turned up in a smile as he shifted me so I was lying on my side, my back against his chest. "I need you," I whimpered as I felt his erection rubbing against me.

Max leaned back, pulling me against him, and lifted my leg over his hip. "I love you, Marley," he said as he slid inside me and slowly started moving in and out of me while our mouths joined together again, saying everything that lingered between us. "And I'll keep loving you for as long as you let me."

Making love to him had become one of my new favorite things.

"Avery is bringing the twins back over," I called to Max from the bathroom as I dried off and got dressed after our shower together. "I think we should have a family meeting—Avery included—and tell them the news." After falling into bed together, and a few rounds of sex, we'd come up with a plan. Or at least the starting point of a plan anyway.

Things were still a bit complicated, but we'd navigate the messiness together, forever.

Max popped his head into the bathroom. "I love the sound of a family meeting." He stepped inside the room and wrapped his arms around my waist as he nuzzled into the crook of my neck. "A meeting with the mother of my children, who is also officially my girlfriend and our kids."

My heart melted at the sound of him calling me his girlfriend. The title was long overdue at this point. "And Avery," I added.

My goal today was to convince Avery to move to Quimby Grove with us for real. Being away from her these past few months had been extremely difficult, but I'd buried it down because I had convinced myself that my time away from her was temporary.

But now, it wasn't.

"And Avery," he echoed as he left a trail of kisses down my neck and onto my shoulder. "I'll let you get dressed. I'm going to put on a pot of coffee." He turned to walk out of the room, but before he could...

"Hey—"

Max stalled, anchoring his eyes on mine, waiting for me to continue. "Yeah, princess?"

A smile crossed my lips at the endearment. "You sure you're ready to take on being a parent full-time?"

"I wouldn't change it for the world," he said. "I know I'm new at this, and I know things won't always be as easy as they've been this summer, but I'm ready to be another constant in their lives, and yours."

"Just checking," I said with a wink. The butterflies in my stomach soared at his response. The confirmation of a real future together was precisely what I was looking for before going into this conversation with the twins.

"Now get dressed and get your fine ass out here," he said, his voice flirty, his gaze smoldering.

I had to clench my thighs to relieve the ache that was building and focus on the task at hand: breaking the news to the kids and Avery.

It was my sister I was worried about, though.

The doorbell rang, signaling their arrival, and I rushed to answer it before Max. I whipped open the door to see Avery holding hands with Izzy and Jax. The kids were looking at each other and talking up a storm.

"Why was the door locked?" she asked as she moved to step inside. When I didn't move out of her way, she studied me carefully. "He's here, isn't he?"

She didn't wait for me to answer before rolling her eyes and pushing past me.

"We need a family meeting," I called as I followed her through my living room.

She laughed. "We don't need a family meeting for me to hear that you've reconciled a day after you decided to leave town."

I narrowed my eyes. "Sit," I demanded. Turning to Izzy and Jax, I addressed them next. "Hey, munchkins, why don't you go crawl up on the couch? I need to tell you something."

"Okay, Mama," Jax said as he grabbed his sister's arm and pulled her behind him.

"Perfect." I clapped my hands in front of my chest. "We're ready," I called out in the direction of my bedroom.

Max walked into the room, smiling as brightly as can be, sidled up next to me, and slipped an arm around my waist. "Hey."

Izzy's and Jax's heads snapped up, looking at their dad. Their excitement couldn't be contained. They both jumped up and barreled into Max's legs, wrapping their arms around him.

"We missed you," Izzy said, tears rolling down her cheeks.

"Hey," Max said, his voice going soft. He crouched down and pulled both kids into his arms. "I love you both. Sorry we had to be apart for a night." He stroked their backs. "I missed you too."

After the tears subsided and they were done giving out their lovins, the kids settled back onto the couch next to their aunt.

"Daddy and I have decided that we want to officially move in together and have the four of us be a family forever."

Izzy blinked a few times. "We already were."

Jax nodded next to her. "We lived with Daddy yesterday."

They weren't wrong. To them, we already had become a

family and lived together. Nothing had changed in their mind, at least not until I'd brought them back here yesterday.

"True," I said, dropping to my knees in front of the couch. "I guess what I'm trying to say is that I want us to officially move to where we were yesterday."

"We'd pack up your bedroom here and add it to your room in our new house, where your bunk beds are," Max added.

"Oh," Jax said. "So we wouldn't sleep here"—he points down toward the floor—"ever again?"

"Correct."

Izzy and Jax shared a look and then shrugged.

"Okay," Izzy started. "Can we go play a little bit before bedtime?"

"Of course," Max answered. "We'll be in after we talk to Auntie Avery."

The kids went over to Avery to give her a hug and say goodnight before they raced to their bedrooms. After they were gone, she looked at us with her brow furrowed.

"Why do you need to talk to me?"

Now wasn't the time to hold back. "I want you to move to Quimby Grove with us," I said. Max stood beside me, nodding his head in agreement. "I can't go without you, Av," I murmured, wiping the tears from my eyes.

She shook her head. "You don't need me there, Mar. I'll just be interfering with your life." Avery's lip quivered, a sign that she was fighting back tears.

Pulling away from Max, I went to my sister and took her in my arms. "That's where you're wrong. I do need you." I kissed her forehead and squeezed her tighter. "You'd never interfere, you know that."

"But I don't have a job or know where I'd live."

"Avery, we can figure all that out later. You can stay with

us. Max has a huge place, and you can work with me until you figure out your next move."

"I don't know..."

I turned, facing her straight on. "This is your chance to really find what you've been searching for, Avery. You can take your time and do that in Quimby Grove. You can find your passion. You can find yourself. And we'll be here every step of the way while we watch you shine." I grabbed her hands in mine. "You can shine in Quimby Grove."

She nodded. "Okay," she said with an exhale. "I'll come but I have to finish up some things here for Events by Halligan." Her gaze darted between me and Max. "Actually... I could use your help with some of it before you head back to Quimby Grove."

"Oh, of course," I said. I turned toward Max and caught him smiling down at Avery and me. "Is that okay?"

"Absolutely," he responded. "Do what you need to do and come back to me as soon as you can."

Knowing that Max and I were going to start a life for ourselves in Quimby Grove with our kids was all I needed when it came to wrapping up my business here. I couldn't wait to tie up the loose ends and hurry back home.

24

MAX

It'd been two weeks since I'd chased after Marley to New York City and two weeks since I'd been able to see and be with her. Marley had stayed behind to wrap up some contracts with her business and help Avery out with packing up their building.

It had also been two weeks since I'd had the twins all to myself in Quimby Grove. They were all too eager to come home with me when I'd offered. Marley had looked like she was going to cry. But ultimately, she knew it'd help her finish whatever she had to do in New York even faster.

The faster we could be reunited, the better.

Everything had mostly gone smoothly back at my place. I'd taken these past two weeks off work, leaving Remnant Hearts in Woody's hands, and fully committed to being with the kids as we continued to grow our bond. I'd be lying if I said I didn't spoil them a bit. I'd gone all out with enhancing the yard. Beckett and I put together a brand-new swing set and hung a tire swing on the big tree out back. The kids helped pick out Halloween decorations, albeit super early, and decorated the porch.

For Marley, the first thing that I changed was to move the painting of her on the beach from the family room to our bedroom. She needed to see it every damn day, a subtle reminder of how I see her and how much of an impact she made on me all those years ago. I finished moving all her things from the guest room into the master bedroom and turned the guest room into an office space for her so she'd have a place to work from home when needed. Whenever she'd get back, I'd give her official free rein over the household to make any changes she desired.

I was making this their home, too. Our forever home, where the four of us would grow closer together and become even more of a family than we were now. Plus, we'd have Avery, who was incredibly important to Marley and the twins. It'd be nice to have some actual family around. I hoped she'd be happy here in our small town.

"Daddy." Izzy grabbed my hand, swinging it and pulling me from my thoughts.

"Yes, my little queen?"

She beamed at my words. "Can we go to Sweet Dreams?" She looked up at me through her long lashes, batting them at me. "We have cravings."

"Oh, you do, do you?" I bent down, tickling her sides. She fell to the floor in a fit of giggles. Her cheeks went red, the laughter taking her breath away.

Jax came down the stairs, looking down at his sister briefly before turning his attention to me. "Did she tell you we have cravings?" He patted his little belly. "It's empty of sugar in there. And food."

These two acted like I never fed them, I swear. "We just had lunch an hour ago," I said, narrowing my gaze playfully. "But now that you said something, I kind of have a craving, too. I guess we should go and grab a snack, just to make it go away.

What do you think?" I placed my hands on my hips, watching Izzy as she climbed to her feet.

"I think that's smart," she said.

"Me too." Jax jumped from the second to last step, his fist shooting into the air. "Let's go," he shouted while they rushed toward the front door, racing to my car. I grabbed my keys from the hook, then locked the door behind me and joined my two favorite people.

As soon as we stepped into Sweet Dreams Bakery, the smell of cinnamon hit us, the scent wafting throughout the store and reminding me of baking cookies for Christmas. My stomach growled as we approached the display.

Erin walked up and greeted us. "Nice to see the three of you again." She peered toward the door. "Not trying to be nosy"—she lowered her voice—"but where is their mother?"

She wasn't trying to be nosy—she was nosey. And I didn't even know this woman.

"Their mother is currently upstate getting ready to move and join us here, actually." I ruffled Izzy's hair as she practically drooled over a beach-themed cupcake. "I'll bring her in with us next time. She'd love this place."

"That'd be great." Erin clapped her hands together. "I'd love to meet her."

"She should be here within a few days. We're excited to have her back." I glanced down at the kids. "Ready to order?"

We ended up getting cupcakes all around and sat in one of the booths, enjoying the full Sweet Dreams experience, unfortunately.

Which was just a whole fucking lot of pink topped with the aroma of all things sweet. It was enough to give me a fucking headache—the color scheme mostly was at fault for that, though.

Jax carelessly unwrapped his cupcake, icing going everywhere, and shoved the entire sprinkled cupcake into his mouth. White icing smeared over the outside of his now full cheeks.

"This is yummy, Daddy." He licked his fingers, giving me a messy smile.

"It sure looks it," I said as I wiped the excess icing off his face with a napkin. I turned to Izzy to see if she needed help too but was surprised by what I saw.

She unwrapped her beach cupcake carefully before setting it back down on the plate and using her fingers to rip the cupcake apart in the middle. After situating her fingers, she flipped the top part of the cupcake upside down and smashed it onto the bottom half so that the icing would be between two layers of cake. She picked her creation back up and took a bite with minimal mess.

"Uh, Izz, where'd you learn to do that?" I tilted my head, impressed by the way she had MacGyvered her cupcake.

She shrugged. "Mama taught me to do it that way so I don't make a mess while eating a cupcake. Mama always said that there's no elegant way to eat a cupcake the normal way, so she taught me this way."

"What else has Mama taught you?"

"That she's okay with a Ring Pop," Jax said before sucking down the last of his milk jug.

That made zero sense to me. I'd never heard Marley mention Ring Pops before. "What does that even mean?"

Izzy scrunched up her face as if trying to remember the meaning behind it. "Um... it's a song. She says that's all she'd ever need if she'd ever find her prince." She nodded excitedly, remembering the song. "We're happy with what we have. We just need each other, I think."

Jax mimics his sister, nodding his head. "We only *need* each other." He narrows his gaze, thinking, and then continues. "And you now. You can be part of it."

"Your mama is a smart woman." I gathered up our trash and tossed it into the bin beside our table. "All you need is your family. Everything else will fall into place." I stared down at the two children sitting in front of me and realized how true that sentiment was. They were all I needed. If they were safe, happy, and healthy, that was all I cared about.

Everything else was background noise.

Today was the day that Marley was coming home to Quimby Grove, where three hearts that belonged to her were anticipating her arrival.

The kids and I had gone to the farmers' market that pops up on the square once a week. We'd picked out a nice bouquet of flowers to put on the table for Marley and some fresh produce to use with dinner tomorrow night.

The kids were excited as we took our turns walking around to each booth on the square. They'd introduce themselves, shove their little hands out for a shake, and say they were living here now.

It was the cutest fucking thing.

Every vendor reciprocated and even offered them samples of whatever it was they were selling. If the samples weren't for children, they'd offer a piece of candy that they'd kept around for the kids of the town.

Quimby Grove wasn't perfect, but it was pretty fucking close.

We'd just paid for some fresh milk when my cell phone buzzed in my pocket. After leading Izzy and Jax to a nearby bench, I pulled my phone out to see that Marley had been my missed call. I dialed her back and waited for her sweet voice to fill the line.

"Hey," she said. "I just wanted to confirm plans for this evening. My train arrives in Harrisburg at around five this afternoon, and then I'll take an Uber to Beckett and Ellawyn's place to pick up the kids."

Woody had called in sick today and was unable to close the bar, leaving me to cover for him. "Yep, and then the three of you will meet me at the bar for dinner before you take them home."

Being away from Marley on her first night back in town was a difficult pill to swallow. But Old Man Woody had been a trooper these past two weeks, and I owed him for that. One more night apart couldn't hurt, and she'd be in my arms by the early morning hours anyway.

"Perfect," she said, her voice growing quiet. "Hey," she whispered. "Any new incidents around town involving us?"

"No, not a one. I think it's safe to say that whoever it was either left town or grew tired of harassing us. I did arrange for some squad cars to add our house into their routes each night just in case, though. We're safe," I promised.

This week was the beginning of the rest of our lives. I'd even taken the kids down to the local elementary school to enroll them in kindergarten for the upcoming school year. We even ran into Kennon as he enrolled his daughter as a new student in the same school. The kids had a playdate together next weekend.

It felt nice to be able to breathe a bit easier these days. I just hoped we could finally move past all this and start our lives together without constantly looking over our shoulders.

25

MARLEY

The sound of the train on the tracks was like white noise, soothing enough to make my eyelids heavy. When I boarded at Penn Station, I opted for the quiet car this afternoon. I hoped to avoid the more annoying passengers that were likely aboard somewhere.

Sometimes a person just needed a calming sense of peace. That was exactly what I craved after a chaotic two weeks in the city. I hadn't slept for more than three hours a night; the fatigue was starting to get to me.

Avery and I had spent these past few weeks together. We had spent the bulk of our time back at the building where I worked for my event planning business. My sister had been great at not taking on any new clients this summer, which resulted in us only having two events to coordinate during the two weeks I was back in town. While I coordinated those and gave Avery a break, she got to work on drafting a communication to my current and previous clients regarding the relocation of my business.

Some of the work I could do remotely, like how I helped

Ellawyn plan a Mr. Claus fundraiser. I'd also expressed that I'd be willing to travel back for weddings and larger corporate events. But I'd been clear that I would no longer be in New York full-time anymore.

After Avery and I put the final nail in the coffin for Events by Halligan, we packed up the office and arranged to have movers come and have it shipped to Pennsylvania. Our biggest nightmare was packing up my apartment, though. I'd focused on my room and closet while she had tackled Izzy and Jax's room, and then we'd tag-teamed the common areas.

It had taken forever.

But the time with my sister had been invaluable. We'd been glued to each other's hip like we always had been, while we prepared to change the course of our lives. I could tell she was nervous about the move, but I had an inkling this was what she needed. It was a gut feeling, and I couldn't wait for her to join me in Quimby Grove in a few weeks.

Leaning my head against the glass of the window, the coolness against my face helped me stay awake. I knew if I fell asleep on the ride, then I'd be even groggier after waking up. I'd rather just stay up and sleep well tonight.

But before too long, my eyelids fluttered closed anyway, the sounds and the sway of the train rocking me to sleep.

"Ma'am." A light touch jostled my shoulder. "We've arrived in Harrisburg."

My eyes were heavy as I tried to force them open and take in my surroundings. I glanced up at an older man in an Amtrak uniform and frowned. "Did you say we're in Harrisburg?" I sat up, reaching for my purse and duffel bag from the floor next to me.

"I did." He leaned his arm on top of the seat in front of me. "I went to wake you about fifteen minutes ago, but you looked so peaceful that I gave you a few extra minutes." The corners of his mouth lifted. "I hope you have a nice time in good ole' PA."

I stood from my seat and stretched my arms out over my head before cracking my back. "You're too kind. Thank you." I grabbed my belongings and gave him a wave. "Have a nice evening."

My feet dragged as I made it through the deserted train station and outside by the rideshare pick-up area. According to the app, I'd only have to wait about five minutes for the nearest car to get to me.

It only took two minutes for the exhaustion to set in and cause me to seek out a bench outside. After I lowered myself onto the seat, I sent Max a text to let him know I'd made it to Harrisburg safely and that I'd be picking up the kids within the hour.

I knew he was at the bar, but I wanted to update him anyway. Being away from him and the kids for so long had been hard. When they left, I knew I'd miss my kids, but I was surprised by just how much I'd missed Max, too.

Okay, maybe surprised wasn't the right word. Instead, I was overwhelmed at just how much I had missed him. I loved him.

Loving him had snuck up on me, surprising me in all the wonderful ways that only love could. My love for him knew no bounds. The feeling was monumental, unquantifiable, and all-encompassing. Even from the beginning, I'd known he was special. He was my soul mate, and I couldn't wait to tell him.

"THANK YOU FOR THE RIDE," I said before shutting the door to the car of my rideshare driver. Instead of going directly to

Beckett and Ellawyn's place, I'd decided to make a quick pit stop at Max's house so I could grab whatever vehicle Max hadn't taken today so that I'd have the car seats. Plus, I could freshen up a bit. I reeked of public transportation. Okay, that was probably a tad dramatic, but I always preferred a shower right after traveling anyway.

Glancing up at Max's—*our*—house, I took in the differences from when I'd last seen it. The front porch had been decorated for fall, and I had a hunch the kids were the culprits of that idea. They loved celebrating everything early. It was a trait they'd learned from their Auntie Avery.

My sister lived for the holidays and birthdays. If there was a reason to celebrate, she'd find it. She especially loved celebrating holidays earlier than necessary, which meant she got in the Halloween spirit by the end of August and into the Christmas spirit by mid-September. She always made the holidays special for us.

As I made my way closer to the front porch, I caught a glimpse of something new in the backyard. I dropped my duffel bag and purse onto the first and then rounded the house to get a better look.

It was a huge swing set, the biggest I'd ever seen on a residential property. It was made of beautiful cedar wood. On one side, there was a miniature rock-climbing wall, a fireman's pole with a knotted rope, and a ramp that led up to a gazebo with little stars cut out of the top with a telescope. Then connecting to the gazebo was a high sky bridge walkway with two swings—a regular swing and a skateboard swing—hung below. The sky bridge was connected to a large play structure with a slide and a ramp to get up and down.

The smell of the cedar was refreshing. I ran my hand over the side of the slide, feeling the smooth texture of the wood. A rustling from the cornfield off to my right drew my attention from the detail of the swing set. The movement only lasted a couple of seconds, if that, before it stopped. An animal savoring the corn most likely.

Laughing at my paranoia, I took a step backward and went to turn around. But before I could pivot my body, a large hand shoved my head into the wooden pillar, hard. I collapsed to the ground, the pain in my head radiating.

The sounds of one person hovered near my head, and in the distance, I heard the shuffling of at least one other person as the stomping grew closer. I fought to keep my eyes open, to remain focused so I could fight. But it was only a few mere seconds before I succumbed to the darkness that was pulling me under...

26

MAX

As the hours passed, the evening set in, and the sky grew darker. With summer about over, the nights were starting to get cooler and the residents of Quimby Grove lived for these few weeks in between summer and fall. They'd walk the town square, popping into the businesses that lined the streets before ending up at my bar for a drink and maybe some food.

These evenings were my favorite.

My bar was busy tonight. The busiest I'd seen it since before the fire. Every tabletop was filled, and there were no barstools left vacant. Folks were standing by the bar, squeezing in to order a drink while they waited for a table to be vacated.

My cheeks hurt from smiling so much from all this past summer had brought into my life. At the top of my list were my princess and my children, followed by a stable business and a roof over our heads. I'd always been content with the life I had lived, but now I had a purpose, and I was thankful every fucking day.

Once the last patron was served, I rolled my sleeves up to

my elbows and stepped off to the side of the bar so I could check my phone and see what time it was. Looking down at the screen, I frowned. Marley hadn't messaged me at all since she'd arrived in Harrisburg. I remembered us talking about her and the kids joining me at the bar for dinner before they went home to bed, but maybe I was remembering it wrong.

I tapped her contact and pressed the phone to my ear, waiting for her to answer, but the call kept ringing and ringing, until eventually, voicemail kicked in. That was unlike her to not be answering her phone, but maybe she was getting in some quality time with the kids and didn't have her cell on her. Seemed possible since they hadn't seen one another for a few weeks.

Ignoring my paranoia, I went back behind the bar and waited on the new faces that had walked in. I'd give her a few minutes and if she didn't call back or answer again, then I'd go home and check on them. I poured a few beers, forcing myself to pay attention to the customers instead of letting my mind think of the worst-case scenario, when I noticed Beckett walking into the bar.

"Excuse me," I said to the group of customers as I rounded the bar, going directly to Beckett.

He ran a hand through this hair, looking anxious. "Marley hasn't picked up the kids yet," he said with a low voice.

Leaving the bar unattended was something I'd never do, but at this moment, nothing else fucking mattered except for Marley. I jerked my head toward the exit and followed Beckett outside.

"Son of a bitch," I said. "She was on her way to pick them up early this afternoon, but I hadn't heard from her since."

Kennon exited the bar and came over to us. "Saw the way you two walked out. What's going on?"

"Marley didn't pick up the twins when she was supposed to," I said to him before looking back to Beckett.

"This isn't like her," Beckett said. "Ellawyn hadn't heard from her since early this afternoon either. Where the fuck could she be?"

My mind raced as I tried to consider where she could be, but nothing came to mind. Marley was still new in town; her only friend so far was Ellawyn. And whenever Marley had been in town over the summer, she didn't have a spot that she'd frequented by herself. She only ever went to my bar, Starlight Books, and home. She'd only been to Illusion once, but again, who could she have gone to see instead of picking up the kids?

"Do you think something could have happened to her?" Beckett asked. "I know you guys were being harassed before she went back to New York. I wonder if someone found out she was back in town or something."

Kennon's jaw ticked. "We need to go."

Everything faded around me. My chest grew tight, my heart beating a mile a minute as the flashes of something terrible happening to Marley popped into my head. I looked all around us as if hoping she'd just pop out of an alleyway.

"I need to go find her." I rushed back into my bar and yelled as loud as I fucking could. "Everybody out, now. I don't care about your tab. Just get out of my bar." People stared at me, stunned. "Get out!" I bellowed.

I didn't wait for them to leave. I simply ran through the kitchen and out the back door, into the alleyway to where I parked my truck. I'd just started the engine when Beckett slid into the passenger seat and Kennon into the back seat.

"We're not letting you do this alone," Kennon said. "Let's go."

Thankfully, High Street was practically empty as I pulled

out onto the main road and sped off in the direction of my house. She had to be there. That was the only other place she'd have gone. I pressed on the gas pedal, tickets be damned.

If something happened to her, I'd never forgive myself.

27

MARLEY

The pressure in my head was unreal, a pain, unlike anything I'd ever felt. A pounding that wouldn't let up. My eyes were heavy, too heavy to open. Maybe if I just slept a little more, the headache would subside. A voice sounded around me; the familiarity sent a chill up my spine as the memories from before came rushing back.

I'd been out back, admiring the swing set. Something had caught my attention by the cornfields, but nothing was there. I went to turn around... and then there was pain, followed by nothing. My eyes fought to open, to figure out my surroundings, but the pain was too strong.

Or maybe I was too scared.

My chest was cold and felt uneven, like I was lying on something. Maybe I was lying on the ground, just not on even terrain. I tried to move my arms to push myself up, but it was no use. My arms were pulled back and unable to budge. I was either handcuffed or someone had tied my wrists together. My legs felt the same except I think my legs were crossed over each other and then secured.

Any movement I made hurt like a bitch.

Footsteps sounded close by, followed by a voice I still couldn't place. "Get here," it spat. "Now. You're the goddamn police—just fucking leave. I'll see you when you get here."

The relief that came had my body relaxing. Whoever was here was trying to get the police to come and help. Maybe the familiar voice had found me like this—outside, bound and tied—and was trying to help.

Thank goodness.

The voice was back, making another phone call. "No, she's passed out cold. This is taking longer than I'd like." There was silence, probably as the person on the other end of the call responded. "You think? Let me check."

The footsteps thundered toward me, getting closer and closer as my heartbeat matched their pace. My heartbeat was louder, stronger with every step that stormed its way toward me. And then, a forceful kick landed on my side, not once but twice.

"You were right. She was conscious."

A scream escaped my lungs while tears streamed down my cheeks. I struggled to roll away from the man, but with the way I was tied, I couldn't. My body curled slightly inward, trying to shield myself. My eyes fluttered, desperately trying to open them while the rest of me drowned in pain. Finally, they opened slowly at first, and after a few more blinks, my vision cleared and I could see around me.

The man had turned away from me, still on the phone, but I couldn't make out what they were saying. He stood tall and wore a black hoodie with the hood pulled up over his head. His hands were covered with blue latex gloves—one hand holding a phone and the other holding a knife.

Tearing my gaze away from him, I took in my surroundings. Tall corn stalks surrounded us in the little space. They'd been harvested either by a farmer or flattened by this sick fuck. I couldn't tell which.

The man pocketed his cell phone before turning his head and looking over his shoulders at me. "How many times do I have to warn you to stay away from here before you get a fucking clue?"

The shadows of his hood blocked my view of any facial features. But at that moment, I didn't need to see him to know exactly who it was. His voice was all the confirmation I needed. Instead of responding, I stayed silent, staring at that black fucking hoodie.

"I tried to get the police to get rid of you," he started as he moved closer toward me. "But those fuckers wouldn't press charges." He circled my body like a wild animal stalking their prey. "I lit that dickhead's bar on fire and left a little note for you. I thought you took the hint when you went crawling back to New York, licking your wounds."

He raised his leg back before using all his force to connect it to my side again in a harsh kick. "But here you fucking are," he screamed, lowering his head toward mine as I groaned on the ground, the pain too much. "And now here we are." He straightened his back and turned away from me. "There's no way out of it this time, Marley."

"W-w-why, Jakob?" My voice broke just as my heart did. Jakob was my past, but at one point he'd been important to me. He always treated me well.

He circled me once more, his face contorted in ways that made it clear that pure evil lived inside him. His eyes were dark, almost empty looking. Devoid of any emotion. He bent down, grabbed my waist, and flipped me onto my back. My arms pushed into the cold ground. The new position had me feeling pain everywhere. Unable to look him in the face, I turned away as tears gathered in my eyes.

He placed one foot on the other side of my body, situating himself so that he was standing over me, and then lowered himself so that he was straddling my hips. He reached out, grabbed the sides of my face, and turned me back toward him until he caught my gaze.

"Because you are mine," he seethed. "You were mine until he entered your life again." He dragged a finger down my cheek and continued downward. "I took care of you and those fucking bastards for a long fucking time."

Bile crept up my throat; his words and contact made me sick. This wasn't the Jakob that I knew. It wasn't the man I'd once cared for. A shudder raced through me when his hands reached my chest.

"You know we were never going to work out," I said. "You worked too much and spent every moment of free time at the bars with other women."

He raised his hand, and then *crack*. The sting of the slap brought fresh tears to my eyes. The pain, when mixed with everything else that was hurting, was too much. I couldn't catch my breath as my world spun out of control. The corn stalks around me had become blurry as they circled around me. Then another crack hit the opposite cheek. My head whipped in the opposite direction; darkness began to take over.

"Tonight, I take back what belongs to me," he said, his voice ominous as he rose from the ground and stepped away from me.

EVERYTHING HURT. My head, my ribs, and my cheeks felt like they were on fire.

Two sets of voices sounded near me, speaking in hushed tones. I forced my eyes open, wanting to see who was there, but the night sky made it harder for my eyes to adjust. Just then,

Jakob came into view, plopping an armful of sticks onto an already huge pile that sat in the center of a metal fire ring before pouring a little bit of gasoline on top.

His eyes met mine. Evil mixed with a smidge of excitement danced within his irises. "She's awake," he called out loudly over his shoulder. He reached into his pocket and waved a matchbook in front of my face before lighting a match and dropping it onto the pile of sticks.

The fire sparked, growing slowly as it made its way up to the top of the stack. The warmth felt nice in comparison to the cold ground. The fire dimly lit the space, making it easier to see. The light reflected off something in the distance, a flicker of light moved across as the figure stepped into the light.

"Hi, Marley," he said as he came further into the light.

Officer Barclay stood near the fire, staring down at me with a smile on his face.

Fucking finally, I could breathe a little easier. A cop was here to stop this nonsense. He must be getting ready to arrest Jakob and free me.

"Officer Barclay," I started as I tried to twist on the ground to see him better. "He has me restrained and it hurts. Can you help me?"

He tossed his head back, laughing. "Of course you're restrained. We can't have you getting away after all the work we've done."

My brow furrowed. "You aren't here to help me?" I couldn't wrap my head around this. A cop was standing here, looking at me, and refusing to help. "Where are the other cops?"

He strode closer to me and lowered himself onto the ground next to me. "There are no other cops coming." He reached out and brushed a strand of my hair out of my face.

"I've been waiting for this moment for so long." He ran a hand up my thigh and underneath my dress.

My body jerked at the touch as I tried to roll away.

"Hands off," Jakob bellowed. "She's mine."

Officer Barclay removed his hand slowly. "You said I could have a taste." He got up and joined Jakob by the fire.

"You'll get your taste. But not until I'm done." He looked down at the fire, almost in adoration before he returned his glance to me. "First, we play with fire, and then we get to taste."

The knot in my stomach tightened. I turned my attention to Officer Barclay, meeting his gaze, and leveled him with a stare. "What do you mean you've been waiting for this? I barely know you."

Jakob knew Officer Barclay, but how? He'd never mentioned him when we were together. But now they were working together to kidnap me? My eyes slammed shut, and the faces of Izzy and Jax came to my mind. They must be so worried. I couldn't leave them.

"Open your eyes if you want story time," Officer Barclay said.

I took a deep breath and willed myself to open my eyes, to be brave for my children. When I did, I saw Officer Barclay with a vile grin. His beady eyes stared down at me as he circled around me.

"I've known Jakob since college. We were thick as thieves. When I found out his favorite girlfriend left him for another man who happened to live in my town, we decided to reunite and get you to leave town and return to him."

"We figured it'd be easy," Jakob added. "Spook you a little bit and you'd leave. Barclay vandalized that business on the square and then questioned you for it. I stabbed that man in the alleyway, knowing your precious heart would stop and try to help." He shook his head as he stoked the fire.

"I worked the scene that day and planted your business cards near that dead fucker's body and wiped them in his blood." Officer Barclay stopped at my sides, glaring down at me. "I had you questioned for that, too. Figured that'd scare you into leaving." He turned toward the fire and bent down, picking up part of a stick that had stuck out, and strode back over toward me.

"No!" I shouted. "Please no," I begged as he got closer to me. The hot end of the stick seared my skin as he pressed it into my thighs. Tears streamed down my face. The pain... The pain was too much. I wasn't sure how much more I could take.

"But even after being investigated for that, you didn't fucking leave." He threw the stick into the fire, watching it burn. "The fire, though, that was all Jakob's idea." He shrugged. "All I did was throw a brick through the door window." He laughed, gazing at Jakob. "Jakob had to fucking rush back to the city to see your sister in time to form a good enough alibi. The fire was a good addition. That one worked."

Jakob's eyes narrowed at me. "Yeah, it worked until today." He turned his attention back to Officer Barclay and glared. "And no more burn marks until I'm done with her."

Officer Barclay rolled his eyes. "She looked too perfect. Just needed to dirty her up a bit."

The pain was pulling me under, in and out of consciousness, and I struggled to stay awake. I thought of Izzy and Jax. I thought of Max and everything we hadn't gotten to do together yet as a family. My heart ached at the thought of losing all three of them. My body recoiled at the realization that I was stuck in this hell with Jakob and one of Quimby Grove's supposedly finest.

A corrupt cop was at the forefront of all this.

He'd been right there this whole time, silently watching me

while he facilitated all the horrible things that I'd gone through since the beginning of the summer.

My eyes grew heavier. The pull was beginning to be too strong to ignore. Maybe just a little rest, and I'd be able to think of an escape plan. I forced my eyes open one last time. The last thing I saw was the two men walking toward me.

28

MAX

The drive to my house normally took about ten minutes. We made it in five.

"Park at the end of the driveway," Kennon instructed.

"Good thinking," Beckett said. "That way we can remain unseen if needed."

Following their directions, I pulled off on the side of the road beside the cornfield near my driveaway. We exited the car and closed the doors slowly and quietly before making our way up toward the house, using the field as cover.

"Let me go first," Kennon said from behind me. "I'm armed." He pulled up the waistband of his jeans, showing his Glock.

I ignored him, not giving a fuck if he was armed or not, and continued walking toward the house. A hand came to my shoulder, gently pulling me back. "What?" I snapped.

Beckett pulled me back once more, letting Kennon take the lead. "You don't know what we may walk into. You won't be able to help Marley if you're dead, man."

I nodded and fell in line behind Kennon. "House first," I whispered. "I have a gun inside, should we need it."

We came up to the end of the cornfield and were standing toward the front of the house, off to the side. There were no lights on in the house and no noise coming from outside beyond crickets chirping.

Kennon stepped out from behind the shelter of the field and jogged toward the house with Beckett and me following behind him. He stopped when he reached the steps and jerked his head downward. In front of us were a suitcase, a bag, and Marley's purse. Panic started to take over. Someone had to have taken her. She had never even made it inside the house. Kennon stepped around the items and jiggled the handle to the door.

It was unlocked.

He eased the door open, stepped inside, and waited for any sign of someone inside. We were met with silence. "I'll check upstairs," he said. "Max, where's your gun?"

"Down here." I stepped around him and headed toward the family room. I'd kept my firearm hidden on the top shelf in a locked box. "I'll grab my gun and check around down here." I turned to Beckett. "Call 911."

Kennon crept up the stairs to the second floor, being as quiet as possible. Once he reached the landing, I turned into the family room and went for my gun while I listened in to Beckett making the call to 911 and telling them to hurry.

We didn't know what we'd find on the property, but we'd need them either way. I reached up, grabbed my lock box, and started to load a magazine into the chamber. I grabbed one more magazine, just in case, and shoved it into my pants.

Beckett had just gotten off the phone and was putting his phone away when I joined him by the front door. "Let's check the rest of the downstairs," he whispered.

We crept toward the kitchen, listening for any movements, but there were none. The house was eerily silent. She wasn't in here. If she were, I'd be able to feel her presence. I went into the kitchen anyway, followed by the half bath and the living room.

There was nothing.

Kennon rushed down the stairs. "Everything is clear up there," he said. "But I noticed something. Come here." He ran toward the front door and went out onto the porch. "Look over there." He pointed out toward the center of the large cornfield. "See that dim light out there? Looks like a fire."

Beckett fisted his hands. "Let's go."

We took off running for the cornfield, but Kennon was faster, sliding in front of us with his hands up. "We need to be quiet when we enter this cornfield. They'll hear us coming, and we can't risk them getting spooked if someone does have Marley out there."

We both nodded and eased our way into the field, going as slow as we could while at the same time trying to hurry. It was torture not to run toward the fire and see if Marley was indeed out there. The slow walk had allowed negative thoughts to invade my mind.

What if something happened to Marley? How could I possibly live without her? The kids would never be the same if they lost their mother. Tears built in my eyes, welling up and threatening to break, but I shoved them down.

Now was not the time to be negative and emotional. I had to hold my shit together. For Marley. For Izzy and Jax. For everybody that I loved.

The warmth of the fire hit my skin as we stood hidden in the cornfield. Someone had made a ten-foot-wide crop circle, and in the center of it stood two men with their backs to us as they looked down at something on the ground.

My hands fisted as I waited for them to turn around. I needed to see what we were up against. Kennon stood beside me, stoic and seemingly calm as he eyed the two men. He pulled his gun out of the waistband of his jeans and turned the safety off, gripping it tightly.

Beckett was the only one unarmed. He stood behind us, scowling. "Stay here. I'll be right back," he whispered before slowly moving along the circular perimeter. Kennon and I stayed put, watching in silence as we waited for his return.

When Beckett came back, he was pale and had a scowl plastered on his face. "It took all I had not to storm through the goddamn corn stalks and kick their ass," he fumed. "Marley is lying on the ground." He ducked his head before meeting my gaze. "She's been beaten pretty badly."

My chest rose and fell with anger. I gripped my gun, removed the safety, and pushed past him.

"Wait," Beckett called. "There's one more thing I need to tell you guys." His gaze darted between Kennon and me. "The one guy—I don't know him. But the other guy... It's Officer Barclay. He's in on this."

A fucking corrupt cop.

It was all starting to make sense now. Why they questioned Marley about the vandalism, why her business card had showed up at the scene of a crime, and how the investigation for the fire had turned up nothing.

It was him pulling the strings and making things go the way he wanted.

Now that I knew Marley was with them, I'd had enough. I

took a breath and stepped out of the safety of the corn stalks. "Barclay," I shouted as I stormed over toward them.

He turned around, a smug grin on his face as he stepped over Marley's body. The other man kept his back turned but bent down and picked up Marley. He hoisted her over his shoulder before he turned to meet my waiting gaze.

My jaw ticked. "Jakob." I stepped closer, standing just on the other side of the fire. The flames danced between us, the heat making it impossible to breathe. "Drop her," I demanded. "She didn't do anything to either of you."

Jakob pivoted his body so he could face Barclay better, which put Marley's face in my line of sight. My stomach twisted when I saw her. Her face was bruised and swollen, with dried blood covering her forehead.

"She did, though," Jakob shouted. "She chose you and now she's mine. Barclay and I will do whatever we want with her."

My free hand fisted at my side, my teeth grinding together so hard I was surprised I hadn't broken a tooth. I kept my gaze locked on Jakob, watching his every move since he had Marley in his arms.

Barclay stepped toward the fire, picking up a stick that had been in the blaze. "We've already had a little fun with her." He stepped up next to her, bringing the stick with him, and lifted it to Marley's thigh, hovering just above her porcelain skin.

As I went to move to beat his ass, Kennon jumped out of the cornfield and right into Barclay. He fell to the ground at the impact and Kennon stood over him, glaring down. "Stay there or you'll never see the light of day ever again." He pointed his gun down at him, finger on the trigger.

Jakob glared at his accomplice. "You're fucking useless," he mumbled before turning back toward me. "One down, one to go, I guess." He looked around the circle we stood in. "And it looks like it's just one on one now."

Beckett stepped out from the field and stood next to me. "Think again." His face was etched in anger, his stance threatening. "Put Marley down," he demanded. "The cops will be here any minute."

Jakob lowered Marley off his shoulders and positioned her in front of him, holding her up by her waist while her upper body slumped forward. He had her blocking my shot. I wouldn't be able to shoot him if I had to. Marley would end up getting shot too if that happened.

My eyes darted to Kennon, conveying a silent message. He glanced down at Barclay, who was still glaring at him. Kennon lifted his right arm and whipped Barclay across the head with the pistol. Barclay's head turned to the side, his eyelids going closed.

Perfect.

Jakob hadn't noticed the hit, his gaze too focused on me as he tried to keep hold of an unconscious Marley. Beckett started walking around the perimeter of the circle, taking Jakob's attention with him and easing him away from the fire.

Jakob reached into his pocket with his free hand and pulled out something small and shiny. The fire reflected across the blade of a small knife. He raised his hand, trying to get the knife to Marley's throat, but was unable to. With Marley being unconscious, her head was still slumped over and in the way.

Jakob shifted her, trying to get the right angle. But instead of focusing on Marley, he kept his attention on Beckett as he made his way closer toward him. When he shifted Marley, he lost his grip on her, and she started to slide down his body. He repositioned his knife, trying to get a better grip while one hand was still on Marley, wrapped tightly around her waist. He raised the knife, ready to strike, when two shots were fired into his chest.

Kennon lowered his gun and put it away as he stared down at Jakob. "He's gone."

I didn't give a fuck about him. I rushed over to Marley as she collapsed on the ground and scooped her up in my arms. I had to hold her—to know that she was truly safe—and that she'd be okay. That we'd get through this together.

"Marley. I'm here, princess." I stood and started rushing out of the cornfield, with Kennon and Beckett leading the way as the sirens grew closer to the house. "I'm here and I'm not going anywhere." I pressed my lips to her forehead and hoped like hell she'd be okay.

29

MARLEY

The sounds of the waves crashing on the beach had soothed something within me. It was as if I could breathe for the very first time. Like all my troubles had just drifted back to sea and I was set free.

The saltiness from the sea lingered with the evening breeze, blowing all around me. The broken bits of seashells mixed with sea glass laid out on the sandy beach like a work of art. The reflection of the moon glistened in the glass and danced on top of the sea.

It called to me, and I listened.

The song and dance of the ocean lead me through the sandy beach to the shoreline where the water washed up toward me. The cold water caressed my feet, soaking the ends of my emerald dress and tugging me further out into the depths of the unknown.

The water crept up my legs, wrapping around my thighs before moving onto my waist the further I waded out into the ocean. The sea was calling me, urging me further away from the shore. The wetness hit my neck, rising toward my mouth, and the saltiness of the ocean seeped into my throat, burning as I swallowed it down, trying to gasp for air. The darkness marked its claim on me, keeping me under as it pulled me further down until I was about to answer.

But something else called for me.

"Marley," a voice sounded from far away. "Come back to me, Marley," it echoed.

I used my arms to turn myself around in the water. Facing the shore, I saw a handsome man on the boardwalk with a guitar. He started running down the ramp and onto the beach. "It's me, Max. Come back to me, princess."

"Princess," I whispered to myself as I swam toward my destiny.

THE BEEPING GREW louder as I fought to open my eyes as if it were an alarm trying to get my attention.

"Come on, princess." A hand I hadn't known was there gripped mine and gave it a long, hard squeeze.

With all the strength I could muster, I squeezed back. "Busker?"

My eyelids fluttered open, meeting those beautiful green eyes I had longed for. The eyes that I'd dreamt of. Max looked exhausted. Dark circles had formed underneath his eyes. His beard was longer than it normally was, and his hair was a mess.

A lone tear slid down his cheek before he dipped his forehead to rest on our conjoined hands. His tears dripped onto my fingers, a physical reminder of how close we were to losing each other. "I'm okay," I croaked, my throat burning. "Water."

Max lifted his head right away and turned to grab a huge water cup with a straw. He placed the straw at my lips. "Little sips for now," he said. "We don't want you getting sick."

The ice water soothed my throat, providing instant relief. I took another sip before letting go of the straw and resting my head down on the pillow again.

"Knock, knock," a voice called from outside my room. The door pushed open and Avery walked in with puffy eyes and smeared makeup. "Marley!" She ran over to the opposite side of the bed and gave me a hug. "I'm so glad you're awake. I was so worried." She studied my face, likely sensing that I needed something. "Ah, I know." She went back over to the door and dimmed the lights in the room and pulled the curtains shut. "There we go," she said as she returned to my bedside. "Better?"

"Much." I grabbed my sister's hand and brought it to my lips. "Thank you."

Avery pulled on the chair that was a few feet away and moved it right up against the railing. "You think I'd miss this? For once, I'm the prettier twin," she joked with a wink.

I laughed, but the pain in my sides instantly made me regret it. "Ouch, don't make me laugh."

"But I mean it, twinnie. The moment I learned that something bad had happened, I got in a car and drove all the way here in the middle of the night. I'm so glad you're okay." She leaned down and pressed a kiss on top of my head. "I love you."

"Love you too, Avery."

Avery looked between me and Max and smiled. "I'll leave you two to catch up. I'll go pick up the twins a while." She bent down and gave me another hug and then left the room without another word.

Max sunk into his chair as he rubbed his hands over his face.

"What happened?" I questioned Max. "I remember everything up until after I was burned with the end of a stick, but after that it's blurry."

He dropped his hands and exhaled. "You're sure you want to know so soon?"

I took a moment and considered his question. Did I really want to relive the worst night of my life? Absolutely not... but I wasn't sure that I'd be able to truly move on from this without the full story, no matter how painful it was.

I swallowed. The burn in my throat returned, a lump forming. "Tell me."

Max laid it all out there for me. From how he, Beckett, and Kennon came to the house and did a search to how they slowly crept through the cornfield, going toward the fire in hopes of finding me. He told me it had ended with Kennon attacking Officer Barclay and how Beckett had distracted Jakob so that Max could have a clear shot at him in case it was needed.

Jakob was dead and Officer Barclay was behind bars.

After Max filled in the missing pieces for me, I felt like a weight had been lifted off my chest. I had no idea that Jakob had been hurting that badly after our breakup. When Avery told me he'd been dating again, I figured he'd moved on happily.

A part of me felt bad that I had caused him so much pain that he felt the need to do everything that he did. But another part realized how this was way beyond the normal feelings that happened after a breakup.

This wasn't my fault.

This was Jakob's fault.

"I'm just glad it's over," I said. "Maybe now the four of us can finally move on and really focus on becoming a real family here in Quimby Grove. Without having to constantly look over our shoulders all the time."

"The time is ours, princess." Max rose from his seat and brushed his lips against mine. "There's nothing standing in our way anymore." He sat on the edge of my bed, scooting as close as he could get. "Fuck, I'm so glad you're okay, Marley." He took my hands in his and looked at me with those glossy forest-green eyes. I practically melted right then and there. "I thought I was going to lose you. I couldn't lose you... I can't lose you—not now, not ever."

My eyes glistened. "Do you know what I thought about whenever I was alone with them?" I braced my hands on the bed by my sides and gently lifted my body up so I could move over a bit on the bed. I reached for Max, pulling him closer to me until I was lying in his arms.

"I thought about you and all the life we still had to live together. I thought about how devastated the children would be if something were to happen to me. I thought about missing out on their lives and the possibility of not being able to be yours for the rest of your life. I thought about how I needed to be strong, because there was no way in hell I was leaving this earth without getting the chance to tell you how much I fucking love you."

Max brushed the hair away from my face. "I love you too, Marley. Forever and ever, and even that's not long enough."

LITTLE WHISPERS PULLED me from my dreams, bringing me back to the reality of being stuck in a hospital bed. My eyes fluttered open, the bright lights overhead blinding me momentarily until my vision adjusted.

"Mama's up," a little voice whispered. "Jax, get over here."

"I got the tiger's lilies." Another little voice sounded from the other side of the room. Little feet scurried across the hospital floor tile, the noise stopping just beside me.

My blurry vision cleared, and in front of me stood my two munchkins, Izzy and Jax. Their eyes were filled with worry, but also a sliver of hope shined through as I surveyed both of my children, making sure they were okay.

"My babies." As soon as I opened my arms toward my kids, they climbed up onto the bed and barreled into my chest.

Loving on my children was worth the pain that shot throughout my body at their impact. I'd take the pain every damn day if it meant I was still here for them. I squeezed them extra tight and gave them too many kisses before letting them pull away.

"We missed you." Jax leaned into me, not giving me an inch of space. "Are you hurt?"

"I am a little sore, yeah. But Mama will be okay." I smiled down at my babies, trying to reassure them that everything was okay. "I missed you both so much, but I'll be getting out of here in a few days."

Izzy sat on my lap, nodding her head. "We know. We're planning a special surprise," she said, beaming. She clutched Effie to her chest for a moment before giving the beloved stuffed animal a kiss. "I want Effie to stay with you tonight." She placed Effie in the crook of my arm and stared down at her favorite toy. "Perfect."

"Here's some tiger's lilies, Mama." Jax handed me a handful of carefully wrapped tiger lilies. He leaned over, inhaling their scent one last time before settling against me with a content sigh.

"Thank you, sweetie. They're lovely."

The kids crawled off the bed and moved toward a corner of the room, where their toys were. They dumped a pile of Legos onto the floor and started playing.

I said a silent prayer for them to remember to pick up all

the pieces before they went home tonight. Stepping on those hurt like a bitch.

"Fairytale Blooms is an awesome flower shop," a familiar voice called out. Avery leaned against the doorframe, looking over at the three of us. "I think it's my favorite shop in Quimby Grove so far." Avery pushed off from the doorframe and came over to sit in the chair at my bedside. "You're looking better. In a few days, I will no longer be the prettiest twin," she teased.

I rolled my eyes, ignoring her self-deprecating comment. "So what I'm hearing is that your favorite shop in your favorite town is the floral shop?"

It'd only been a few days since the incident, but Avery hadn't left my side, or Quimby Grove, at all. If she did leave my hospital room, it was to do things that would help out, like picking up the kids and staying with them in the evening until Max could get there. She'd been a huge help to us, and I needed to finally get a commitment out of her on when she planned to officially move here. I wanted her here as soon as possible.

"You could work there, you know. Speaking of working there, when are you moving here?"

Avery groaned and tilted her head back to look at the ceiling. "Even in a hospital you're still pushy as fuck," she grumbled. "There's nothing holding me back in New York. I just need to pack up my apartment." She brought her gaze back to me. "Just need to figure out a life for me here first."

I waved her off. "Oh my gosh. I'm so glad you'll be living here as soon as possible. Don't worry about figuring out a life for yourself. We'll figure it out, I promise. There are so many opportunities for you here."

"I hope so."

Avery might not have been sure of herself, but I was. And man, oh man, did I have an idea for her once she was settled into Quimby Grove. With being on the mend physically and Avery moving here, I was beyond thrilled and ready to be out of this hospital.

All I needed was the green light from the doctors and I could finally move on from this and start looking forward to the future.

30

MAX

"Are you sure you have everything?"

"For the thousandth time, yes." Marley narrowed her eyes and flipped me off. "How could I possibly forget anything with you constantly checking?"

"I'm glad to see you finally back to being your old self—a pain in my ass." I grabbed her duffel bag and placed it over my shoulder before going to Marley's side.

After a few days in the hospital, Marley was finally breaking out of the joint and ready to come home. It felt as though a lifetime had passed since the incident with Officer Barclay and Jakob. Marley had landed in the hospital, of course, and now that she was released, she was planning on going up to New York in a few weeks to help Avery pack up her apartment, despite Avery's protests for her sister to stay home.

Little did Marley know, I was also protesting her traveling to New York anytime soon. Marley had been lucky she'd escaped the cornfield without any substantial injuries. The worst injury she'd had was the cut on her forehead, which had needed stitches, and the concussion that followed. Everything else beyond sore muscles had healed a few days ago.

Marley was almost as good as new—physically speaking—but the trauma of what had happened wouldn't be disappearing anytime soon. But she had a large support system by her side and one of the best therapists that Quimby Grove had to offer.

"You love when I'm a pain in your ass, busker." Marley took one last look around her hospital room and nodded her head. "We're good to go." She laced her fingers with mine and looked up at me. "Take me home, Max. Take me home."

Marley rode shotgun in my truck with the windows down, her hair whipping all around her with a smile as the wind captured her sunshine-blonde hair. She turned the radio up and sang along with the song, bobbing her head the entire time. It was fucking attractive, that's what it was.

I could watch her like this all day.

She was happy and carefree for the first time in months. She was fucking perfect, and she was all mine.

As we approached my driveway, I eased off the gas and flipped on my turn signal before easing onto the dirt driveway and taking my time to drive us up to the house. Marley sat up straight and rolled up the window before turning her attention to her feet.

The house must have been bringing up painful memories from a few days ago. I slowed us down a bit more. "You know we don't have to stay here, right?" I glanced over at her. "We could move. I wouldn't have a problem with that."

Marley met my gaze and shook her head. "No, no way. This is your father's house. We can't give this up."

"I'd do anything for you, Marley. The memories of my dad live in here." I tapped my temple. "And in here," I said, tapping my heart. "I don't need a whole house to remember him."

"I know, but honestly, I don't want to leave. The kids like it here. I do too. It'll be hard at first, but I can get through it with time."

This woman was amazing and so selfless. "I appreciate that, princess, but let's just see how it goes. If you feel like it's too much, we can make other arrangements and discuss it further then, okay? But in the meantime..." I'd just made it to the front of the house and threw my truck into park. "I worked with the farmer who owns the land surrounding our house, and they agreed to cut the cornfield down. Look." I pointed out her window. "Hopefully this change makes coming home a little bit easier on you."

Marley's mouth dropped open. "Max..." She got out of the truck and walked to the front steps of the porch. "This does make it easier." She tangled her fingers in mine. "I love you. Thank you."

"Come on." I pulled her up the steps and into the house. It was unusually dark, especially since Avery and the twins were supposed to be home. "That's weird..." I turned to the light switch and flicked it on.

"Surprise!" Balloons and confetti flew out of the family room as our friends rushed into the entryway.

"Oh my god." Marley held a hand to her mouth as tears fell from her eyes. "What's all this?"

"It's a welcome home party," Ellawyn explained as she and Beckett made their way toward us, each holding two champagne flutes. "Here you go," Ellawyn said, offering Marley a drink and then handing the other one over to me before taking another flute from Beckett's hand. "Welcome home, Mar!"

Marley blushed and took a sip of her drink. "Thank you so much. You didn't have to do all this."

"It was all Avery and Kennon, surprisingly." Beckett pointed into the family room, where I saw Kennon fighting with Marley's sister as they each held an end of a welcome home banner. "They've been fighting about that fucking banner for the past twenty minutes."

"This would have been done ages ago if you could keep your side level," Avery snapped loudly, causing Kennon to growl at her.

"It would have been done a hell of a lot sooner if you'd just go find something else to fucking do besides get on my fucking nerves," Kennon barked.

Marley watched her sister with sparkling eyes as she laughed at their interaction. "That's hilarious."

"Mama! Daddy!" Jax ran in between Ellawyn and Beckett and launched himself into my arms. I bent down and picked him up. "Welcome home, Mama."

"Thanks, munchkin." Marley looked around. "Where's your sister?"

A sly smile slid across Jax's face. "I don't know," he said, the last syllable slightly higher than the rest.

"Well, why don't you go find her and tell her to come and enjoy the fun down here, okay?" I kissed his cheek and then placed him back down on the ground.

Jax nodded and took off running up the steps in search of Izzy. Those two were up to something, but I had a feeling it was a surprise for Marley, so I decided to just let them do their thing.

I snaked my arm around Marley's waist and led her into the family room, where everyone had congregated once again. "Avery, why didn't you tell me you were planning this?"

We sat down on the couch, watching as Avery dropped her

end of the banner. "All right, Kennon, since you think you can handle it on your own, go for it. My sister needs me."

She stepped up to him and patted him on the chest twice, while Kennon mumbled something about stubborn-ass women, before joining us on the couch.

"I just wanted to do something nice for my sister," Avery said, shrugging. "But I promise it's just a little get-together with some cake. I know the kids have something planned."

Marley's eyebrows shot up, but Avery refused to share any information. Instead, she served everybody a slice of cake while we all just sat around and enjoyed one another's company.

Ellawyn took a bite of her cake and then pointed her fork at Marley. "Marley, what's next for you? Do you have enough event planning business here in Quimby Grove to keep going?"

"I'm actually booked out for several months!" Marley smiled as she pulled out her phone to check her calendar. "I have a few weeks off now so I can help Avery pack for her move to Quimby Grove and so I can get the munchkins ready for their first day of school."

"That's great," Ellawyn replied as she leaned into Beckett's side. "I'm happy for you, Mar."

Kennon stared at Marley. "Seriously? Your sister is moving here?" He cast a glare over at Avery, who just shrugged and smiled sweetly at him.

"Yes, I am." Avery gave him a little wave.

"Great," Kennon groaned.

"Fight nice, children," Beckett joked. "The six of us are now our core friend group. Can't go making waves on day one."

Everyone in the group laughed except for Kennon, who remained quiet and unmoving. That guy was in for a wild ride if he was going to be spending any considerable amount of time with this crowd. Maybe it'd do him some good. The guy seemed like he could use a solid friend group, a support system.

After about an hour, our guests said their goodbyes and left the four of us to enjoy the rest of our evening together.

"That was sweet of everyone." Marley lingered by the staircase, waiting for me to join her. "But I'm dying to spend some time alone with Izzy and Jax."

"Me too. I can't believe they've been playing in their room this entire time." I came up behind her and gave her ass a playful smack. "Let's go investigate, princess."

She grabbed my hand, pulling me behind her. "You'll pay for that later tonight, busker."

"Don't threaten me with a good time."

Marley was adorable when she tried to be tough, but really, it was just a fucking turn-on. I'd beg on my knees for forgiveness and spend the entire night worshipping her and reminding her that she was home and that she was mine.

It was something to look forward to.

"It's awfully quiet in there," Marley whispered as we stood outside of the children's bedroom. She turned the doorknob and opened the door quietly.

Marley gasped as she stepped inside the room. "Oh my goodness. How'd you do all this?" She covered her mouth as she scoped out what the kids had done.

The room had been transformed into one big fort. Comforters, throw blankets, and sheets were tied together and strung up from the ceiling, with the ends tied to other various pieces of furniture or toys on the floor. A small flap was across from us with a sign that said, "enter if you want lovins." The lights in the room were out, but there were small glowing lights coming from inside the fort.

"Come in already," Izzy shouted from inside their homemade fortress. "But you have to crawl."

Marley and I both dropped to our knees and crawled underneath the opening of the fort. Marley laughed and pointed toward the two mattresses pushed together in the middle of the floor, with the two larger bean bag chairs next to them. In the center of the mattresses sat Izzy and Jax, each holding a star projector between their legs. The projectors were turned on—one displayed a starry night, while the other was showing us the northern lights. Off to the side of the mattresses was a plate from the kitchen, filled with various Ring Pop flavors.

"You guys made our favorite song a reality?" Marley crawled past me and settled onto one of the mattresses. "And brought Ring Pops?" Her hand went to her heart as she took in the space. "This fort does feel like a castle."

"We did, Mama." Jax inched toward his mother and sat on her lap. "To celebrate you coming home from being sick. Auntie Avery helped us."

"Did she? That was nice of her." I joined them on top of the mattress and lifted Izzy into my arms. "This was so sweet of you two."

"Are you surprised?" Izzy beamed at her mother as she leaned back against my chest, getting comfortable.

"I'm so surprised. I love it so much." Marley squeezed Jax as she smiled at Izzy. "Thank you both so much."

This was the second time this song had been mentioned as Marley's favorite, and I still hadn't heard it. "Okay, someone needs to play whatever song this is and finally clue me in." I tickled Izzy's sides. "Are ya going to share it with me?" I asked as I moved down to her kneecaps, tickling underneath them.

Izzy gasped for air as she burst out laughing. "Yes, yes, we will play it," she said with a squeal. "Mama. Play it."

Marley played the song on her phone while we each grabbed a Ring Pop, cuddled together on the mattresses, and listened. The song was a sweet one, the message being that the couple was happy with what they got—they didn't need fancy things like a diamond ring or a lot of money. They didn't need a huge house. They didn't need diamonds when they were each other's rock. They just needed each other. They'd be okay with mattresses on the floor, a fort, and a Ring Pop.

It was a sweet sentiment.

It was perfect.

Because as long as I had Marley—and the kids—I'd be okay. They were all I needed in this life. Not money, or fancy material objects, and not crazy success. If I made my family happy day in and day out, kept them safe, and always showed them how much I loved them, that was all that mattered.

They were all that mattered.

They were my family, my entire world, and after spending years trying to chase what I'd lost, I'd make damn sure I never lost them again. I'd spend the rest of my life making up for the time that we'd lost and showing them just how much they meant to me.

Today marked the beginning of the rest of our lives.

And I couldn't fucking wait.

THE END.

EPILOGUE
MAX

A fit of laughter sounded from upstairs, followed by the light thud of two sets of feet running across the floor. "Are you two ready?" I called out from the bottom of the stairs as I checked the time on my watch. "We're going to be late." The kids and I were planning a surprise, and if we didn't leave soon, we'd get caught.

We couldn't afford to get caught.

Not now.

Marley was booked with back-to-back consultations at Starlight Books until late this afternoon, which was perfect. But if we didn't get a move on soon, we'd run out of time.

Jax appeared at the top of the stairs. He took a deep breath before he barreled down toward me. "Ready!" He jumped up and down, the tips of his untied shoelaces hitting the floor.

"Oh no, looks like we've got some untied laces. Plop down on the stair there and see if you remember how to tie them tight while I go get your sister."

"Yes! I'll fix it," he said, nodding his head. He sat down on the bottom stair. With his little tongue poking out the side of his mouth in concentration, he reached for the laces and started singing his shoe-tying song.

"Be right back," I called. I raced up the stairs, looking for Izzy. When I reached their bedroom, Izzy was sitting on her unmade bed, fidgeting with her wrists while wearing her fancy white dress. Her eyebrows were raised as she kept turning her wrist this way and that way. "Need help, Iz?"

She looked up at me and exhaled. "I wanted to wear mama's pearls for the wedding. They match my dress." She looked down at her wrist again and frowned. "But I can't get the bracelet to stay on."

"Sweetheart, you do know that today isn't the actual wedding, right?" I took the ends of the bracelet between my fingers and secured the clasp on her tiny wrist. "This is just your dress for our top secret engagement plans tonight."

The bracelet was so big that it didn't even need unclasped for her to slide it on. It slid around her dainty wrist as she held her arm up and examined the pearls. "Oh yes, the engagement." Izzy tilted her head to the side, staring at me with furrowed brows. "My dress for the wedding will be just as pretty?" She stood from her bed and placed her hands on her hips. "Sparkly, maybe?"

"Of course," I agreed. "A beautiful dress for my beautiful girl." With a hand on her back, I guided us back downstairs so we could head out.

Jax stood by the door, looking so grown and handsome in his little tux and blue bowtie. "Daddy, we ready now?" With his hands stuffed in his pants pockets, and a grin spread wide, I couldn't stop smiling down at my little man.

"Yeah, we're ready. But first, we need to capture this moment." I couldn't stop myself from taking a second and snapping a quick photo on my phone. There'd never be too many photographs of my children.

Izzy moved in front of the door to stand next to Jax and slung an arm around his neck while he did the same to her. Their faces were lit up with excitement. After sliding in behind them I wrapped an arm around them and held my arm out in front of us so we could smile into the camera.

Blonde hair filled the screen with bright smiles followed by giggles. "Okay, one...two...three...say cheese!"

"Cheese!" The kids laughed through toothy grins as I pressed the button to snap the picture.

"Perfect." I stood and grabbed the car keys from the wall. "Okay, let's go before Mama gets home and finds us."

Marley

I'd just pulled up to the house after long afternoon filled with meeting clients and found Max's jeep gone. I frowned at the house. I'd been hoping that we'd cook an early dinner together and I could snuggle up on the couch to read and relax.

Today had been a long ass day and I wasn't quite up for the task of cooking alone. Maybe we could just grab dinner out or Max could bring something home.

Not feeling like getting out of the car yet, I sent him a text to get an ETA from him.

> Hey, I just got home and noticed you're not here. Where are you and the munchkins?

> Want to meet for dinner?

MAX
> Go inside to the family room. I've got a surprise for you. All will be revealed soon, Princess.

> **MAX**
> P.S. I love you.

I turned off the truck, grabbed my purse, and practically dragged myself through the yard and into the house.

Soft music sounding from the family room pulled me further into the house and toward the source of the lovely musical notes.

The room was dimly lit with twinkling string lights hanging across the shelves, illuminating the space like a fairytale. A garment bag hung from one of the shelves with a note pinned to it's front with my name written in Max's messy scrawl.

With shaking arms, I carefully unpinned the folded piece of paper and opened it.

> *To my forever Princess,*
> *Please meet me at the place where we were finally reunited. I'll have a car pick you up in an hour. Don't worry about what to wear - I've taken care of it for you.*
> *Love you and see you soon,*
> *Your Busker.*
>
> *P.S. I'll always chase you but I'm hoping that this time I won't have to.*

Instant tears.

Just instant fucking tears filled my vision and I couldn't wait to go see my man. Especially for what seemed to be a special date night. Not wasting any time, I grabbed the garment bag and rushed up the stairs to our bathroom so I could quickly shower and make my hair presentable before the car arrived.

Wanting to sneak a peek, I unzipped the bag and unveiled the beautiful dress Max purchased for me.

It took my breath away.

I couldn't wait for Max to see me in it.

And out of it.

MAX HAD GONE OUT and made me feel like an actual fucking princess with all that he'd planned.

I was currently riding in the back of a limo with a full bottle of chilled champagne and wearing the most beautiful emerald cocktail dress. Along with the matching heels that he'd hidden in the bottom of the bag.

Be still my fucking heart.

I was no princess but I hoped like hell that when the clock struck midnight that he'd still be my Prince Charming.

"Ma'am," the limo driver called out. "We've arrived at The Vault. Please wait for me to come open your door for you."

I threw back the last of my drink and placed the flute into an empty cup holder.

The door beside me slowly opened and a waiting hand dropped in my line of view followed by a familiar face.

"Avery." I took her hand and let her help me out of the limo. "What're you doing here?"

"We're just here to be with you. To love you and to have a good time."

I'd been too busy staring at my sister to notice that we were surrounded by other people, too. Beckett and Kennon held open the doors to The Vault while Ellawyn stood off to the side with tears in her eyes.

My heart was about to pound out of my chest, I was sure of it.

"Go on in," Avery said, guiding me toward the door with a hand on my back. "Your future awaits."

With a deep breath, I walked through the double doors and into the building. The space was quiet, almost too quiet until I'd finally heard it. "Ring Pop" played quietly from the second floor of the building.

I climbed the stairs, eagerly awaiting to see Max.

Needing to see him.

When I reached the landing, everything but them disappeared. The space was filled with dozens of tea lights with Tiger Lilies—among other beautiful arrangements—lining the perimeter of the space. But in the center, down on one knee, was Max. He was so fucking handsome in his tux. But what was even more cute was how he was sandwiched between our beautiful munchkins.

Izzy and Jax each had a Ring Pop in their hands, both of which were a different flavor. The kids held out their arms, proudly displaying their lollipops. Max opened a black velvet box with a beautiful diamond ring inside.

"Marley Halligan," Max called out. "Will you marry me and make our family of four official?" He jerked his head toward the kids. "We weren't sure which flavor to get, so we got a couple."

I rushed toward them and leapt into Max's arms just as he stood to catch me. "Yes. A million times yes."

His strong arms spun me around as the kids jumped up and down screaming with joy. A round of applause could be heard in the background.

But all I saw was him.

He and the kids were all I'd ever need.

THANK YOU FOR READING

Thank you so much for reading Max and Marley's story. Every reader is so special to me and I'm eternally grateful that you took a chance on a new author. If you enjoyed their story, please consider leaving a review. Reviews mean so much and are such an easy way to support authors that you enjoy.

ACKNOWLEDGMENTS

To all the readers who enjoyed Finding Starlight and couldn't wait for Max's story —I hope you enjoyed it.

To my friends who continue to support me in this endeavor, you mean more than you know. Kate, thank you for literally everything. It'd be too much to type. Forever my best friend. To Jaime for always being the person who makes sure shit makes sense and for truly being one of my biggest cheerleaders, even on your wedding day. To Miranda for always being so damn supportive and reading everything in the worst possible state. To Kathy and Summer for beta reading for me again, too. It means the whole damn world. To Kiira for reading Chasing Redemption at the last minute, right before Christmas, and providing her feedback. I owe you so much and I'm so thankful that you took the time to help me out. You're wonderful and your comments were amazing. To all of my other author friends who continue to show their support for me and my books: THANK YOU. We're part of an amazing community and I wouldn't have been able to do it without you.

To my lovely editor, Amanda Cuff, for dealing with me pushing back my release twice and thus rescheduling our editing session. Ugh! I'm still so sorry and appreciate you so much!

To my ARC readers, I appreciate your willingness to sign up to ARC read Chasing Redemption and your patience when

I pushed back the ARC date. Thank you so much for wanting to read my little book baby. It means the world.

To my son, Kohler. For being the most amazing kid ever.

And lastly, a huge thank you to the readers once again. Your support and your love of Quimby Grove mean the world to me.

ALSO BY SHANNON NIKOLE

<u>The Quimby Grove Series</u>

Finding Starlight

ABOUT THE AUTHOR

Shannon Nikole is a lover of books, art, true crime, ghost hunting, and all things Disney. She runs on sarcasm and Pepsi Zero. When she doesn't have her nose in a book, she can be found getting into shenanigans in Pennsylvania with her son.

    Stay connected by joining my Facebook reader group: Shannon Nikole's Shenanigans and joining my newsletter.

- facebook.com/shannonnikoleauthor
- instagram.com/shannonnikoleauthor
- goodreads.com/shannonnikole
- tiktok.com/@shannonnikoleauthor
- bookbub.com/authors/shannon-nikole